God bless you brotha

Mike Root

17 July 1991

REV

a novel by

Mike Root

This is a work of fiction. Any resemblance of any of the characters
to persons living or dead is strictly coincidental.

FIRST EDITION

Copyright 1988, by Mike Root
Library of Congress Catalog Card No: 88-50590
ISBN: 916383-65-2

UNIVERSITY EDITIONS, Inc.
59 Oak Lane, Spring Valley
Huntington, West Virginia 25704

Cover by Vicky LeMaster

Dedication

To the men and women who opened their cruisers and their lives to Chaplain 8. Their professionalism was unparalleled and their friendship was unwavering.

To Deborah, Elizabeth and Jonathan who became temporary orphans as their daddy juggled vocation and avocation.

To Donna, who loved and supported me through it all; who cried with me when I was overwhelmed, and who prayed for me when I forgot who I was.

CHAPTER ONE

I feel like one of Pavlov's dogs. Everytime the phone rings I get a terrible, sinking feeling in the pit of my stomach. After years of being called to the scenes of hundreds of fatalities, homicides, and suicides, one would think I'd be more calloused.

It was 3:15 in the afternoon on a hot and muggy June day, Friday the 13th. I had spent a frustrating and depressing three hours making hospital visits and talking to a car salesman. I'd had some wild idea that it may be time for me to purchase a new car, but one look at the window stickers made me feel like time and inflation had just passed me by.

When I walked in the door of my house, my wife said two things, the second of which contributed to the first. "You look like you've been through the ringer," and "Officer Bitalli called ten minutes ago and wants you for something." That rang the right bell and the dreadful, sinking feeling edged its way into my stomach.

"This is Chaplain 5. What's going on?" I asked the desk person who'd answered the phone. "Got a juicy one for ya," he smirked. "A suicide at 3654 Digby Glenn Road. They want you to come to the scene."

"Is that north or south of Route 37?" I'd learned the hard way that turning the wrong direction during rush hour could have permanent consequences.

The line was muffled as he asked someone else the same question.

"North," he said finally.

"Tell 'em I'm on the way, would ya?"

"Will do. Good luck!"

I ran to the bathroom, washed my face, recombed my hair and tucked my shirt-tail back in. I almost looked official. But before I could get out the door the phone rang again. I thought I'd better answer it because it might be the P.D. again.

"Hello."

"Hello, Pastor Temple?"

I never liked "Pastor", but I also don't like preaching on the phone. "Yes."

"This is Thomas Mills from Hallelujah Ministries. Are you familiar with our ministry?"

No, and I don't want to know about it, I thought to myself, but to him I just said "No."

"We have developed a low cost, high quality procedure for recording the entire Bible on cassette tapes. These tapes are . . ."

I couldn't believe I was listening to a sales pitch when the police needed me and a family in pain had asked for me. Yet on he droned. He believed in his ministry and I didn't wish to be rude. I also didn't want to be negligent.

5

"I appreciate your calling, but we have several sets of the Bible on cassette. We even have one in our church library for members to check out and use. But I appreciate your calling and . . ."

"Well, let me tell you about a new translation of the Bible that has just been put on tape. I think you will find it . . ."

"I'm sorry," I interrupted, "but I got an emergency call just before you called and I need to respond immediately."

"If I could take just a few seconds of your time to explain our new tape set, I feel sure you'd like to listen to them. I'd like to send you a set, with no obligation to purchase, so that you could examine them. We would bill you in thirty days for . . ."

This was crazy!

"Listen! I'm in no mood to make decisions about ordering tapes. I've got a suicide to deal with and I must go now. Send me some information in the mail and I promise I'll look at it."

"Can I just call you back in a couple of weeks and explain this ministry to you?"

What ever works! "Yes, you do that. Thanks for calling." Click. Boy, it sure is hard to be a nice guy sometimes.

Digby Glenn Road is one of those old, winding country roads that has become a major thoroughfare for residents and an embarrassment for the Highway Department. It's dangerous and destined to stay that way because it would cost the county a fortune to purchase the land necessary to straighten it out. The houses that front Digby Glen are all small framed country houses build thirty years ago when it was a small, seldom traveled rural road. In short, it is one of the worst roads in the county to have to be traveling slow on as you attempt to read numbers visible on their mailboxes, so I had to slow down a little more to catch the number on the front door.

Traffic was backing up behind me. The road was so curvy I had to watch it and missed a few houses. I just prayed I hadn't passed up 3654.

The pick-up truck behind me started blowing his horn at me. Obviously he didn't know I was a Police Chaplain, or care that I was having a difficult time finding the house.

Why should he know or care? He had a cold beer waiting for him at the Seven-Eleven. He had a family who was expecting him home any minute. He had a pay check to get to the bank before it closed. He wanted to go faster and some Jerk was out for a Sunday afternoon drive.

I've been in his seat before. I grip the steering wheel, swerve back and forth so they'll see how irritated and impatient I am. I grit my teeth and mentally call them every name I can think of and not feel guilty about. It is personal. They're purposely trying to aggravate me; upset my world which I rule from my crushed velour throne. It's me they're after. It's a vicious, premeditated attack on me and I will not be pushed around by some nut who doesn't know how to drive. I'd like to rear end that piece of junk, then jerk that wacko out of the car and beat him to a pulp. I'd like to . . .

I wonder if anyone I've ever followed was on his way to a suicide? I made a mental note to be more understanding the next time I found myself behind a slow poke.

Suddenly, I noticed the house number out of the corner of my left eye. At the same time I saw I was going to pass it by. Miraculously, there was no oncoming traffic. I swerved quickly to the left, turning into the driveway of the house next door. It was a good move since there was no more room in the driveway of 3654. It held a pick-up and a Chevy Cavalier, which presumably belonged to the residents, a police cruiser, plus two unmarked cars. One belonged to the I.D. team and the other belonged to the homicide investigators. They always work together though they are separate departments. Homicide does the investigating and working of the case, while Identification processes the scene, taking pictures, gathering evidence, checking the body and so forth.

3654 was a picturesque, white frame cottage with blue shutters. It was in the middle of a two-acre tree shaded lot, exuding hominess and orderliness. With a white picket fence out front, it could have been used in "The Little House on the Prairie."

I walked through an arched arbor of morning glories and followed a red brick walkway up to the front porch. The screen door framed the white shirted torso of Investigator Bowen, who quietly slipped around the door to brief me before I entered the house.

Bowen is a large, intimidating fellow with an egg-shaped head. His crew cut red hair gives him a permanent glow of Irish anger. His gruffness is belied by a rather mild mannered voice. I had worked with him a couple of other times and I always found him to be a respectful, compassionate cop. Of course, I'd never let another officer hear me describe him that way. To them I'd say he's a good man and a good cop. Anything else would be damaging to his image.

"Hey, Jim. What ya got"? I whispered.

"A fifty-eight year old female shot herself in the head with a .357 magnum. She's on the floor in the back bedroom. Her husband and father-in-law are in the living room. They liked the idea when we offered to call you," he said reassuringly. I think he remembered the last time he called me out, relatives of the deceased blamed God and me for everything.

The husband is pretty talkative. He heard the shot and had to kick in the bedroom door to find her."

"It's clearly suicide then—no doubts?" I needed to know

these things.

"Oh—no question. The investigation will be strictly routine from here on out." He leaned forward a little and lowered his voice even more. "By the way, the father-in-law is 79 and has cancer. He has only a few months to live."

"Wow—that's rough!" I said. "What are the names"?

The victim is Helen Martha Watson. The husband's name is Bob Watson."

"Let's do it." I said confidently.

Jim held the door open for me as I stepped up into the living room. It was small but cozy. The early American couch, three chairs, braided rug and end tables were in good condition. Two men sat cross-legged on the couch. One, a sixtyish, balding fellow was wringing a handkerchief in his hands. He was obviously very distraught. The other man, who must have been the father-in-law, as he was clearly older, calmly puffed on a three inch cigar.

I looked at the first man and introduced myself as he rose to shake my hand. "Bob, I'm Mark Temple, a Police Chaplain with the Lexington County Police Department."

"Thank you so much for coming over." he muttered. "This is my father, Robert, Senior." I shook his hand while signaling for him to keep his seat. He gave me a gentle smile and a soft, "Hi."

Sitting on the edge of the chair next to the couch, I started the task of making contact and building trust.

"Bob, I'm really glad to meet you, but I'm sorry it had to be for a reason like this." With red eyes and quivering lower lip he nodded his head and said, "Me too."

"Is there a minister or close friend I could call to come and be with you"?

"I don't know . . . I mean I'm not sure. Helen used to go the Providence Baptist Church years ago. But, they changed minister and she hadn't been back in a long while. I've already called her brother who lives over in Essex. He's going to go by and see her mother and tell her what's happened. I just couldn't be the one to tell her. I mean, I don't think I know how. She's not in good health herself, and well, he's the better one to tell her.

"Helen has really been having a hard time lately. She just spent four days at the hospital on the—what is it?—mental ward—psychology ward? She thought the water we use was poisonous and that some bugs were destroying the house, and well, it bothered her that my father was dying and she, well, didn't want to believe it.

"You know, when I first got in the room and saw her lying there, I thought to myself, just pick up that gun and end it all, but I thought, that's no answer. Oh, what's my son going to think? He's overseas in the Army and it was his gun she used. I should never have let him keep it here! But I guess it doesn't

8

matter. She'd have done it some other way. I just never knew that she . . ."

Bob needed to talk so I just let him ramble on. Actually that's a lot easier than trying to help someone who won't talk. You sit with them wanting to say something that will help, something that will make everything better but you don't know what to say. So you sit and hope they'll give you some idea of what you can do. If they just sit in silence, about all you can do is sit with them, and that gets very awkward after awhile.

Bob talked and I listened, Occasionally, I offered a few words of advice and comfort. The biggest pitfall that catches survivors is the temptation to blame themselves for what happened. The "if only" guilt inducer has sent many a person to a early grave or mental hospital. Fortunately, they both seemed very receptive to my comments.

Looking through the window behind them, I saw the ambulance pull into the front yard. They are usually sent away while the police investigate the scene, and then called back when it's time to transport the body to the county morgue. From experience I knew having the family watch as a loved one is carried out for the last time is a traumatic experience. So I got up and went back to the bedroom to tell Jim I was going to go out back with the two relatives until they transported the body.

The bedroom was small. It was especially small looking with four police officers in it. The original case officer, Mike Bitalli, was in the basement. They were having a difficult time finding the bullet. It had entered the wall and somehow ricocheted down. On the floor at the front of the bed lay Helen. Her pale white legs were covered by a blue and yellow flowered dress. Her arms and legs were almost as white as the lace which trimmed her dress. Her head was covered by a towel, but the towel wasn't large enough to cover the pool of blood which formed a crimson circle around her. Even though my view of the room was obscured and amounted to only a peek, I could see it was quite a mess. I could see blood, pieces of skull, and globs of brain matter on the bed, walls and ceiling.

When I stepped back into the living room, the Watson's were moving a chair from the way of the ambulance crew who were trying to get a stretcher through the angled doorway entrance.

They seemed more than happy to step out back out with me. They knew what was going to happen and didn't care to be in there. We sat in lawn chairs looking across a small, well-tended garden. Bob continued talking and I continued listening.

I excused myself from them when I saw the ambulance leave. When I found Jim in the dining room, he looked a little concerned. I asked what was happening, and he wrinkled his forehead and said, "We need someone to clean up that room some. The husband shouldn't have to do that himself."

This wasn't the first time I'd been faced with that problem. So I said, "Let me go see if I can find a neighbor who might do it."

I went out the front door and crossed the yard to an elderly couple who were sitting on their porch. I introduced myself and asked them if they knew the Watson's very well.

"Great people." said the man in a husky voice. "If we both didn't have heart trouble we'd be over there helping Bob, but we've both just taken some medicine and need to calm down first."

Not exactly the kind of people who need to clean brains off the wall, I thought. We'd have to call the ambulance back for them if they saw that room.

"I'm sure he understands. Are any of the other neighbors home that you know of"?

"Let's see. The Johnson's and the Marble's work downtown and don't get home 'til round seven. Heck of a long day for a person, but then most folks round here works like that. Then—I think the Burton's, the folks on the other side, are in Florida on vacation. Ain't that right, honey—yes, I think that's where they are. Why"?

"Oh, just routine checking. No problem. Thanks a lot. You all have a good day."

"You too, Reverend."

Bob and his dad were still around back when I got there. I asked Bob if he had a bucket I could use to clean up a little bit in the bedroom. "I'd hate for you to have to do that," I said, "I thought I'd get the worst of it and maybe when your brother-in-law gets here, he can do the rest of it." He was very appreciative. He didn't know if he could ever go back into the house again. He said I could use the buckets on the back porch and any towels that were in the hall closet.

Grabbing a bucket as I went into the house, I came into the dining room where Jim, Mike and the other three officers were talking. I could tell by their eyes that they were aghast about my intentions. Before anyone could speak, I lifted up my bucket and declared, "I can't find any neighbors, so I thought I'd go ahead and clean up the worst of it. I've had some experience doing this before."

One of the I.D. men asked me if I needed some rubber gloves. When I said yes, he produced a half a dozen pairs. Putting one pair on and setting the others aside, I filled the bucket half-way with cold water, grabbed three towels and stepped into the room.

Other than the large pool of blood where the head had been, the spots were not that obvious. As I stood just inside the doorway, I was at the foot of the bed. The large pool was about three feet to my right. It covered about two square feet of carpet and a small part of a throw rug at the foot of the bed also. I could see blood and brain matter on the dresser and chair to my right which were just inches from where her head had laid. On the bed in front of me were three six to eight inch long blood smears with quarter sized pieces of skull at the far end of each. There were four or five streaks and splotches of blood and matter on the wall to my left and several more angling towards the corner. I could clearly see the bullet hole in the wall. She had sat on the floor with her right shoulder leaning on the foot of her bed. She held the gun in her left hand, and fired into her left temple with the gun pointing somewhat upward. She then fell straight backward to my right.

There was a time when I would have stood there transfixed with shock. A time when I would have tried to get out of doing this. Now, it really didn't bother me much and I didn't allow myself to think about it either. I knew I had to just get in there and get it done.

I placed a wash cloth on the floor to kneel on and soaked a towel in the clean bucket of water. After wringing it out I spread it over the large pool of blood and tried to scoop it all up. When I applied pressure my hands slipped across the blotch like grease. I scooped a lot up and dropped the towel and contents into the bucket. The remaining water immediately turned red. I soaked another towel in the red water and scrubbed some more of the pool away. I dropped that towel into the bucket and carried the bucket across the hall to the bathroom. Setting it into the tub I turned on the cold water and pulled out the towels. I rinsed them and squeezed out as much excess water as I could. Since they were still terribly messy, I went out on the porch, got an old five-gallon plastic bucket, and placed it in the tub. I dropped the towels into the five-gallon bucket and dumped the other bucket out in the tub. Blood and water ran everywhere. Large globs of coagulated blood clogged up the drain and the tub began to fill with red water. I reached into the drain and took out large handfuls of the coagulated blood, dropping it into the large five-gallon bucket. No one would want to keep those towels anyway. Finally I was able to drain the tub and wash down the sides of it.

Armed with some clean towels and a fresh bucket of water, I went back to the room. I put the throw rug, the bloody bandages that were laying around, and the chunks of skull in a paper bag. I sopped up some more of the floor stain and scrubbed down the dresser and chair. Under the chair was a pair of moccasin house shoes that had a little blood on them. When I pulled them out, I could see that one shoe was filled with blood so I just dropped them into the larger bucket also.

Next, I started wiping stains and matter off the walls and ceiling. It was uncomfortable work by the very nature of what it was, but it was also an unair-conditioned house. I was sweating, thirsty and trying to be casual about washing brains off the wall. Mike walked in before he left and said, "I wouldn't have your job for anything." I laughed it off with, "Oh, I've had to do worse," and then I got depressed as I remembered when that was.

On the wall just above the bullet hole there was something protruding. It looked like a gouged place in the sheetrock, but upon closer inspection, I discovered it was a piece of skull embedded in the wall. With gloved hand I grabbed it, and wiggled it loose, and pulled it out. It was about an inch long and as thick as a pencil. It was hard, gray, and only two hours from life. It dropped in the bucket with a plop that signaled an end to that clean-up detail. I dropped the stained towels into the big bucket, poured the contents of the cleaning bucket down the drain, washed out the tub, stuffed the rubber gloves into the big bucket and washed my hands.

Looking in the mirror of the bathroom I seemed a little pale and harried. I guess detachment is not one of my better acts. I felt drained. I felt unclean. I felt insensitive. Yet, I felt good and even a little proud. I was doing something that very few people could and would do. I was helping. I was making a difference. How many times had it been necessary to remind myself of that?

By the time I returned to the back yard, Bob's brother-in-law was there. They seemed to have things well in hand so I gave them a little advice about guilt, about arrangements for the funeral, and about the bedroom clean-up. I gave Bob my card and told him he could call me anytime for any reason. He thanked me profusely and I bid him sympathy and farewell.

I'd been gone from home for only three hours. In some ways it was just another chaplain call and just another suicide. Yet those "just anothers" have a way of burning their way into your memory and becoming interruptions that last a life time. It was a part of me now. Just like the hundreds of other "calls" which have been a part of my life for the past six years.

Six years. That's all? Just six years? Before that I'd never seen a dead person who hadn't been fixed up by a mortician. But since that time I've seen everything. I have seen more in one year than the average officer sees in an entire career. In six years I'd gone from rookie to expert. So much has happened. And to think how much I feared going to my first roll call.

CHAPTER TWO

A cold sweat and white lips betrayed my facade of confidence as I stumbled down the stairs behind the Station Commander. It was his distasteful job to introduce me, the new station Police Chaplain, to the 4 to 2 shift of police officers, which in this case was E squad. I say distasteful because I was the first Chaplain this Sub-station had ever had, and until further notice, I was an outsider, a civilian, a questionable entity, and possibly, an undesirable.

Word of my arrival undoubtedly preceded my triumphal entry into the inner sanctum of the roll call room. Still trailing the cautious Captain, and a good ten feet from the roll call room, I heard the first reaction to my presence. "Who the heck needs a Chaplain?" declared a youthful voice from the room. The answer from a second officer did nothing to slacken the oversized knot in my stomach. "Somebody's got to pray for your rear-end when you die from AIDS.", explained a gruff voice from deeper inside the gathering. "Lord help me," I thought, "what am I getting myself into!"

What I was getting myself into was the crowning paradox of my life. What was a pacifist fundamental preacher doing volunteering to be a Police Chaplain? A technical answer could be found in one of the many Counseling and Psychology books gathering dust in my church office, but basically it was a compromise with my conscience. I grew up wanting to be a soldier, a cop, or a billionaire. The decision I made in college to be a minister changed everything, especially the latter. Being a very diligent student of the Bible, I concluded that I must be a conscientious objector to military service, a decision that was quite painful for me. I had dreamed all my life of spit-and-polish, glories of war, and duty to my country. As a child, playing war was the number one game in my neighborhood. And growing up in Washington, D.C. I was keenly aware of military history. I always wanted to be a soldier. Secondly, I made the decision during the height of the Vietnam conflict. I not only supported our government's actions, but my older brother was on his second tour of duty in that far off war. I wanted to be there and experience the thrill of fighting like my brother. Thirdly, John Wayne wouldn't have liked my decision.

Okay. That's not exactly what you'd call a theological reason, but I'm a non-typical theologian. Trying to be like Jesus caused me to be a pacifist, but it was wanting to be like John Wayne that made it difficult. From "The Sands of Iwo Jima" to "The Alamo", the Duke was my hero. He was in fantasy the father I never had in reality. He was in control. He was tough. He was always right. To this day I cheer and cry my way through "The Green Berets" and then thank God that I have never been placed in a position where I had to kill my enemies. Some might call that hypocrisy but a lifetime of identifying with the Duke is not erased because you give your heart to a King.

Standing in the doorway of the roll call room. I felt like a missionary of sorts. Ready to be Dale Carnegie, Billy Graham, and Frank Furrillo rolled into one. The ten faces looking at me were pleasant and some were even smiling. But, there was an icy tint of suspicion in nearly every eye. Eyes that seemed to exude cynicism and caution were giving me a silent third degree. "What's in this for you?", "Are you some kind of religious fanatic or something?", and "Who do you really work for and report to?", were questions, I later discovered, that concerned them when they saw me for the first time. You'll look long and hard before you find a group that has a stronger "us and them" mentality than police. Everyone except fellow officers is an outsider and therefore not to be trusted. It's a paranoid fraternity which accepts being hyper-critical of one another, but tenaciously defends even the worst cop from outsider's accusations. It's like what my older brother would tell the other big kids on our block when we were youngsters, "He's my little brother and only I can pick on him."

How can I describe the roll call room? It's simple yet complex. It's nothing, and yet it's everything. Originally it was a small basement bedroom in a relatively small house. Since the County converted the house to a Police Station, the basement became a small roll call room in a small Police Station. At one time, a half dozen teenagers could have stretched out in it and had a good bull session. Now it held a Captain, a Sergeant, a Corporal, ten officers, and a very nervous Chaplain. We all sat in ugly scarred desks that had been discarded from some County High School and were meant for Munchkins, not men. Nearly one-fourth of the room was overshadowed by one of those grotesque gray government desks which haunts schools, basements, and offices across the country. If everyone stretched their legs out in front of their desks the entire squad could have played footsie with one another.

On one wall there was a large blackboard, which had school crossing assignments scratched on it. Cops place school crossings in a very special category along with hemorrhoids and jock itch.

A bulletin board was fixed to the opposite wall. It was bare except for two small training posters. One poster had two detainees pictured on it showing the right and wrong way to take I.D. pictures prior to incarceration. The other, somewhat larger poster, reminded the officers of the proper verbal procedure for halting a suspect. In bold letters it read, "POLICE, STOP". It had been altered to cop specifications. Someone had taken a black marker and written "Bang" just before "POLICE STOP."

Clearing his voice to get their attention, the Captain said,

"This is Rev Temple, our Chaplain. He has volunteered his services to the County to be of service to you. He has ride-along privileges with everyone. He can use the radio and will be on 24-hour call to assist with fatalities, homicides, suicides, police shootings, and any crisis or disaster where his presence might be needed."

I was impressed. The job had never been placed in such a neat nutshell before. He said it with such authority and conciseness that it came across as unalterable department policy. However, there was a tinge of bureaucratic disgust in his voice. Just a hint of "Here's another piece of garbage that has rolled down from the idiots in the Ivory Tower." I would soon discover that the guys in blue saw themselves as having three primary enemies. These included the crooks, the courts, and the Department command structure, better known as the Ivory Tower. In terms of aggravation and stress, the Department policy makers head the list.

He continued, "Let me make something clear. The Rev here is a Chaplain to the police, not the community. He is here to help you." I wished he had said "us". "He is empowered to do any police work when he is with you that will assist you in carrying out your duties. He's trained, qualified, and willing to help. So don't hesitate to use him." It was all I could do to keep from laughing when he described me as trained. The three day seminar I had attended was a joke. It did nothing to prepare me to be a police chaplain. It dealt primarily with communication skills which seemed rather elementary to me.

"Rev, would you like to add anything to that?" he said turning to me. Here it was, my turn to speak for the first time to the troops, and I felt a strong urge to yell out, "Don't call me Rev!" I really dislike titles. They either alienate others or they give you a false sense of self-importance, and I couldn't afford to have anything get in the way of building trust with these guys. I had a feeling I'd been tagged with a name I'd never get rid of. Rev. What a name.

I had spent a great deal of time thinking about what I would say to them so I was somewhat prepared. "The Captain pretty well covered the job description, but let me clarify a couple of things and at the same time ease some of the concerns about me that you may have.

"First, I want to emphasize the fact that I am here to help you, not to complicate your lives. I don't work for or answer to Lexington County. I do not report to anybody about anything." I could see the Captain arch an eyebrow when he heard that.

"When I am riding with you, you are the boss. Whatever you need me to do to assist you I will do it. The heart of our relationship will be confidentiality. I will never betray the confidence you place in me

"It is also important that you know that I will not talk religion at all unless you bring it up for discussion. I will not use your cruiser to make you a captive audience."

Pretending to be wiping sweat off his forehead with his index finger, Sergeant Hinckley said, "Thank God!" They all chuckled a bit at his comic relief, and I responded with "At least you didn't say 'Thank Buddah'", to which they crackled even louder. That really helped me to relax a little bit and caused that big knot in my stomach to loosen up a tad. However, I did notice that Sergeant Hinckley didn't laugh.

"One more thing. If you really would rather not have me riding with you, feel free to say 'no' when I ask you. I won't be offended," I lied. I felt obligated to give them a way out. Besides, I'm not sure that I wanted to ride with anyone who might truly be belligerent towards me.

The Corporal, who was a tall, muscular, sandy-haired guy with a calm and pleasant look on his face, asked, "should we call you Pastor, Reverend, Chaplain, or what?" He seemed to be sincere and interested in finding an answer.

"I prefer Mark. Chaplain Temple is how I'd like to be introduced to citizens when we're on the street. The dispatchers have been told to use Chaplain 5 as my call designator since this is Station 5. I'm not too keen on titles. I'll answer to 'hey you' if it makes you comfortable." He nodded his head and seemed to like my answer.

The Captain waved a hand on his way out the door shouting over his shoulder, "Call me if you need me." and he was up the stairs. Sergeant Hickley picked up his clip-board and cleared his throat, signaling that it was time to get on with roll call. Looking at me he groused, "Are you going to ride tonight?" I really hadn't thought about it, but I quickly said, "Yes". Directing his gaze at a young fellow with rosy cheeks, he said, "Bud, why don't you take the Chaplain with you tonight." With an exaggerated nod of his head and a friendly smile on his face, Bud responded with a lively, "You got it!".

The rest of roll call went rather quickly. The Corporal read the Daily Activity Board, which was a computer printout of all the arrests, activities, and car thefts that had happened since they left work the day before. The Sergeant then read a couple of memos from the Supervisor's Board. These were the infamous departmental memos which on a daily basis did more to stir up animosity than any other aspect of police work. Today's memos, fortunately, were mild and noncontroversial. The last thing done before hitting the street was the giving out of area assignments. Bud drew area 52, a large residential section in the heart of Station 5's patrol area.

The scramble to clear the station was something akin to a Chinese fire drill. The combination of a station that was too small and men and equipment that were too big made for some interesting two-stepping in the hallways, which also were lined with lockers. Lockers slamming, night sticks hitting things, boots pounding up the rickety stairs, shouting, cursing, phones ringing, cruiser sirens tested, radios crackling, and a cacophony of indescribable noises were the identifying sounds of tax dollars at work at the police station.

One would think these guys were getting ready for a month of work instead of just one night. Most of them had to have at least two briefcases to carry all the papers and forms that they needed. Some of them had as many as five and six cases to load up in the trunk of their cruisers. Bud had three. Two briefcases and one large gym bag with flashlight and traffic vest sticking out of the zippered top. I even had a briefcase to hold all the equipment that had been issued to me at Headquarters. I had a traffic vest, a five celled plastic flashlight, a yellow full-length rain coat, a portable radio, notebooks, rubber boots, and my old orange hunting hat for rain since they didn't issue hats to the Chaplains. It was ugly, but it would do the job.

With one hand on the steering wheel and the other holding the microphone, Bud squealed the cruiser out of the police lot and marked "in service" with EOC, Emergency Operation Center. Before he could place the mike on the hook, I asked him to let EOC know that I was with him. He smiled big and said, "Oh yeah."

"Scout 52," he yelled into the mike.

"Scout 52," they responded.

"Be advised that Chaplain 5 will be riding with me."

"10-9 your last." They wanted him to repeat himself.

"Be advised that Chaplain 5 is with me."

"CAPTAIN FIVE is with you?"

He swore under his breath. Then to EOC he slowly declared, "That's Charlie-Henry-Adam-Paul-Lincoln-Adam-Item-Nancy-5!"

"10-4," came the curt reply. It was followed by a series of clicks on the radio. Bud explained that the clicks were all the other officers keying their mikes and creating a kind of applause or laughter on the radio. It was against department regulations, but it was impossible to know who had done it. A small victory for the cop on the street.

Officer Bud "Cowboy" Cabot was the perfect person for my first ride-along experience. At twenty-five, he had been on the Department for six years, four as a sworn officer and two as a cadet. He was young enough to be gung-ho, yet experienced enough to be cynical and suspicious of outsiders like me.

Still, within minutes, he was relaxed and open. We talked about several things of mutual interest. Like most, he was astonished that a preacher liked hunting, fishing, camping, and

17

guns. I live for hunting. Squirrels, rabbits, dove, quail, and especially deer fall victim every year to one of my well-placed bullets or arrows. I may be a conscientious objector to war, but not to putting meat on the table. The woods, the stalk, the challenge, the kill, and the bragging rights are all things I love. I can shoot just about any kind of rifle, pistol, or shotgun there is. My real passion, though, is bow hunting. I love slinking thought the woods completely camouflaged and armed only with a weapon used by Indians. It's a real back-to-nature high for me. And since one must get so close to his prey before shooting, the challenge is much greater than gun hunting. Bud felt the same way.

Just the week before I had gone to a target range with a member of my congregation who is a gun collector. It was quite a thrill for me to practice with his Ruger Mini 14, 9mm Luger, S&W .357, and a classic Army Colt .45 automatic. But the best part of the experience was firing his Thompson Sub-machine gun. It was a beautiful piece of ordnance. Well balanced, smooth actioned, and mean. The sense of power that it gave the holder was phenomenal and scary. It was difficult for me to ignore the death and destruction which this invention had wrought, but I did. I didn't want to spoil the fun. Needless to say, Bud was impressed with my armament orientation.

Building a relationship is difficult in the best of situations. Being a preacher and trying to gain acceptance from the police is a little like getting Miss Piggy to accept a BLT. Cops and Minister's are both societal symbols of right, protecting mother and child from the crushing avalanches of scum, sin, and Satan. Yet, depending on the cop, it could be harder for him to befriend a preacher than a crook. In fact, since they have seen their share of Elmer Gantry's, "crook" is a word some would use in describing preachers.

Suddenly Bud swung the cruiser around in a screeching U-turn that slammed me against my door and drained the color from my face.

"Expired inspection sticker," he yelled, as the car leaped up behind a blue, late-model Cadillac. I was astonished that he had seen an expired three inch sticker on the windshield of an on-coming car in the opposite lane, passing each other at 50 mph, and while embroiled in a discussion of compound bows.

He flipped three toggle switches on the console between our seats. Two turned on the rotating roof lights and the flashing lights on the front grill. The third switch was the siren which throbbed in my ears. My heart was pounding and my hands began to sweat. Bud was completely blase.

Immediately the big Caddie pulled off to the right shoulder of the road and slowly rolled to a stop. In that same instant two thoughts crossed my mind which caused me to panic slightly. The

18

number of cops killed each year during traffic stops is second only to domestic disputes. Here I was in the middle of a traffic stop and I had no idea what I should do.

Bud snatched the mike. "Scout 52." EOC acknowledged him and he continued. "I'm 10-31 on Virginia Henry-Adam-King-4-7-8 at Waterford Road just south of Flint Road." He dropped the mike in the seat and hopped out the door without any words of direction for me. Instinctively, I grabbed my portable radio, climbed out, and cautiously walked up on the right side of the Cadillac.

The only person in the car was the driver, but he took up enough seat space for two people. To say he was obese would be kind. His bald head was resting on fold after fold of overindulgence. He looked like the Michelin Tire Man, and he talked like he owned the company. I couldn't hear the conversation he was having with Bud, but it took no superior detective skills to discern his discontent over being stopped.

With the man's license and registration in hand, Bud walked back to the cruiser. As I slid in beside him he growled, "I would have let the Fat Cat off the hook if he hadn't been such a pain in the neck. Now he's gonna help finance the County." He ran the license plate, checked for an outstanding warrant, and groaned when the searches came back negative. A ticket for an expired inspection sticker was all the damage he could inflict.

"Please press hard. There are five copies." This courteous statement is music to the ears of an officer whose authority has been challenged. It is capped off by a smile and, "Have a nice day." That seems to really rub salt in the wound of a motorist who has been belligerent. I couldn't help but savor the small victory too. We'd stuck it to a fat cat who thought he was above the law. I was soon to discover that many people who drive luxury cars seem offended when stopped by the police. And that has a direct impact on their chances of being let off with a verbal warning. The word is nil.

Off we zoomed to our next adventure, picking up our conversation on archery like nothing had ever happened. "Hey, I think I'm going to like this," I thought to myself. *Excitement—adrenalin—fun.* That was soon to change. Innocence and ignorance go hand in hand. When one changes the other does, too.

A cute little blond in a red VW dared to drive through our county and run a red light on Rt. 3. We saw her do it, stopped her, and she admitted doing it. There's something extra exciting about catching a law breaker red-handed. I was almost giddy with anticipation. But, instead of dispensing justice, Bud galantly gave out mercy. I suspect that it was more the result of batting eyes than a big heart. More due to a halter top than to chivalry. But he was happy with himself, and who am I to cast stones.

19

As he dropped back into his car seat he explained, "That's what we call selective enforcement."

We rode in silence for awhile, because I was straining to find another expired inspection sticker and I couldn't concentrate on that and talk at the same time. Bud broke the silence by broaching the subject of religion. He was not only a religious person, but he attended church services whenever he could. Before I could pick my jaw up off my lap, he mentioned his religious affiliation and it was the same as mine. Now my chin was scraping the floorboard and I was speechless. The Lord really has a way of slapping us out of our misperceptions. I was on a quest to save the uniformed infidels and the first one I ride with is a fellow Christian. Not perfect, but then, who is?

Before my response took form in my mind the radio cracked with urgency. Scout 50 was pulling over a 280Z that was on the hot sheet. He was just down the highway from us so Bud peeled rubber as he informed EOC that we'd provide back-up.

With lights flashing we pulled in behind Scout 50 and jumped out ready for action. Scout 50, which was Mike Bitalli, a seven year veteran, had already taken the license and registration from the driver and was running a check on the car and suspect. On the passenger side of the Z a young woman sat sideways with the door open, with a cute three or four year old boy on her lap. They were all black, clean-cut folks who hailed from a neighboring state. Bud and I walked over to the Z. He watched the driver and I knelt down beside the woman and child to see if I could help allay their fears.

The woman talked incessantly. I was sure that was due to nervousness. She claimed to have just hitched a ride with the driver and she really knew nothing about him. It was obvious that she anticipated his arrest. She was very friendly, but it was her little boy who really caught my eye. He had on a New York Yankee hat, a red and white striped T-shirt, blue jeans, and tennis shoes. His smile was captivating as we talked about his future with the pros. They didn't even notice when Mike and Bud got the driver out of the car, cuffed him, and placed him in the back seat of Mike's cruiser. It turned out that the car was not stolen after all, but the driver was wanted for a larceny of gas in an adjoining county.

The lady showed a trace of panic in her eyes when Mike asked her for her driver's license. He had decided to run a warrant check on her, too, and she was visibly apprehensive. The little fellow was a delight. For his sake, I hoped his mother had a clean record.

Mike's shadow loomed over my left shoulder, so I stepped back a little to let him get closer to the mother and child. In a soft, but firm voice, Mike announced, "I'm sorry, Ma'am, but you're wanted in Maryland for two counts of passing bad checks."

She sucked in her breath in shock. The little boy immediately sensed that something bad was happening. He reached around his mother's neck with his small arms, and with fear in his voice, cried, "Momma, Momma, Momma . . .". His eyes bulged with fright and his cheeks glistened with tears. I wanted to reach out and take him in my arms, wipe away the tears, and tell him everything would be all right. Some store had been victimized by this woman's thoughtlessness or maliciousness, but the real victim was this little fellow who had no control over the events which were scarring him for life. I didn't know whether to cry or cuss. Neither were viable options. So I stepped aside and let the cops collect them.

Mike arranged for the 280Z to be impounded. We transported the prisoner and her child to the station where they were held until the warrants and Child Services arrived. We didn't stay around after the transport because Bud was needed on the street. I was glad to drive away from all the mess. The woman would get what she deserved, I guessed, but that little New York Yankee never would. As we pulled out of the parking lot I kept remembering the slogan which we sarcastically shouted to one another during high school football practice when one of us was rattled by a good hit. "We're having some fun now, aren't we!"

By the time we finished our steak sub at the local Italian greasy spoon, I was feeling ruthless again and ready to fight crime. I let Bud know that he couldn't be too much of a hot dog as far as I was concerned. I was ready for action and he accepted the challenge to find some.

"What are you going to do if I get us into a fight? You can't preach your way out of a situation where a Toad wants to break your neck." In police-speak, a Toad was a crook, low-life, or undesirable.

Full of bravado, or something, I answered, "Don't worry about me, I can take care of myself just fine. I was raised in the city, boxed in the Golden Gloves, and I've had self-defense training. If you get into trouble, I'll be there to help before you can say, 'signal 13'." That's the radio signal for "officer needs help". It's what brings the cavalry from every corner of the county.

He grinned and I swelled. Then he dropped the bomb on me. "What if some Toad tried to kill us? Would you hesitate to ice him?" He said that with one of those "Let's see what you're made of" looks on his face.

I had known it was just a matter of time until someone asked me that question, but I had hoped it wouldn't happen so soon. Certainly not on my first ride-along. Long before, I decided that I couldn't allow them to know that my convictions

21

forced me to be a conscientious objector even when I wished I could be otherwise. I knew I would never be accepted by them if they discovered I was a C.O. I had struggled for half my life with that controversy, and it couldn't be explained in just minutes between ratio noises. So I gave him my canned answer.

"I will do everything in my power to stop anyone who would harm me or any officer I happened to be with."

He saw no hidden meaning to my answer. "That's all anyone can ask for," he said. As far as he was concerned, the subject was settled. From his point of view, I'd blow away any Toad who drew on us. From my point of view, that wasn't within my power. Truth is often obscured by semantics. Yet what ate at me more than the verbal gymnastics was the nagging question: Could I let a cop, a friend, die rather than shoot to protect him?

By midnight it began to drizzle. We had written two more traffic tickets and stopped twice for coffee at the 7-11 store. On Rt. 14 we came upon a car on the shoulder of the road which seemed empty. Disabled cars are Legion when it is late, but this one had legs sticking out the open back door. What was it, I wondered. A victim of a robbery? A lover? A corpse?

It was a drunk. He was passed out cold in the backseat of his car. That's better than driving under the influence and not nearly the offense. I held him up while Bud checked him for weapons and I.D. His breath could take the wrinkles right out of your shirt, but his body odor would put them back. We handcuffed him and tried to tell him that he was being arrested for Drunk in Public, but he was too far gone to understand us. We placed him in the back of the cruiser and called for a wrecker to impound his vehicle.

"Scout 52. I'll be 10-15 to ADC with a 6X," Bud relayed to EOC. The Adult Detention Center is what the county calls its jail. It sounded more like a place for immigrants than miscreants, but one look at the bars, steel doors, and security systems and one knows it's a jail.

The prisoner was unloaded in a secured parking area under the jail. We took him into a holding area where Bud wrote up the paper work and appeared before a magistrate to get a warrant for DIP. The magistrate was behind a counter protected by a thick plexiglass window. He told the drunk that he would have to spend a few hours sleeping it off in jail. Later he would send someone to interview him to determine his level of sobriety before he could post bond. The drunk just wanted a bed.

When we opened the doors of the cruiser, we were assaulted by the acrid smell of urine. The drunk had left his mark all over the back seat and a puddle on the floor. Bud was beside himself with anger. And that guy beside him was using some heavy expletives. We marched back into the holding area and he grabbed some paper towels from the finger printing room.

Fortunately, our weak-bladdered drunk had been taken up to his cell, or we might have had some police brutality take place. Maybe some Chaplain brutality, too. I was a little perturbed myself.

Most of the damage was wiped up or soaked up, but the smell lingered on. We were in a Johnnie-On-The-Spot with lights and siren. Needless to say, we drove back to our area with the windows down. Before long it smelled like the stale smoke and sweaty vinyl I remembered.

At the station, guys were amazed that I had ridden the entire ten hour shift. So was I. I had put in seven or eight hours at the church office before coming over to the Police Station, and it dawned on me that I'd had a long day. Something told me that I'd have a lot of long days as I spread myself between church, station, and family.

"I really enjoyed having you with me tonight, Chaplain," said Bud as he carried my briefcase to my car for me. "I'll pass the word around that you're O.K., and that you're a good ride-along. Any maybe I'll see you at church on Sunday, too."

Shaking his hand I replied, "It was my pleasure, Bud. Remember, I'm available anytime you need me. Remind the rest of them to call me if something big goes down."

"Will do!"

"See ya later. I'll ride with you again real soon. I want to be where the action is."

Riding home it came to me that I hadn't seen my wife and children all day. And now at two A.M. they would surely be asleep. Was it worth the sacrifice? The cops weren't sure they wanted a chaplain. The church and my wife weren't sure I ought to be a chaplain. I had doubts about my ability to juggle my time, my talents, and my convictions in order to be a chaplain. Yet it was a dream come true for this closet soldier. It fulfilled my need for an adrenalin fix. I provided a service, a need, to a group that for the most part was alienated from society. Of course, they didn't know they needed me, but they would. Right then that circle was small. Just Bud. But that would change. I just knew it.

I discovered another occupational hazard for police chaplains that night. I couldn't unwind and fall asleep until 4 o'clock.

CHAPTER THREE

"Abduction, rape, and robbery—22:30 hours in Station two's area—last night." The sergeant had undivided attention now as he read the Daily Activity board. Certain words like 'abduction', 'murder, 'suicide', 'child missing', or 'signal 13'—officer needs help', are guaranteed to silence the rumble of roll call every time. We all waited for the gruesome details.

"Victims were Shirley Johnston, black female, D.O.B. of 6-3-59, and Josephine Matthews, black female, D.O.B. 1-27-58. Both have D.C. addresses.

"Victims called the P.D. from a phone booth on Van Buren Parkway. When Officer J.K. Smith arrived they filed a report claiming to have been abducted by two white males. They were taken from 14th Street in downtown Washington to a secluded area in McLean. They were then raped and their money was taken. The two men then released them on Van Buren. The suspects are described as being . . ."

The sergeant was drowned out by a chorus of groans and hoots from all the troops. How could they be so insensitive to what happened to those poor girls, I thought to myself.

"Oh sure, a couple of nuns!", exploded one usually calm cop.

"They were covering their rears from their pimp," said another. That helped me to start seeing the light.

"A couple of whores got picked up, turned a trick, got ripped off, and dumped," sneered the Corporal looking at my dumb-founded face. "And they got what was coming to 'em."

The tone of these "Choir Boys" was swelling to a dissonant chord. The cracks were a combination of amusement, disgust, and self-righteousness. I wasn't sure if I should scorn the street walkers or rebuke the conclusion leapers. I chose to quietly adopt the Fifth Amendment.

It wasn't long until they had vented their moral outrage, some in a rather vulgar vein, and returned their attention to the roll call routine.

In the past week I had ridden with about half of the men in E-Squad and A-Squad. Tonight I would be with B-Squad for the first time. These were all experienced officers with a number of years on the department. The youngest guy on the squad was a three year veteran named John Davis. He was an All-American looking fellow, who looked like he lived in a Harvard frat house. A college graduate who lettered in tennis and golf, John was on his way to the top in the department. Good looking, easy going, well liked, and the first man in B-Squad to have the Chaplain ride with him. It had something to do with gravity, because I heard one of the older officers whisper to him about things rolling down hill.

I was looking forward to riding with John. He was something

of an intellectual and I felt we would have some interesting discussions. For one thing, I wanted to know if there was more of a story behind his nickname, "Pretty Boy," than the obvious. Everybody had a nickname. Most of the ones I'd heard sounded like Mafia nicknames like John "Pretty Boy" Davis and Ron "the Pervert" Mitchell. Some were poetic, like Deke the Skete, Earl the Pearl, and Dave the Rave. Others had names that came off park benches or bathroom walls, like Killer, Thunder, Blackie, Hardnose, and General. So far I had been called "Rev" more that anything else, but a couple of the guys liked "Padre" and "Parson" a little better. I didn't like any of them, but then, that was the nature of nickname.

Everyone with whom I'd shared a cruiser was in my circle now. Each one started out reserved and suspicious, but eventually ended up enjoying the help and company I gave them. Nothing major had happened yet. I was still revelling in neophyte bliss. I'd directed traffic, carried DWI's off to jail, interviewed suspects, lost a foot race with a fleeing shoplifter, comforted victims of minor traffic accidents, helped break up a beer party some high school kids were having, and generally had a good time playing police. The guys really appreciated my willingness to help with everything. Word was spreading that I was an "all right guy". Except, inside me, things weren't all right.

What would I do when things "hit the fan", and they would. Two questions kept echoing in my mind. How far could I go in backing up a fellow officer, and what would I do when I was called on to help at the scene of a death? I'd conducted many funerals and visited the bereaved, but never at the scene and surrounded by men who were judging my every move. Not only did I not want to disappoint the grief stricken, but I didn't want to fail the officers who had been told they could count on me. It was just a matter of time before I would be called on to test my mettle.

John was not as talkative as I'd hoped he would be. Clearly, he was sharp and very conscientious. The routine complaints and traffic stops were handled courteously and professionally. He could have been used as a textbook example for the Police Academy classes. John was the epitome of the new breed of cop that the Department wanted. The days of "Dirty Harry" and "This is my town" approach to police work were gone. The Burger Court was hard on hot dog police. Street cops had to be Public Relations representatives, psychologists, and lawyers. The job was not to fight crime but please the tax payers, who elected the Board of Supervisors, who control the P.D. budget, which the Chief desperately wanted increased, who issued the orders that inevitably ended up as Departmental Memos to be read in roll call and obeyed by all.

At about 10 P.M., in Dave the Rave's patrol area, a burglar

alarm sounded at a driving range on Breedlow Road. When Dave arrived, a silver Toyota pick-up truck was pulling out from the parking lot. Dave immediately turned on his lights and siren, and marked in pursuit with EOC. It was a short-lived pursuit. At the first traffic light, the fleeing truck ran the red light and for no apparent reason lost control, and swerved off the road to the right striking a large oak tree head on. The suspect jumped from the truck and fled into the woods in front of his truck. Rather than chase him in the woods in the dark, Dave stayed with the wrecked truck, which had a stereo and TV in it from the range. Dave casually called EOC and had them send some backup units, a supervisor, and K-9. John and I were the first back-up unit to arrive.

Within minutes we had the area cordoned off. It was a small section of woods with roads on all four sides, so it was easy to cover. Now it was up to K-9. We listened to our radio and watched our assigned road.

"We're on a hot trail," the voice on the radio announced. The K-9 officer was using the override channel which was only heard by us and not EOC.

"There he is . . ." We waited in pained silence for several moments. What's going on—let's do something, I thought impatiently.

"K-9 three. Everything is 10-4. We have the suspect in custody. We need a unit to transport him to the hospital for minor injuries. My partner left his calling card on his leg." The air waves were filled with the clicking of keyed mikes.

John and I cleared the scene and continued to patrol our area. We both had a good laugh thinking about the K-9 officer's comment. John said that he knew the K-9 officer and he probably commanded his dog to bite him "Just for the fun of it." Talk about seat-of-the-pants justice . . .

Turning the cruiser down a secluded dirt road, John said, "Let's check on one of our prominent Toad families." Soon we came up on a small house with peeling white paint and dingy blue trim. Actually, to call it a house was being kind. Most people would call it a shack or even a dump. No one was sitting on the puny porch, which may have been due to the questionable stability of the two old rockers that resided there like ancient sentinels.

"This is the hole of the infamous Cooper clan," explained John. "They are criminal entrepreneurs of the first order. They supply the county with most of the PCP, Mary Jane, and cocaine which circulates in the drug world. We tried to burn 'em on several occasions, but all we've been able to do is get the oldest of the three sent up for six months on a minor distribution charge. Bud's the one who got him, and they've vowed to pay him back some day. And you know Bud. He's been hassling them every chance he gets just daring them to do something."

"If they're such big drug dealers, why do they live in such a dump?"

"Everyone asks that," said John. "It's believed that they have several other houses, some say they are mansions, out of state in Florida, California, and New York. The mother lives here with the youngest toad named Brian. The two bigger toads, Ralph and Jerry, come and go all the time. Sometimes they're gone months at a time. Probably buying dope in Mexico or South America. Who knows. But one look at them and you'll know they're toads through and through."

"I can hardly wait to see 'em," I said with sarcasm, but I was really serious. It would be interesting to see some real hard core crooks.

My imagination and education were interrupted by the radio. As always it had been noisy all through our discussion, but the urgency in Sergeant Scott's voice captured our attention.

"Car 5. There is a 9-1 on Route 3 just east of Golden Oak Road. Notify Fire Board, and send another Unit for traffic control."

A 9-I is an accident with injury, and from the tension in his voice it must have been a bad one. But since we were so far away from that area, we knew we wouldn't be called. At least, that's what we thought.

Five minutes later the Sergeant was back on the radio.

"Car 5. Change that to a 9-F, and send another unit for crowd control."

A fatality. But still it was another unit that was called.

Then it hit me. A fatality! That's when I'm supposed to be called! Lord, what am I going to do if they call me? My heart started pounding so hard I just knew John could hear it.

"Want me to start over that way in case they need you"? he asked. I tried to act calm, but I wanted to yell "No."

"They probably won't need me," I hoped, "but let's ease over in that general direction to be on the safe side." The safe side to me was China, but I knew that I couldn't run from the inevitable. If it wasn't this call, it would be another.

Not two minutes later the call I'd dreaded came.

"Car 5, We need another unit for crowd control. And have the Chaplain respond. The parents of the victim are at the scene."

My heart dropped. My first call for my first fatality and the parents were already on the scene. Not only that, but half the squad, two sergeants, and the station Captain were there also.

John drove Code 3 (lights and siren) down the mostly deserted streets. I prayed. I had no earthly idea what I was going to do when I got there. What a stupid idea it was to be a Police Chaplain. I had a police badge and a license to play cops and

27

robbers, now I had to pay the piper. This was my show-down at the O.K. Corral. I had to prove my worth to a bunch of officers who were not sure they needed me around. And right then, I wasn't sure I needed them or this.

Some memories are vague and cloudy when you recall them. One memory has been etched into my mind with the clarity of Waterford crystal, and that's the scene we witnessed as we came over the rise in the highway that looked down on the scene of the 9-F. It was a tapestry of red lights. The five police cruisers, two fire engines, ambulance, and flares, put a festive pall on the macabre site. The spotlights mounted on top of the fire engines lit up the woods and a small creek to the side of the road. A large crowd had gathered on the shoulder of the road and were being somewhat contained at a respectable distance from the scene by an officer.

John dropped me off in the middle of it, then went to assist with the crowd control. As I started towards the focus of the spot lights, I was met by Sergeant Scott and the Captain.

"We're glad you're here, Rev, we really need ya," said Scott. Taking me over to the edge of the small creek where everything was awash with light, he explained the situation to me.

A couple in a 1967 Nova SS were east bound on Rt. 3, a four lane highway, when they started to race another car. The Nova was in the fast lane, and after passing the other car, it changed lanes crossing in front of the other vehicle. Due to their inebriated condition, they lost control of their car, left the road to the right, went air born across the creek, and crashed into the trees on the other side. They were not seriously injured, but when they left the road they struck a sixteen year old boy who was riding to get a pizza at the Pizza Hut up the road. It was several minutes after the accident before Sergeant Scott discovered the boy's body in the creek several yards away from the wrecked car.

He showed me the car off in the woods to our left. It was truly strange to see taillights through the tree about four feet off the ground. One of the officers was busy taking pictures of it from various angles.

Then he walked me over to the creek, again to our left but only a few feet away, and pointed to an odd shape down in the creek water that at first looked like rocks. It was the young boy. Twisted like a rag doll, he was lying on his back with his head wrenched up and over his left shoulder. His left arm was bent back behind him as was his left leg. The shadows danced across his black skin giving him an inhuman appearance.

"Why hasn't he been taken away," I asked.

"We have to process the scene, and since he's dead, there's no hurry. The fewer things that are moved the more accurate the pictures and the evidence."

28

I was amazed at how calm they all were. There was a dead boy lying right there, and everyone was busily doing their jobs. There should have been dramatic music in the background, but instead there was the incessant roar of the big motors of the fire engines.

"The boy's name is Markus Franks. His mother and sister are over by the Captain's car," he said pointing back to the right. Out in the road, which had been closed down except for one lane, was the Captain's white Malibu. Behind the open back door, on the driver's side, stood a heavy set, black woman with both hands up to her face. Beside her stood a young girl of about fourteen, who was holding onto her mother, shaking with anxiety. Behind them both, stood a huge fellow with an Afro, who looked angry enough to kill.

"That big guy is the stepfather. We had to pull him off the driver of the Nova a while ago. He also wanted to go down into the creek to find out for sure if it was Markus. We haven't got a positive I.D. yet, but we feel pretty sure who it is. Come on. I'll introduce you to them."

As we walked over to them the mothers eyes widened with anticipation of news.

"Mrs. Franks, this Reverend Temple. He's our Police Chaplain, and . . ."

"Is it Markus? Please tell me. It must be him. He came this way twenty minutes ago and he hasn't come back yet," she blurted out at me.

"We don't know, Ma'am. The officers are still investigating the accident. It may be some time before we have all the information." It wasn't much, but it was all I could think of to say. The Sergeant left us, giving me a "you can handle it" nod.

"The best thing you can do right now is stay calm. You have to have hope too. You need to help each other be strong." I talked in a soft calm voice myself, remembering that it was important to model the kind of behavior I was asking for. The stepfather silently gritted his teeth. I could see his jaw muscles rippling along the sides of his head.

She did begin to relax a little, but she never took her eyes off the creek. Just when I was getting the young daughter to look at me and talk some, the rapport was shattered by a scream from the mother. She saw an officer come up out of the creek with a twisted ten speed bike and she immediately recognized it as her son's.

She tried to run over to it, but I held her in place behind the car door. When Sergeant Scott saw her reaction, he held up a hand and indicated that I should hold her there.

She began yelling, "Markus. Markus. That's my baby down there. I need to go to him." The daughter was crying and the stepfather became even more agitated.

"I must know," she said gripping the car door and looking intently toward the creek.

Through soft, but insistent, talking, I was able to diffuse the tension for the moment. The stepfather was inching his way around us. I could see a plan of action formulating in his eyes, and I knew that I'd have to do something to restrain him from going down into the creek. There was no way that I was going to grab him and hold him in place like I was doing with the ladies. An old joke crossed my mind that had a punch line which was apropos. 'He goes any where he wants to.' This guy was twice my size, and if he decided to go into the creek, well, let the cops handle it.

I decided to solve this mess with some preventative action. I stepped in front of the distressed stepfather, and looking him in the chin I suggested, "Why don't you stay with your wife and daughter, help them, and I'll go talk to the investigators and see if we can't settle this now?"

Looking past me to the creek, he grunted something that I interpreted as approval, and stepped over beside his wife. I turned and walked to where Sergeant Scott was directing things.

"What's the normal procedure for getting a positive I.D. on the victim," I asked, hoping I used all the correct terminology.

He paused for a second and replied, "Well, before long we'll transport the body to the hospital where the Medical Examiner will clean it up a bit, and then we'll have the family come in and I.D. the body. Or, at least a member of the family."

"Is that a law, or a required way that it has to be done?"

"No, not really. It's just the standard procedure. Why?"

"Well, this is not a good situation, keeping the family hanging around and not knowing for sure if it's their relative. Why not let the stepfather go over there and give us a positive I.D. Then I can get the family back home, and there will be less confusion around here."

Scott was a very sensitive and sensible man. He described himself as a lay-Methodist preacher. I knew that he, like myself, felt for the boys family. But he had a reputation for being a "by-the-book" supervisor, and he was mentally computing what the repercussions would be if he changed the S.O.P.

"If that were my boy down there," he said, scratching his chin, "it would take an army of cops to keep me away from him. Give me a minute to set it up with the I.D. guys, and have them turn off the spotlights. We'll lead him over there with flashlights. I'll wave when we're ready."

He quickly turned and went towards the fire engine. I returned to the family, who were anxiously waiting for me.

Standing between them and the scene, I got eye contact with the stepfather and said, "In a moment we'd like for you to go with the Sergeant into the creek to see if you can identify the

30

victim. Can you do that?"

He grunted and slowly nodded his head yes. I thought I detected a noticeable shiver in his shoulders, but it may have been just the shadows. His wife gripped his right arm with both hands and rolled her forehead back and forth across his biceps. The young girl had sat back down on the car seat with her feet on the pavement and her head in her hands.

Looking over my shoulder I saw that Scott was half-way to us, and he signaled for the father to come on over. Before I could turn back around to the family, the stepfather was past me and on his way to the sergeant.

Standing beside the mother and daughter, I watched as the two men disappeared into the shadows. The entire creek area was black with darkness now that the spotlights were off. There was only the red glow from the cruisers, fire engines, and flares. Maybe it was my imagination, but it seemed to get glaringly quiet too.

In the creek, flashlight beams and reflections danced around like giant lightening bugs. But it wasn't the beauty of nature we were watching. It was the horrifying result of man's irresponsibility. These were not actors in some television drama, but real people with real feelings and real loss. A large hammer was pounding in my chest and every time the thought would cross my mind 'what if that were my child lying in that creek,' the hammer beat with a vengeance. So I tried not to think about anything but doing my job. I had to help these folks, and to do that, I had to be strong, compassionate, and in control. How can you stay detached when your job is to care? I could tell that was going to possibly be the greatest challenge I'd have as a chaplain.

The lone figure of the stepfather walked from the shadows of the creek towards us. With head bowed, the once proud and erect black man was noticeably smaller. His arms were hanging at his side like loose rope. He seemed to have lost all his strength and vitality. As he circled us. causing us to pivot with our backs to the catastrophe, the mother and daughter held their breath in anticipation of his pronouncement.

With quivering lower lip and a whisper he said, "It's Markus."

There was an instantaneous surging of bodies coming together and an equally instantaneous wail of grief. With arms and heads entangled they became a huddle of mutual pain. I stood there feeling more helpless than I'd ever felt in my life. Surely there was something I could do or say that would make everything all right? But there was nothing. They would determine what happened next. All I could do was stand there and wait for them to recover from the initial shock. For now I was just a witness to writhing, an intruder on the periphery of private misery.

31

To stand by quietly and say nothing is hard. Through the years I've seen doctors who couldn't just bring the bad news but felt compelled to explain all the reasons for the death and all the things they did to try and prevent it. They couldn't just stand there and let the family grieve and accept their own helplessness. Police can't just notify people that a loved one was fatally injured in an auto accident. They continue to tell all the details and the facts. That's not the time to tell them that "the so-and-so who caused it was drunk and uninjured." It's hard to be helpless.

After about five minutes the father looked up at me with mournful eyes that said, "What now?"

"There's nothing that you can do here" I said. "I think it's time for you to go to your home. You can help each other better there and you'll probably want to make a few phone calls to relatives too. Where's your car?"

He pointed up the road beyond where the spectators were being contained. Placing my hands on the ladies' shoulders I guided them in that direction. It was slow moving at first because they still clung to each other, but after a few steps they settled for being arm-in-arm.

As we passed, the crowd became silent and stared intently at the stricken family. The people were curious, but sympathetic. Some, maybe friends, were even crying for the family's loss.

A short way past the spectators, the father pointed, for my benefit, to a pale green pick-up truck parked on a side street. When we got to the truck, I helped the mother, then the daughter, into the passenger's side as the father got in behind the wheel.

Through the open window the mother asked, "What's gonna happen to Markus?"

Assuming she was talking about the body and not asking a spiritual question, I answered, "In a few moments he will be taken to the county hospital. By law, the Medical Examiner must determine the exact cause of death." The word 'death' almost got stuck in my throat. "What you need to do tomorrow morning sometime, is call a funeral home and they will take care of everything for you. There's no need for you to go down to the hospital at all."

She must have still been in shock, because her face was blank, registering no reaction to my comments, just mumbling a hushed, "O.K."

"If you have any questions about anything else, or if I can help you in any way, just call the police station and ask for the chaplain. They can reach me any time day or night."

The father leaned over and said, "Thanks. We appreciate your help. We're gonna be all right."

I guess I was shocked to hear from the man for the first

time, because before I could say another word, he'd started the truck and pulled out into the flow of traffic.

A plethora of emotions plundered my mind. I was numb from the overload of new experiential information that had so rapidly been crammed into my brain. Yet, I was soaring from the adrenalin high. I was relieved to have the family out of the way, but my heart was aching for them and I wished there was something more I could have done for them. I was elated because I'd done my job, but crushed because I was powerless to help where it really counted. To say I had mixed feeling would be a terrible understatement. It was like hitting a home run that gave someone in the grand stands a concussion. Do you cheer or cry? Praise, pray, or spit? Maybe all three.

I volunteered for this? I could cruise through life doing my pastoral duties and never do anything more painful than eulogize some elderly Christian who died in their sleep. Don't I want a nice peaceful parish where I can grow white, wide, and wise? No. There are plenty of pious polyester preachers standing in line for jobs like that. I want to make a difference, and no one is standing in line to help folds scrape their child up off the highway.

Walking back down to the scene of the accident, the red lights cast a surrealistic murkiness which fed the introspective state I was lost in. The luxury of tuning out the tragedy was short lived, however. At the same moment I returned, a car screeched to a halt across the highway and discharged a teenage girl and an elderly couple who charged across the road, oblivious to on-coming traffic, screaming, "Markus, Markus!"

The skinny, old man with a cane, the short, heavy-set old woman, and the wiry, fifteenish girl somehow made it past the one open land without becoming like Markus. I grabbed the young girl and held her until the older couple caught up to her. By then Scott was there to corral them. All three were hysterical and each one talked as if the other two weren't there. Piecing it together, we discovered the couple were the grandparents of Markus and the girl was his cousin. A neighbor of the Franks had called, told them about the accident, and they came right over. They asked a battery of questions which we politely ignored as we herded them back to their car. I told them that the family was already home by now and that was were they needed to be.

Scott stopped the traffic while I directed them into their car. Then I, in true traffic cop style, guided them onto the highway and down the road. Everyone cut loose a huge sigh of relief as their taillights disappeared over the hill. I was too drained and numb to spend any more time empathizing. It was time to switch channels and find some cartoons.

"Hey Rev!" came a voice from the shadows. It was Sam

Hicks, the County's accident investigation expert. "We're gonna nail this sucker good," he said with a big smile showing from under his bushy mustache. "He was drunk as heck and he was at least twenty miles over the speed limit."

Not only was I intrigued, but I was ready for an escape from my present ruminations. "That right? How You gonna prove it in court?"

His eyes sparkled. "Elementary my dear Chaplain." The English accent was decidedly more Hollywood than Holmes. "The pecker-head blew a point two-one on the breathalizer. The measurements and calculations on the skid marks show that he was doing nearly seventy when he left the road and hit the kid. And this little baby here will show that he was doing over sixty when he impacted the trees cross the creek."

In his hands he held a small object about the size of a pie plate, except it was more oblong. Stepping over next to him I recognized it as the speedometer panel of a car—the panel that has all the mile per hour increments painted on it.

"Is that from the Toads car?" I couldn't believe that he just tore it out of the guys car.

"You bet your a-a-a . . . , I mean your life. On impact, the speedometer slams against this plate and scratches the paint permanently recording the speed at impact. What's even better, when you put this under a blacklight, the fluorescent paint from the speedometer needle lights up around the P-O-I, point of impact, like a neon sign."

"All right! Stick it to him!" I was impressed.

"We ought to save the citizens a bundle of money and just shoot the turkey. I recognized the guy right away. This is the second person he's killed with a car. Two years ago he drove up into a man's front yard and killed him. The man he killed had just cleaned his plow for smarting off to him. So he jumped in his car and ran him down. The courts, in their infinite dip-stick wisdom, gave him three years of prison and he was out in nine months. Maybe they'll really put him away this time. Still, one double-o-mag from my 870 would be a lot cheaper."

The smile had disappeared and the sparkle turned to glaze. People who believe that cops stay emotionally detached from their cases have never been around them very much.

"We could just give the stepfather ten undisturbed minutes with the guy. That would do the trick." I said that with a laugh, but to my sudden dismay, I realized I was serious in my heart. My laugh caught in my throat. I didn't believe in violence, vengeance, and hate. Was I starting to be like the cops instead of leading them to be like me? Maybe I really didn't know myself as well as I thought.

Trying to recover from the slip, I quickly added, "But, as much as we don't like it, the jerk deserves a fair trial and he is still innocent until you help prove him guilty."

"Sure, Rev," he groaned. "It's just a crying shame that the courts didn't do their job right the first time. They ought to be out here and see what their 'justice' did for this boy and his family. And the worst part of it is that they'll probably screw it up again this time."

"Hey, have some faith, Man. Maybe he'll go up before a 'Hanging Judge'", I said with an obvious positive voice, and a friendly pat on his shoulder.

"Wishful thinking, Rev. Hey, the guys were talking about you a few minutes ago. You done good tonight. Just about the entire station was out here at one time or another, and they all saw the way you helped out. I'd say you just made yourself valuable to us tonight. Next time I'm out patrolling, why don't you ride with me a while. We'll shake up some Toads and stroke some good citizens for speeding."

"That sounds great. You've just been moved to the top of my Ride-along Victim list. I'll catch you at the station tomorrow or the next day, and we can wreak havoc throughout the county."

Walking away from Sam, I wanted to say, "Thanks for the compliment," but somehow that seemed a little too effusive for the moment. Yet, I was ten feet off the ground because what he'd actually said was, "You're accepted now," and that was worth more than a medal. For the time being, the calamity of the accident was shelved and replaced by a feeling of pride, warmth, and victory.

The sergeant, corporal, and two officers turned towards me as I approached them. They had been having a casual bull session as they watched the rescue unit load the boy's body into the ambulance.

"I was some-kind-of glad to see you arrive tonight Chaplain," said Sergeant Scott. "You did a good job of taking care of the family for us so we could get this mess finished up."

"I'm glad I was able to help. I didn't do much to help them, but if it made your job easier—well, I'm glad I could be here." That was profound, I thought to myself. Why is it difficult to accept compliments?

"I should have had you come over and calm down that crowd of spectators," said the corporal. "They were really a pain in the neck. I thought they were going to assault us when we wouldn't let them get closer to the gore."

One of the officers chimed in, "What would the Chaplain do, have a prayer with them? I can see it in the paper now, 'Police Chaplain Beat Up By Angry Crowd.'" They all chuckled.

I reached over and took Scott's five cell flashlight from under his arm. Holding it like a club in my right hand, I struck my left hand with it twice. Then with as serious a look as I could muster, I said, "No one beats up on this Chaplain."

"All right!" hooted the officer. They all loved it and they all laughed.

"The radical Rev with the mean flashlight," said Scott.

The other officer who hadn't said anything yet, was Nat Kawalski, a former New York city cop. He was tall, broad shouldered, dark-complected, and quiet, but he was about as gung-ho as a cop could be. He loved his job and literally bounced when he walked. We'd talked a couple of times in the station, but it was brief, as we passed in the hall. I had decided that he probably didn't care much for having a Chaplain around.

Speaking with a heavy Bronx accent, Nat said, "Well, Chaplain, I don't know about the other guys, but I think you were worth your weight in gold tonight."

The others nodded their heads in agreement.

It was nearly 3 A.M. when I walked into my darkened house. I had to step over several Matchbox cars and trucks to reach the bed where my son slept. I kissed him lightly on the forehead. My daughter was lying on top of her Cabbage Patch doll so I had to move it before I kissed her on the cheek.

I managed to slide into bed without waking up my wife. The last thought I had before I passed out from exhaustion was that my circle of acceptance with the Police was decidedly larger after tonight's experience.

CHAPTER FOUR

The townhouses on both sides of the street were burning. The flames seemed to be leaping for the sky from the backside of the homes, giving them a ghostly silouette on the street side. Debris with odd jagged shapes cluttered the side-walks, yards, and streets. Everything had a reddish hue as the smoke and flames danced phantom-like apparitions over the scene. It was war.

In the middle of the street, a lone figure lay sprawled out, motionless, and wearing a Police uniform. I raced to his side and rolled him over.

"Oh my God! It's Bud! He's hurt! But I don't see any blood. His pulse? Check his pulse. All right, he's alive. But what happened? What do I need to do?"

For some reason I was dripping with sweat, and had black smudges all over my face and hands. My heart was pounding like a drum. I could feel the skin stretched around my eyes as they widened to their maximum.

Panic had it's icy fingers in my stomach. I had to do something quick. Bud's life depended on it. Should I go get help? No! I couldn't leave him alone. I had to protect him. From what? I didn't know but I had to stay by his side.

Frantically surveying the scene to see if someone was available to help, I caught some movement at the far end of the street. I started to yell for help, but instinctively I knew that the faint figure coming our way was the enemy.

His profile became clearer as he slowly, with measured steps, came down the center of the street, the battle-zone. He was tall, with a lean muscular build that gave his silhouette clean, sharp lines. His long arms were down and about at a thirty degree angle from his sides. Almost as an extension of his right arm, I could clearly see the barrel of a .44 magnum.

"This is crazy. Didn't I see this in a Clint Eastwood movie once? This is for real. He's going to kill us both. What do I do? I could run. No. I've got to protect Bud. With what? His police revolver."

I reached down and took Bud's gun out of his holster. It was just like one that was part of my gun collection. A S&W model 15 with a four-inch barrel. A nice shooting piece, and quite accurate. It felt good in my hand,. The cold metal slid around in my sweaty palm so I gripped it tighter.

Looking back at our protagonist, I was surprised to discover how close he was. Still just a shadowy figure, he was only twenty steps away. With each step he began to bring his cannon up to a shooting position.

"I've got to shoot now or die. But I don't want to!"

Fifteen steps.

I grabbed my gun with both hand and aimed it at the man.
Twelve.

"Pull the trigger now! Do it for Bud!"
Nine.

With teeth clenched and muscles tensing in anticipation of the pistol's kick, I squeezed the trigger.

Click. Nothing. An empty chamber.
Six steps.
Click. "My God what's happening!"
Five steps. "Why can't I see his face!"
Click. Click. Click.

The huge barrel was only inches from my gun. I knew it was about to explode and take my head off. I squeezed the trigger for the last time.

KA-boom! White-red-flashing!

I was sitting up in bed when I awoke. My left hand was knotted up in the sheet and my right hand was in a fist. The fingernails were digging into the palms, almost bringing blood.

It was all I could do to be civil at the breakfast table. It wasn't the family's fault that I was being haunted by a dream, but it was hard not to be grumpy. The kids just assumed that I was behind in my sleep. My wife knew that something was eating at me.

After herding the youngsters off to school, I recounted the dream to my wife.

"The worst part is that I don't know if it was a nightmare because I was going to kill a man, or he was going to kill me, or because the gun wouldn't work."

"Well Honey," she said in her soft soothing Georgia accent, "it sounds to me like you were doing the only thing you could do. You couldn't let a bad guy hurt one of your guys could you?"

The only thing my wife knew about crime was from watching T.V., and she had the emotional security of seeing the whole 'cops and robbers' business as simple Black and White morality. Plus, we'd had Bud over for dinner a couple nights before, just after my first fatality, and she took a liking to the young, bouncy boy cop. Like our church family, any officers she met she considered "one of ours".

"I suppose you're right." I said, giving 'suppose' a strong questioning emphasis. "But it goes against all I believe for me to intentionally take a life. Life is sacred. I'm supposed to be a 'Peacemaker' not a 'Widow maker'."

My eyebrows were furrowed as I spoke with deep conviction. She knew quite well how I felt. We'd been together too many years and she'd probably heard too many sermons from me on the subject. Yet to her, there was nothing taxingly complex about my problem. She was only vaguely aware of the conflict in my heart between a cultivated conscience and an intrinsic machismo.

In her own inimitable way the solution was obvious.

"Honey, maybe you don't need to be a Police Chaplain."

I didn't want to hear that, but I had to slowly nod my head in agreement and whisper, "Maybe.".

All day long I went through the motions of doing my job. The morning was spent visiting in the hospitals and the afternoon in shuffling paper at my office. Fortunately, nothing required deep thinking because I was lost in thought trying to interpret my dream. I needed Joseph to come out of the Bible and help me. Was God trying to tell me something? Was it a prediction? Was it a sign of a psychological problem? Or maybe it was just a bad dream.

I decided the best way to get over this "dropped pass" was to get back into the game. So after dinner with the family, I went to the station and had Bud called in off the street to pick me up.

As I opened the passenger door of the cruiser, Bud was pulling all his paraphernalia from the passenger seat to a disorganized pile in the middle.

"Hey, Rev," he said with a mischievous smile on his face."You got your Killer flashlight with ya don't ya?"

"You bet your badge I do, and it's loaded for bear too."

I'd learned something very important about cops. Rumors and stories travel through a Police Station faster than gossip at a ladies quilting Bee. It had been a week since the fatality and not only did everyone know about the help I gave, but everyone knew about my flashlight comment. They were really getting a kick out of teasing me about it too. I'd been called "Father Flashlight", "Kilowatt Killer", and "The Five-Celled Conan". One night when I was out riding with one of the guys, a Corporal called for me over the radio to come help with a family dispute. At the end of his transmission he added, "And be sure and bring your flashlight with you." That attracted a few seconds of clicking.

I feigned irritation to the cops, but I loved it. One of the truest forms of acceptance is 'kidding'.

"Let's go pillage and plunder, and, in general, make life miserable for Toads," said Bud as he whipped the cruiser out into the flow of traffic.

"Ah, a man after my own heart," I said in my atrocious W.C. Fields voice. "Let us make the world a safer place for women and children." I was feeling better already.

After a few minutes of searching the highway for a law breaker, we settled into an easy patrol in a residential area. That allowed us to talk with fewer distractions.

"You've been the number one topic of discussion around the station lately," offered Bud.

"I hope it hasn't all been bad."

"No, it's been pretty favorable. I think most of the guys have decided that having a Chaplain is a pretty good idea. Or, at least they've decided having you around is a good idea. We were all paranoid about getting a Chaplain because we assumed we'd get some stuffy old pain-in-the-neck clergyman, who'd preach at us about drinkin', smokin', and cursin'. We didn't want no wimpy Chaplain either. I like having you ride with me cause I know you'll jump in there and help and not just pray. I mean, nothing against praying, but sometimes you need a hand, not talk."

"Well I'm glad you brought that up. I've been meaning to talk to you about your drinking, smoking, and cursing. You want to pray about it?"

Expletive.

"See!" I slapped him on the arm as we laughed at my sham.

Two traffic tickets and one false burglar alarm later, Bud dumped a little cold water on my good feelings.

"Just to warn you, Old Hardnose said the other day that he didn't trust you and that he didn't plan on using you for anything. He's just a real cautious guy and I think, I'm not absolutely sure about this, but I think he's had some bad run in in the past with a preacher. Anyway, he doesn't care much for any preacher and for now that includes you."

I didn't know what to think about that. I wasn't terribly surprised. Sergeant Charles E. Hinckley was not well liked by anyone. He was gruff, crude, and demanding. Hence his nickname, Hardnose. Sometimes he was called Hardhead and sometimes he was called Heartless, but at all times it was behind his back.

The worst part about his being outside my circle was the influence he had on his squad. If he didn't need me that was one thing, but his squad needed to feel free to call on me if I could assist them.

"I've ridden with several of the D-squad guys and they seemed to be pretty receptive to me. Do you think he'll influence them to not call on me?"

"Naw! They all like ya just fine. They're use to ignoring him. They're the ones who gave him the name Hardnose. He's a smart supervisor, and he's got a lot of good things to teach, but everyone knows to take what he says advisedly. He can be mean but he really knows his stuff. He's a guy I'd want to back me up in a tough situation. Don't worry about it. He'll come around in his own sweet time."

"Yeah, I guess I'll have to work on him a while." I said feeling in my heart that it was a hopeless cause.

"Whoa!" yelled Bud, but he did just the opposite as he floored the gas pedal. "Is that a Cooper Toad that just ran that stop sign up there?"

I didn't think he wanted an answer since he had a sinister smile on his face.

Cooper? Weren't they the family of drug dealers who vowed vengeance on Bud for hassling them so much? Weren't they supposed to be dangerous? Did he really run a stop sign? I had been so busy talking that I didn't see it.

The vehicle was a faded maroon Dodge van adorned with bright yellow lightning streaks down the sides. It had a Confederate flag covering the back windows and a personalized license stamped DUDE. From the roar of the motor, it probably had a souped up engine.

In obedience to our lights and siren the van pulled off on the right shoulder of the road. As soon as Bud notified EOC of our location, and reported the van's tag, we hopped out of the cruiser. Bud inched up on the driver's side with his hand resting on his revolver. I walked up on the passenger side armed menacingly with my faithful five cell.

The driver was a young guy with sandy blond hair and a reddish beard. His lip curled in a vicious, rebellious disdain for the officer who was taking his driver's license and vehicle registration. He said nothing. He just looked straight ahead and gritted his teeth.

The passenger's seat was occupied by an attractive, curvaceous brunette. Even with her face twisted in a sneer, she was very pretty. Her designer cloths, jewelry, and hair accentuated her looks and identified her as a chic lady. Like her driver, she acted like I wasn't even there.

I walked back to the cruiser, and sat down on th edge of the seat with the door open. Bud was filling out a traffic summons and enjoying himself.

"This here Toad is Brian Cooper, the youngest of the clan. I've tagged all three of em now at least twice. Brian has got the cleanest record, but he's so heavy into drug distribution he ought to have a Columbian name. From the fat cats to the kids, he supplies the goodies—he and his brothers. When your kids are offered drugs in the halls of their elementary school you can be sure of where it came from." He nodded his head towards the van.

"Why are they so hard to catch?" I was appalled.

"They're good at it. They've been at it a long time now and they've learned how to cover their tails. That's why I hassel 'em every chance I get. I figure they may make a mistake, and when they do I want to be there to bust some heads."

"Aren't you concerned about their threat to pay you back? If these guys are that well organized, it would be nothing for them to arrange for a hit."

"Naw. These guys are a bunch of hot air bullies. I wish

they'd try something. I'd love to use them for target practice. In fact, I think we need a closer look at Mr. Cooper. I think I detected the smell of alcoholic beverages coming from him."

He bolted out the door and stormed up to the van. I quickly retraced my steps back to the passenger side.

Bud politely asked Cooper to step out of the van, but there was an obvious 'refuse and make my day' tone in his voice. He escorted the much shorter man to the area between the van and the cruiser. Cooper did everything he was told but he clearly was steamed about the whole thing.

After having him do a couple sobriety tests, the kind that make you feel like a ballerina or a slob, Bud let him go with only a traffic ticket. The slamming of the van door was followed by the famous "Have a nice day".

Back on patrol I asked Bud, "How is it that a low-life like that has such a beautiful girl with him? That seems to happen a lot. We see Toads and the pretty girls see Princes." I chuckled to myself thinking about my analogy.

"They definitely don't hang around them because they're such good looking and lovable guys. These guys give them all the dope and money they need and in return the girls give them, well, let's just say they satisfy all their fantasies. Plus, drugs and money are power. There are always good looking chicks who like to be close to power. You and I are just in the wrong line of work if we want to attract girls."

"Speak for yourself. I'll have you know that after I preach on Sunday the ladies are all over me. Of course they're sixty and seventy year old ladies but, hey, life's full of small thrills."

"You can keep that small thrill," said Bud with mock seriousness.

After wreaking havoc on the citizens of our fair country for a couple more hours, I was ready to call it quits for the night. It was about 1:30 in the A.M., and all was quiet on the county's western front. There was no traffic on the road or the radio, and I was talked out and sleepy.

"Let's mosey toward the station. I'm ready for a little 10-42 action." 10-42 is 'out of service at home'.

"You got it. It is kinda boring tonight. I'll just let EOC know what we're fixing to do so they won't assign us some rinky-dink complaint before I get you back to the station." He reached for his mike and, without my seeing it, switched to channel 8, the override channel that doesn't go through EOC.

"Scout 525," said Bud

"Scout 525," responded a familiar voice I was too sleepy to fully identify.

"Scout 525 will be 10-6 transporting Chap 5 to Station 5."

"10-4 Scout 525. 01:33."

Since we were on the extreme western edge of the county, it

was a good fifteen minute drive back to the station. Five minutes into the return trip, however, the radio cracked with the voice of Sergeant Scott.

"Scout 525, stand by for a special assignment."

"Scout 525. 10-4 go ahead."

"Scout 525, proceed to Oakview Shopping Center and prepare a landing zone for Chopper One. It's a VIP deposit. You copy?"

"Scout 525 direct. Hold us in route."

Now I was wide awake, "Do what?", I asked, displaying my ability to make insightful inquiries.

"For some reason, they're using the PD chopper to transport some VIP to Oakview. This time of night we often use shopping center parking lots to pick up or drop off people. Usually it's for a medivac after a 9-I or something like that. But, we do all kinds of things for VIP's too. Once I had to set up a landing zone for a drop and it turned out to be the Governor."

This was starting to sound interesting. The adrenalin was flowing at the prospect of getting to met the Governor or a Senator. "How do we set up a landing zone? Aren't there lights in the parking lot?"

"Only about a third of 'em are on this time of night. The most important part is laying out a large circle for them to land in that will keep them away from electrical and guide wires. So we'll make a circle with flares about forty yards in diameter. Boy, I'm glad I stuck an extra case of flares in the trunk today."

Oakview was back in the area we just came from, so we were there in five minutes. It wasn't much of a shopping center with only a medium size Kroger, a Peoples Drug, and a small dry cleaners. It did have a large parking lot with widely-spaced pole lights. As Bud predicted, only about a third of them were on. So most of the empty parking lot was dark or in shadows. On one side of the lot was a rural road and woods. The other side had a large open field that rose up to a short ridge.

Coming to a stop in the middle of the parking lot, we quickly checked for wires. Finding none, we popped the trunk and took out a case of flares. Just as Bud tore open the waxy cardboard box lid, his portable radio came to life with the voice of the Sergeant again.

"Scout 525."

Pulling his radio out of his belt holder, Bud answered, "Scout 525."

"Scout 525, I need you to respond to 516 Pine Branch Court ASAP. Can the Chaplain handle the landing zone by himself?"

Bud just looked at me questioningly and I said, "Sure".

I panicked for a second then decided that it might be interesting to be the only one here to receive the VIP.

"That's 10-4 Car 5. Chap 5 will cover the landing. I'll be in route."

As he ran around to get in his cruiser, Bud shouted, "Put a flare about every two feet and don't let 'em go out before you replace them with a new one. Got your portable?"

"Aaa, no!" I grabbed it off the front seat and shut the door as he squealed away leaving me alone in a huge parking lot with a radio, a flashlight, and a case of flares.

I stood there a second thinking about how quiet and spooky it was. Then I shook my head free from those thoughts and went to work lighting flares.

I could only carry five or six flares with me at a time. Even that required some amazing contortionist moves to prevent igniting more than one at a time. I laid down the few I had then ran back to the case and grabbed another handful. It took several minutes to lay out about thirty flares. Each one had wires that had to be bent, giving them a frame to stand up on.

I stepped back to view my creation. It was more an oval than a circle. I ran around and repositioned several flares. Now, that was more like a circle.

I walked around the outside perimeter of the glowing circle, occasionally checking the sky for a helicopter. I'd been present before at a medivac and I knew at night you always heard choppers long before you saw them. Still, I couldn't help but search for the incoming VIP.

Where's Bud? Why's the radio so quiet? I hit the squelch switch to test it and it was 10-4. I was proud of my landing zone. I knew I'd get a few that-a-boys for it.

I was tempted to call the Sergeant on the radio but I had very little experience talking on it and I didn't quite have the jargon right yet. Besides, if there were a change in plans they'd call me. They needed to do something soon because the first flares already needed to be replaced.

How long had I been there, I wondered. They were thirty minute flares so I must have been there at least that long.

One by one I started placing new lighted flares beside the old ones. I hadn't gone far when I lit the last flare. There are only fifty to a case. What was I going to do? Call for some more flares? What if they went out before the chopper arrived?

I started to pace and panic. The only choice I had was to call for some more flares. The radio was quiet. Maybe they called the whole thing off and forgot to tell me. And where was Bud?

I jerked the radio up to my mouth, but before I could speak into it, it spoke to me.

"Chaplain," the voice was Scott's. "Go to channel 8."

I was careful to respond properly. "This is Chaplain 5, go ahead."

"We wish to commend you for a job well done. I've never seen such a pretty circle of flares. Please turn towards the field

44

to your right and receive your applause."

"What?" I turned toward the field and on the small ridge sat ten Police cruisers. In unison they turned on their head lights, emergency lights, and honked their horns.

I'd been had.

When we got back to the station there was more laughing and back slapping than at a political convention. I did more than anybody. I knew this story would be all over the county in a couple of hours, but I didn't mind. I felt like I deserved it for being so gullible about seeing a VIP.

"Chaplain, you've really got a flair for Police work"

How many times did I hear that.

"I understand you saw the light tonight"! Others were singing "You light up my life."

"Need a ride home Rev? We can call in a chopper for ya!"

They all had fun at my expense and I didn't begrudge them their reward. Wherever there's an expense there's a debt and I wanted them to be indebted to me. Right now it was for a good laugh but later it might be for life.

Getting into my car to go home I took a deep breath and relaxed a minute. It had been an interesting night and I'd remember it for a long time to come.

As I reached forward to turn the ignition I noticed something on the passenger seat. It was a flare. One of them had used a slim-Jim to get into my car and place it there. It had a small stick'em note on it.

JUST IN CASE YOU NEED A LIGHT TO GUIDE YOU BACK TO THE STATION TOMORROW. GOOD NIGHT REV.

CHAPTER FIVE

"Listen up. We've got an important memo from the Ivory Tower," said Hardnose Hinckley, as he wrapped up the 4 to 2 roll call.

Changing into his official "from-the-top" voice, he read, "Be advised that from this date on the Department will no longer be responsible for any damage to citizen's vehicles as a result of officers helping them get into cars in which they have been locked out of."

As expected, he was interrupted by hoots, groans, and various curses. Just about everyone carried a Slim Jim with them because slipping car door locks was the most often "citizen needs help" call they received. Many of them took great pride in their ability to 'crack' any door made. Plus, it was the source of many "that-a-boy" letters from the public, every one of which became a permanent part of the officer's Department file.

Several decibels louder, Hinckley continued with the memo. "Due to a large number of requests from citizens for payment of damages to their vehicle doors, the County has paid out a considerable amount of money. We do not wish at this time to discontinue this practice of helping 'locked out citizen', but from this date on you will perform this help using your own discretion. The County will not cover any damage you cause to said vehicles. Any and all damages incurred will be the responsibility of the officer who caused them."

There was some statistical garbage on an attachment to the memo, but the guys were beyond listening to a rationale for the directive. To them it was just another pain in the neck from the jokers in white shirts. The 'Desk Patrol' or 'Brownnose Brigade,' as they were called, were not considered 'real cops' but rather mutants. Every street cop who was promoted to white shirt rank, vowed to his compatriots that he'd never change. "I'll always be a street cop at heart", they'd say. Then in the scramble, to impress the Chief, they straightway forgot the slobs on the street and jumped on the bandwagon of making life miserable for the troops.

With a half grin on his face, the Sergeant pointed his finger at one of the rookies and said, "Translating this memo for the public you say . . ."

The squeaky-voiced rookie put a bogus smile on his face and said, "Sorry Ma'am, but we are not responsible for any damage we do to your vehicle with this Slim Jim . . ."

"No, no, no!" interrupted Hinckley. "That still has your tail in a sling."

One of the older cops from the back joined in without being called on. "Sorry, Ma'am, but I don't have a Slim Jim. I'd be happy to call a locksmith for you. They only charge a hundred and fifty bucks to come out this time of night."

"Now you got it!" cheered Hinckley. There was scattered applause and laughter.

"Anyone have anything further? . . . Corporal? . . . Chaplain? . . . O.K. Let's do it."

Before I had a chance to tag someone for a ride along, the imposing frame of Sergeant Charles "Hardnose" Hinckley loomed over my right shoulder. When our eyes connected, in a muted voice, he said, "Can I talk with you a minute in the Supervisor's office?" He turned and headed that way before I could answer him. What was I going to say, "No, I don't want to talk to you because you don't like me and you're undermining my efforts with the troops." I don't think anybody ever said "no" to Hardnose Hinckley.

Hinckley had a Tom Selleck mustache and that's where the similarities ended. He was twice the size of ole Magnum, and Magnum's pretty big. With a thick stock of wavy coal black hair that enhanced his intimidating presence, Hinckley could easily have been mistaken for a tank or at least the right side of the Redskins offensive line. At 6'6" and 275 pounds, he was in control of every situation he was in. Or at least it seemed like he was. He ran a tight squad and had a couple of Valor awards. Other than being somewhat reserved, he was a Cop's cop. He chain-smoked Winstons and had a few cold ones after each shift at the Police Association Hall.

"Close the door," he said as I walked into the office. He was behind one of the ancient gray metal desks, reclining in a rickety chair that I fully expected to see shatter any second. We were alone, with billowing swirls of cigarette smoke looking for a clean Chaplain's sports coat to sink into.

"Listen Chaplain," I wished he'd said Mark. The way he said 'Chaplain' sounded cold and formal. " . . . you know that cops are overly paranoid of outsiders. Well, the guys seem to like you well enough, but there is some concern over all the notes you take in your 007 book. They want to know who it's for and what you plan to do with it. It may sound silly, but I thought you should be told."

Unbelievable! I was dumbfounded. I noticed how neatly he separated himself from the guys who "seem" to like me. And his concern that I be told was as phoney as a Nerf nightstick. Of all the things that could put a snag in my circle-building, my 007 book had been beyond consideration.

The 007 book was a 3x8 notebook issued by the PD to be used by officers for taking field notes. It was a mini steno pad just perfect for scribbling a few notes and then sliding into your back pocket. On the top of the front cover was printed the stock number which was 007, hence the name.

"I'm almost at a loss for words Sergeant Hinckley." I could

be formal too. "I'd be more than happy to show my chicken scratching to anyone who'd like to see it. Since it was my plan to turn in a monthly report of my activities to the Captain each month, I had to have something to keep records in. This is it." I held up my 007 book. "I record who I ride with, which roll calls I attend, when I'm called out, and how long I work. And of course, if I have to take notes at a crime scene I use it then too."

"Well,' he replied, "I personally didn't think there was anything to the rumor, but it's always better to get things out in the open. If guys think that what they're doing is going to be reported to HQ or even the Captain, they'll avoid you like the plague."

Cops live in a world of facades, falsehoods, and pretense. His commitment to 'openness' would have been laughable if it were not so pitifully hypocritical. I wasn't being harsh in my judgment of Hinckley. I had been around them for nearly a month now and I knew that "getting things out in the open" was definitely not S.O.P. for cops. Perception was everything, and right then, I perceived a petty misdemeanor being jacked into a capital felony.

"Hey—I appreciate you pointing this out to me," I said. "Maybe I'll go to each squad's roll call and straighten this out once and for all. I'll just pass my 007 around the room and we'll get this behind us pronto."

Sitting up in his chair a little and clearing his throat he said, "That might be a good idea, but it's probably not worth making that big a deal out of it. I'll just get the word out to the few who were concerned and that should take care of it."

"No." Did I actually say that Hardnose Hinckley?

"I've got to make sure that this is cleared up completely. I've got to have the trust of the men or I can't do anything as a Chaplain. Everything I do depends on them having confidence in me. If that's destroyed then so is the job. No, I'll take it to the roll calls and squelch this as soon as possible." I stood to leave and quickly saw that he had a mild puzzled expression.

"Thanks again for helping me out by telling me about this," I said while opening the door." I'll catch ya later."

Kerplunck. The door shut behind me.

I couldn't be certain what the extent of the problem was, but I felt sure the Sergeant was imbued with a sense of having opened the proverbial worm can. Was he trying to stir people up against me? Was he involved in some kind of one-upsmanship with me? Or was he simply trying to resolve a potential problem? It was hard to tell with him. He had no way of knowing that Bud had warned me about his anti-chaplain sentiments.

For the time being I was confident I'd never get a call for help from Hardnose Hinckley. I was wrong.

As I went from roll call to roll call the next three days, most of the guys were thunderstruck when I brought it up. The closer they were to me, friendship-wise, the more vociferous they were.

"Now that's a crock of bull if I ever heard it," snarled Deke the Skete.

"Some guys are so freaking paranoid that the word 'Bug' will never mean insect to 'em," said Pretty Boy Davis.

"Sounds like someone's got a personal problem," said Bud with a sly grin.

A few of the guys just sat there, seemingly unimpressed with the whole thing. I didn't know if that meant they were suspicious or blasé. Everyone wanted to know who told me I was being scrutinized because of my 007 book. It remained a secret between Hinckley, Bud, and myself.

Within a couple days it was all history. I never heard another word about my 007 book. The 007 book was the most used piece of Chaplain equipment I had. Some of the guys rather enjoyed my taking down complaints that came for them over the radio. They didn't have to take their hands off the steering wheel. Many times they would refer to my notes when we took a break to write up a report. So, it wasn't a matter of hiding the "problem" from anyone. I had my 007 with me everywhere I went. I couldn't help but conclude it was all a matter of connivance rather than paranoia. I needed to keep a cautious eye on Sergeant Hardnose Hinckley.

CHAPTER SIX

One sparkling Tuesday morning, after I had two cups of coffee and helped to get the kids off to school, I decided to soak my sleepiness away in a long hot shower. Leaning against the wall and bending over slightly, I let the pulsating spray drum on the area between my shoulders. It was soothing and invigorating. I was luxuriating in one of life's simple activities. Humanity started changing from a nocturnal gray to a pale shade of pink. I had sent my son off to school with a "Go get 'em tiger" when I felt like a ragged-out alley cat. Now I could feel the stripes coming back to the surface.

My wife knocked on the shower door and jarred me out of my feline feelings.

"You're wanted on the phone," she yelled over the noise of the shower.

"Tell 'em I'll call 'em back in a few," I replied grumpily. Can't a guy even take a shower peacefully?

"It's EOC."

"Oh. O.K." My heart leaped. I turned off the shower, grabbed a towel, and ran to the phone, dripping water everywhere.

"This is Chaplain Temple. Whacha need?"

"Chaplain, the supervisor wants to know if you can respond to Jonestown Middle School on Red Apple Drive. A fourteen year old boy is in front of the school with a knife to his throat. He's threatening to commit suicide if anyone comes near. So there's kind of a stand-off now. Can you respond?"

"Sure. Can you send a unit to pick me up? I need a couple minutes to get dressed."

"We will start a unit that way immediately. Thank you."

Quickly slipping into one of my old polyester suits, I stepped out the front door just as a cruiser pulled into my driveway. It was Thunder. Patrolman Matthew Kilpatrick was not called Thunder because of his size, personality, or voice. His sobriquet came from a much less auspicious source than that. It had to do with the proclivity he had to provide noxious gases. It was the only thing he did that was earthshaking. His short thinnish stature did nothing to prepare you for the raucous reverberations he emitted constantly. It was further amplified by his utter complacency when it happened.

I had ridden with Thunder once before, and I used him to get a good laugh at roll call that day. I had known in advance that I was going to ride with him, so when I was asked in roll call who I was going to ride with I pulled out a surgical face mask, put it on and said "Guess." That brought down the house, Thunder included. Later, I apologized to him and he said he thought it was the funniest thing he'd seen in roll call in ages.

In spite of his reputation, he was a very polite and considerate cop. He was totally committed to his family which explained why he never stayed around after work for choir practice. He wanted to get home to his wife and kids. I was very impressed with his clearly-defined and prioritized life. As a cop he was a coaster. He did what was expected and no more. His stats were adequate, but he took almost no initiative, and that made for a boring ride-along. I had to remind myself that I was there to be with them, not hunt for Toads.

With lights and siren bellowing "Get out of the way" we flew down the road to Jonestown Middle School. There was something about Jonestown and suicide that sounded terribly familiar but I couldn't figure out what it was. Thunder couldn't tell me very much because he had been on another complaint. He said that it must be a circus because everyone in the County was there.

Driving through a picturesque tree-lined neighborhood, we could see the school down the street. Circus was an appropriate description. I could see four fire engines, seven county cruisers, three State cruisers, and two ambulances. There was no way to tell how many unmarked units were present.

Twenty-five or thirty police and firemen were in a large circle around a small stand of trees in front of the school building. The street and a circular driveway created a little park, and that's where all the attention was focused.

Thunder let me off at the driveway and I walked up it to where the Sergeant, Lieutenant, and several others were huddled. The single-story red brick school was to my right and the small wooded area to my left. I could see the boy in the center of the woods, leaning against a tree. From forty yards away I could see the huge butcher knife tight against his throat. He was extremely agitated, moving around, keeping his back covered by the tree, and the cops covered with his wide eyes. He was shouting obscenities at us or maybe the world.

"Hi Rev. We got us a real Signal 34 here," said the Lieutenant. As Assistant Station Commander he was very supportive of my work. I had to jiggle some brain cells to remember what Signal 34 meant. Mental Case.

"We're kinda at a loss for ideas," he said. "We've got to do something pretty quick because the teachers are keeping kids away from the rooms in the front of the building by keeping them in the hallway. So that's not gonna work for long." He scratched his head and squinted his eyes.

"We've thought about hitting him with a blast of water from one of the fire trucks and then cuffing him before he recovers. But, there's too big a risk that they'll miss with their first blast and the kid will slice his throat. Everyone has had a crack at talking to him and all he does is swear like a sailor. You want to

51

give it a try?"

I took a deep breath and looked around.

"Yeah Bob, I'd like to try it. He probably won't listen to me either. Could we get everyone to back off a little? No wonder he's uptight. He's got an army of cops around him, a couple K-9's, and the Fire Department to boot. Maybe he'll calm down a bit if we give him some space."

"We can do that, but you've got to watch your as—rear. He may be freaked out on drugs and decide that knife would look better in you than him."

"I got my track shoes on. Don't worry."

Using his portable radio he told everyone to back off some. Immediately they began to back up about thirty yards

The boy stopped his ranting, but increased his vigilance. He sensed that something was about to happen.

"What's his name," I asked.

"Billy," said the Sergeant, "His teacher said he had some kind of run-in with his parents before he came to school this morning. She thinks it was about drugs, but she doesn't know that for sure."

"Have you been able to get in touch with his folks yet?"

"We've been trying, but all we have is a home phone number and no one is answering it."

"Well, here goes nothing." I don't know where I came up with such a great line. I could have been a little more positive about it.

I had taken three steps toward the boy when it struck me how dramatic the whole scene was. There was no traffic on the street. A host of public servants were watching me in silence, tensed and ready to come to my rescue if need be. In front of me was the culprit, the cause of all this commotion. A blond-headed, baby-faced fourteen year old boy, who had an argument with his folks and now was seeking some revenge or more precisely, some attention.

I found myself feeling sorry for the boy. He just needed someone to talk to. Someone who cares about him.

"DON'T COME ANY CLOSER YOU — — — — — — — — — — — — — — OR I'M GONNA CUT MY THROAT! I SWEAR TO GOD I WILL!"

Poor little boy? I was about fifteen yards away from him now and I could see that the knife was pressed so hard against his throat that it should already have been cutting him. He had it in both hands. One on the handle and one on the blade. He almost gagged when he talked because of the tightness of the knife against his throat.

I froze. In a calm voice I said, "Billy, let's talk about this. I'm sure we . . ."

I DON'T WANT TO TALK TO NO — — — — — — — —

52

— COPS! GET OUT OF HERE OR I SWEAR I'LL DO IT!"

"I'm not a cop, Billy. I'm a Chaplain, a minister, a preacher. I want to help you get through . . ."

"GET THE — — — — — AWAY YOU — — — — —! I'M SERIOUS! I'LL KILL MYSELF IF YOU — — — — — COPS DON'T GET OUTA HERE!"

I started to say again that I wasn't a cop, but how could I prove it. I was in a suit like several of the plain-clothes cops there. I had fairly short hair and I was so clean-cut looking I squeaked when I walked. I almost wished for a monk's robe or a white reverse collar.

He was getting more and more hyper. His foul ranting was non-stop, and the knife blade was visibly tighter. With my hands up, in what I hoped was a peaceful gesture, I started backing up towards the Lieutenant.

When I returned to where they were standing, I said, "Whoa. I'd say he's a little upset. He sounds like he went to the Charles Manson school of 'Respect for Authority'. I've been cursed at by some of the best but I believe he could make the Hell's Angels blush."

"Now Rev," said the Lieutenant in a patronizing tone, "we rarely run into Mary Poppins in our line of work."

"One of the EMT's said that as tense as he is, if he jerked that knife across his neck it won't cut very deep. He'd probably miss his jugular completely," offered the Sergeant.

"And when the kid's head rolls off his shoulders we'll just say 'oops that wasn't supposed to happen'," frowned the lieutenant.

Grand plans were not formulating in my mind. I had a fleeting vision of being a hero. I could see myself inching my way up to the boy and at the propitious moment, giving him a hard right to the solar plexus, disarming him, and restraining him until the guys could cuff him. But, the cold reality of becoming a pin cushion had me leaning towards the fire hose idea. There was a wildness in the boy's eyes and voice that gave credibility to the risks involved in approaching him.

"Bob, I'd like to try and get closer to him," I said. "I'm not sure, but when I was talking to him I thought it looked like he had the dull edge of the knife against his neck and the sharp edge pointing out I'm not positive, but he was pressing it so hard that it was cutting off the air flow when he talked. It should have been cutting into him if it was the sharp edge."

"If we could be sure of that Rev, it would be worth the risk to rush him before he turned it around."

Before I realized what I was doing I offered an approach. "If you'll go with me Bob, I'll try to see how close I can get to him. And if I can tell positively that the knife edge is not against him, we can grab him real quick."

He looked surprised. "Don't you realize that if the edge is not towards him that means it will be towards you. Us. No, I've been stabbed before and I don't want to be known as the Lou who let the Chaplain get sliced up like Christmas turkey."

Made sense to me. I wasn't the least bit offended.

"Let's close the circle in on him slowly," he said like he was thinking out loud. "As we get closer to him we'll watch the blade. If he starts to turn it to the sharp edge we'll back off and regroup. If we can tell for sure that the dull edge is against him, we'll take him."

He said the last three words with such conviction that everybody started putting the plan into effect, assuming that it was decided.

Within minutes we formed a large circle around the boy. It started with everyone about thirty yards away from him. I was between the Lieutenant and one of the plain-clothed detectives. Without being instructed to, I started talking to the boy, trying to keep his attention on me.

"Calm down, Billy. No one's going to hurt you. We want to get you some help. Relax and put the knife down. Don't make a bad mistake. I care about you . . ."

He was screaming warnings and obscenities at us, but at least he was looking at me. He was pulling the knife harder and his voice was a staccato of strained words and retching.

As we eased up to the ten yard mark, his yelling became a screechy whisper due to the pressure he put on his throat. I could see saliva foaming from the sides of his mouth. His eyes were bulging and his face was turning red.

Many of the officers stopped in place as the circle got smaller. This allowed it to shrink in size and number. As the circle narrowed to about twelve feet, Billy began to cry hysterically. I could see that the sharp edge of the knife wasn't against his neck, and I could also see that he was going to give up. All at once his eyes rolled up and his knees buckled. He slid down the tree but was caught by five officers before he hit the ground. Even though he was somewhat unconscious, they had to pry the knife from his hands. To be on the safe side, they put plastic flex cuffs on his hands and his feet. Six of them picked him up, carried him to one of the ambulances, and strapped him down on one of the stretchers.

Watching the ambulance zoom off to the psycho ward, I wondered what would become of Billy. Somewhere there were some parents who were going through their daily routines completely unaware their son was being carted off to the County rubber room. I just hoped they cared.

"Just another excellent piece of Police work," said the Lieutenant as we walked over to his unmarked car. "Let's go get some lunch, Rev. It's on me. We can go to the Deli and get a sliced roast beef sub. Maybe we can get a discount if we bring our own butcher knife." He laughed as he held up the knife which had just been the center of attention. "This one wouldn't cut hot butter. It has absolutely no edge at all."

Driving back through the peaceful neighborhoods with bright sunshine filtering through the big shade trees and flowers blooming everywhere, I felt like it had all been a weird dream. Life went on like it never really happened. Mothers pushed strollers down the sidewalks. Sprinklers were already broadcasting life to grass that was fighting a brown-out. Birds sang, traffic buzzed, and the Lieutenant droned about how pitiful his garden was.

There was no sense of having avoided a serious crisis. There was no crying, hand-wringing, or concern. Everything was business as usual. Forgotten. History.

But what about Billy? What's going to happen to him? How will his family react? Should I be with him—them?

I had to remind myself that my job was to help the cops, not the public. That was a concept I constantly forgot. Others did too. As a minister, I was available to anyone who needed me. As a Police Chaplain, my primary obligation was to help my officers. If that meant helping a citizen, that's what I did, but only to the extent that it helped the police. That may seem somewhat cold and selective, but if a chaplain followed up on every citizen contact he made it would soon cause him to bog down and be unable to assist the ones he was primarily responsible for. They essentially became a second congregation for me, and in terms of receiving attention, a minister's congregation must always come first. The heart of the Pastor concept rests on that idea. It's true even for churches that don't believe in calling their minister a Pastor. They just dropped the title but still require the pastoring.

I spent the afternoon working on my sermons for Sunday. I couldn't shake the image of Billy being hauled off to the ambulance. After chewing on it for thirty minutes, I finally decided to call and find out what his status was.

"Lieutenant Wilson, can I help you," said a tired voice on the station phone

"Hey Bob. This is your favorite Chaplain. How come you aren't on your way home?" It was 4:15 P.M. and he usually left sharply at 3:30 each afternoon. You could set your clock by him most days.

"Mary Beth had to leave early so I've been covering the desk. Smith is late for some unknown reason. He's probably trying to find a store that sells those gosh-awful cigars he smokes. If he doesn't get here soon I'm gonna send the wagon after him."

The station communication personnel, called PCA's for Police

Communication Administrators, changed shifts at 4:00 and PCA Dick "Dip-Stick" Smith was undoubtedly unaware that the Assistant Station Commander was covering for his tardiness. He'd be up a very famous creek when he came in to work.

"Well, I'll know what it's about if I get a call about a Signal—36 at the Police Station. I hate to bother you, but I was wondering if you had any further word on what has happened to the kid from Jonestown this morning?" "Are you ready for this, Rev? Within one hour after we cuffed him, he was declared fine by a family psychiatrist, and released to the custody of his parents. The kid's folks are lawyers and they live in one of those mansions on King's Table Drive. Can you believe it? The Kid disrupts half the county for most of the morning and nothing's going to happen to him, except he has to visit his shrink a couple of times. He probably staged the whole thing just to get out a day of school."

"What a bummer. At least the County is the proud owner of a butcher knife."

"Only until they ask for it back," he said with disdain.

"Well, hang in there in spite of all the injustice that surrounds you. Take it out on Dip-Stick. You'll feel better." Everyone gave Dip-stick a rough time. He seemed to thrive on it too.

"You can depend on that. See ya later, Rev. And, ya did a good job this morning."

CHAPTER SEVEN

The seven men sitting around the imitation mahogany conference table were as different as the Seven Dwarfs. The only characteristic the dwarfs shared was being dwarfs. The only area of commonality we had was being Police Chaplains for the County. We were meeting in the HQ conference room to discuss a plan to unify the approach we took to being Police Chaplains.

Since our training had been minimal, almost non-existent, we each attacked our job being guided by our consciences, personalities, and religious biases. Still, this meeting was as close to being ecumenical as any of us would ever be. In an effort to maintain its image as a progressive organization, the County had asked for volunteer chaplains. Yet, they really didn't know what to do with us or about us. They evidently wanted to keep a little distance between us and them. I think it was a matter of not wanting to take responsibility for what we did just in case some self-righteous Rev bombed out with the troops or got burned doing something he wasn't supposed to.

Any recognition or appreciation we received came from the street cops, not the Department. It was like the recording you used to hear on Mission Impossible. "We will disavow any knowledge of you" if you fall on your face. The bad part was we received no support, no guidance, and no reimbursement for expenses incurred. The good part was that we were free to do the job any way we saw fit, and the "hands off" policy placed us firmly in the camp of the cops, not in the Ivory Tower.

Like the cops, some Chaplains were gung-ho and others did the bare minimum. Some of us put in an extraordinary amount of time. Others attended a roll call, rode with someone for a couple hours, and called it a week's work. Of course, all of us were on twenty-four call, and could be called on to cover for a Chaplain who was out of town.

Two of us were rapidly getting a reputation throughout the Department for being gung-ho. Cops loved to hear stories about a Chaplain helping out in a fight or using an 870 to back up an officer. I'd been in a couple of wrestling matches, one with a Toad who resisted being cuffed after a DWI arrest and one with a big biker who freaked out at the jail before we could give him to the Sheriff's Department, who ran the jail. I prayed I'd never have to grab for the 870.

Because we were so different, I was not filled with a strong sense of comaraderie as I sat in conference with six "men of the cloth". There was one Catholic priest, two Episcopalian priests, two Methodist pastors, and two of us evangelical fundamental preachers. We were in suits, while the others wore clergy garb.

It's true confession time. I've never cared much for preachers, priests, or pastors. The clergy was a man made institution that set some very fallible men on pedestals as being super spiritual. Jesus went to the drunks, whores, and thugs of society with his message. The ones who thought they were super spiritual he called snakes and hypocrites. Pompous profiteers of salvation have dispensed guilt, false security, and self aggrandizement with such alacrity that a real man of God has to spend more time proving his motives pure than presenting His message.

The biggest obstacle to my becoming a preacher wasn't the low pay, the enormity of the task, or the wiles of the Devil. It was preachers. The preachers I'd seen were, for the most part, egotistical, overweight, over-rated, and wore twenty-year-old cheap suits. They damned any of us who smoke, drank, or cussed. They invented sins like dancing, mixed swimming, and good night kisses. For every sermon I heard on Grace or the Love of God, I heard twenty on the Deceitfulness of Sin and The Judgement of God. Then I met Brother Joe.

Brother Joe was a little over-weight and his suits bordered on being obsolete, but his spirit was genuine gold. A smile and a kind encouraging word were freely given to everyone. He was positive and patient as he taught me the Word of God. What impressed me the most was his humble, unpretentious preaching. I remember him describing preaching as "one beggar telling another beggar where to find food". He made you feel good about your decision to be a Christian instead of making it a burden. He accepted people as they were, in spite of their faults, my faults. He never badgered, he only instructed and encouraged. He was a giver.

I became a preacher because I wanted to be a giver like Brother Joe. When the Captain warned me, prior to taking me down to roll call, that I'd be hearing a lot of dirty jokes and foul language, I answered in true Brother Joe fashion, "Captain, I wasn't born yesterday and there are few things that I haven't heard many times before. Besides, I don't expect cops to be angels or even to pretend to be when I'm around. Just because I have chosen to not do some things that doesn't mean I expect everyone else to live by my choices. I won't think less of them because they do things I wouldn't do. I like to be a good example but not a judge."

I'm not as open minded when it comes to Preachers. I expect more because we have publicly proclaimed a higher calling in life. Some of the Chaplains would drink, smoke, and cuss right along with the troops. I didn't, yet I don't believe that any Chaplain was any closer to his men than I was. They respected my convictions which they discovered from observation, not because I preached to them. They enjoyed testing my consistency. Smoking and drinking were no temptation to me because, being athletic, I wanted good health. It took several years, but I finally removed cuss words and swear words from my vocabulary. The hardest area was dirty jokes. Not mine but theirs. I couldn't very well leave the room when somebody started to tell a joke. I couldn't scowl or fret, and I couldn't laugh too much and encourage more. I developed a technique of lowering my head and making them wonder if I was laughing. Sometimes no matter how much I didn't want to laugh out loud, the joke would really break me up. It was just part of rolling with the punches. I never appreciated, however, and never will, the complete disdain many had for the name of God. Many of the guys did make an effort to tone it down when I came around. I had some subtle ways of making them more aware of it. Someone would exclaim, "Jeeesus Christ!" and I'd respond "No, I'm just a representative, not the real thing." And, I always said it with a smile.

At the meeting one of the chaplains offered his sure-fire way to get accepted quickly by the cops. "First thing I do when I get in a cruiser with a guy, is I tell him a dirty joke. That really loosens him up." Everyone gave one of those deep intellectual chuckles that is more polite than heartfelt. I've never been a prude but I wanted to suggest "What's wrong with a clean joke? Aren't they funny any more?"

The rest of the meeting dealt with the pros and cons of monthly reports, standardized Chaplain outfits, and monthly meetings. The last item for discussion was a theoretical proposition about arming Police Chaplains. It was a fairly heated debate. Most of the arguments centered around whether the practical advantages in terms of self-defense and police back-up offset the social concerns of a man of peace, love, and forgiveness carrying a gun. It was bad PR but good use of manpower. Then we got into the implications of training, County liability, and personal conscience. The two Episcopalians were split on the issue. I had to agree with the younger one who argued, "I feel that it's our job to show an alternative to violence. We are the real Peace Officers. Wearing a side-arm would seriously damage our influence."

"Well for one thing," said the older priest, "it wouldn't have to be seen. It could be concealed like it is with the detectives. And secondly, what are you going to do if the officer you're with gets shot and you're the next target? Or what if he's just wounded? You can sacrifice yourself but what about him? If you're unarmed you're up the creek."

They talked on for a good while. I say 'they' because I just listened. I didn't want to reveal my CO feeling just yet. If they knew, it would only be a matter of time before every cop in the county would know. I didn't want my guys to know. Besides, they said nothing new. I'd wrestled with it for so many years that I could have given them a dissertation like they'd never heard.

We were all better off because I didn't.

I suppose I was being modestly deceptive with my officers because I hadn't told any of them about my being a CO. In fact, they saw me as being the "Dirty Harry" of the Chaplains. I was aggressive, physical, and willing to help with anything. And occasionally, I forgot who I was, or rather who I represented. Like the night we tried to stop the carload of foreigners on Route 14.

We attempted to pull them over for speeding but they didn't respond to our lights and siren. They didn't speed up or try to get away either. They just kept on trucking down the road.

"Scout 540. I'm involved in a slow pursuit West-bound on Rt. 14 just passing Maple Drive. It's an '80 Ford Fairmont with Diplomat tag David-26117." reported Pretty-Boy. We were in the Paddy Wagon so it was a good thing that it was a slow pursuit. It rode like a tank and was about the same size.

Within seconds, a back-up unit was behind us. Pretty-Boy told them to cover the backside of the car while we cut them off from the front. He pulled up along-side the Fairmont and I could see one oriental male driving and three more in the back seat. I signaled for him to pull over and the driver smiled and waved back at me.

"He's either drunk or he doesn't understand what we're doing, or both," I said.

"Hang on Rev. We're gonna stop that Knuckle-head or flatten him."

We pulled past him some, then started to force him off the road to the right. He finally came to a stop on the shoulder of the road, sandwiched between us and the back-up unit.

As I took my position on the passenger's side of the Fairmont while the two officers were talking to the driver, I noticed something very strange about the guys in the back seat. The three oriental men had a blanket across their laps and they were struggling to get their pants on. All three of them.

I met my two guys at the front of the car. The four guys in the Fairmont were from the Army of the Nationalist Republic of China. Supposedly, they were here as special guests of the Pentagon. They didn't speak a word of English.

"Did you see those guys in the back seat?" yelled our back-up. "They're a bunch of freaking queers!"

"This is a mess Rev. They don't understand a word we're saying and they have diplomatic immunity anyways. What do you think we should do with'em?" asked John.

Well, I was still appalled at what I'd seen. So with very little forethought I said, "Let's throw a grenade in there and blow the foreign faggots back to Formosa."

I regretted saying that the moment I said it. It was the wrong thing to say. Of course they loved it, and of course it was the talk of the station within minutes. The next day, when I came by the station to attend the afternoon roll call, I arrived late so I just stood in the doorway. Immediately everyone got quiet and looked at me smiling. Before I could ask "What?", I noticed a new sign on the bulletin board. Someone had made a Xerox copy of Time Magazine's Man of the Year cover picture of China's Chairman. Then with a marker, they'd written across the top of it "Frag the Foreign Faggots". What could I do but laugh and shake my head. If they only knew.

The Chinese had been let off the hook, but I was on a big hook. There was no way that I could let them know about my non-combatant convictions without losing their trust. I was "one of the guys" and "one of the guys" means you might own a T-shirt that was inscribed with "Kill 'em All And Let God Sort 'em Out".

In the few weeks that I'd been a Chaplain, I had become pretty close to most of the troops. There were a few exceptions of course, not the least of which was Hardnose. Between ride-alongs and off duty events, most of them had come to think of me as an insider now. I had gone on a family picnic with E-Squad, which allowed me to meet most of their wives or girl friends. The only problem had been a minor one. My kids just sat there while everyone else was eating. They were waiting for someone to offer thanks for the food.

I went to the Police Association Hall with C-Squad one night after finishing up the shift at 2 A.M. We played pool and threw darts until 5. I'm pretty good at pool but I was stomped at darts.

Another night I played basketball with most of D-Squad which led to my being invited to play on the station team during the upcoming tournament with the other stations.

On their day off, I went with B-Squad to their Sergeant's place out in the country. We spent a couple hours target practicing with our pistols. I had a Smith & Wesson model 15 which was the same gun they carried. The only difference was that mine had a two inch barrel while they had four inch barrels. At twenty-five yards I was all over the target while they stayed pretty well within the silhouette's body area. When I pulled out my Berretta 380 I put thirteen rounds in the kill zone.

It was with A-Squad that I went off the deepend. I gambled. We left the station at 2:15 A.M. and went to one of their homes close by. Then we played dime and nickel, dealers choice, until 6:30. As I drove home and saw the sun rising in the east, I couldn't help but wonder what would happen if word ever got out at church that the preacher had gambled. Wouldn't the muckraking church publications have a field day with that. Especially if they knew that I'd won more than anyone else. A whopping $4.75.

One sticky June afternoon I was returning to my office after running a bunch of errands. I flipped my portable radio on just to see what was going on. After a few crackles the voice of Sergeant Scott came through. He was in mid-sentence, ". . . and I've been trying to raise the Chaplain but we can't find him."

"10-4, Car 5. 15:21", said EOC.

I was so surprised I almost had a wreck. I quickly rolled down my window, stuck the small antenna of my portable out, pressed the transmit lever and said, "Chaplain 5!" Nothing happened.

I pressed the button harder and spoke louder and still no response. The only reason I had a portable was because it was so old that no one wanted to use it. So the Captain let me use it. Usually it functioned adequately, but it was somewhat temperamental. Maybe the battery was down.

I kept trying to use it but all I got was frustration. Should I find a phone and call EOC? I decided that I could drive to the station in the same time I did that.

When I got to the station, the desk PCA told me that I was needed for a fatality at Rt. 45 and Glencove Rd. That was about two blocks away from where I had been when I first heard Scott call for me. Now I was about five miles away.

The ambulance was leaving just as I got there. A gray five-year-old BMW had veered off the road to the right and smashed into the rear of a disabled flatbed truck. The car had been pulled back away from the truck, but I could see that the flatbed had taken the roof of the car off back past the front seat.

Walking up to the BMW, my nostrils were assaulted by the acrid smell of burning flares, car exhaust, and spilt gasoline. When I looked into the car I got a faint whiff of perfume. The roof had been pealed back about two feet and the hot sun beat down on the brown plaid upholstery. Windshield glass sparked from the floor and seat. A small pool of blood on the passenger's seat, an opened purse partially spilt, and a set of keys dangling from the ignition gave it an eerie battle-zone quality. Somebody's afternoon drive had turned into tragedy.

Sam Hicks, who was well into his accident investigation, came over to were I was standing by the car.

"Nasty one ain't it Rev? The driver was killed instantly. She was an eighteen year old girl name of," checking his 007, "Linda R. Cardoza."

"Run it down for me Sam. How'd it happen?"

"Looks like she was toolin' down the road when she reached down to get something from her purse or something, and drifted off the road to the right and when she looked back up it was too late. She never even had time to hit her brakes. The flatbed caught her right across the forehead killing her instantly. She was so close when she looked up that she never had time to duck back down or she might have lived."

62

"Has anyone notified the parents yet?"

"Naw. We need to finish up here first then we'll go to the hospital and call them to come over."

The next hour was spent directing traffic, measuring distances, taking pictures and replacing flares, which I was real good at. After the wrecker had taken the BMW away, I followed Sam to the hospital. On the way, I heard Sam ask EOC to call the family of the deceased and have them meet us at the emergency room. It's policy to never tell someone over the phone that a relative has died. They always just say that there has been an accident and could they please come to the hospital. You never know how they will react to a notification, so it's best to do it in a controlled environment where help is available.

We decided to wait outside the emergency room since it was so crowded. It wasn't too unbearably hot as we stood in the shaded ambulance drive-through. Both of us were a little antsy and we joked to cover up our nervousness.

A shiny new red nine passenger Suburban pulled into the Short Term Parking space. A silver haired distinguished man in a yellow knit shirt got out of the driver's side and ran around to help a portly woman get out the passenger's side. Anxiety was written all over their faces. There was no question about who they were.

"Are you Mr. and Mrs. Cardoza?", I asked extending my hand. "This is Officer Sam Hicks and I'm Chaplain Temple." Mrs. Cardoza gave an audible gasp when I said "Chaplain". People expect to hear the worst when the Chaplain is called in.

I ushered them into the small counselling room around the corner from the Emergency Room. They sat on the love seat while Sam and I sat in folding chairs. They stared at me intently, hoping against hope that I wasn't going to tell them that what they feared most really had happened. But it was time to drop the bomb so I ignored my heart.

"There was an automobile accident involving your daughter Linda, and I'm sorry to have to tell you, but she died as a result of the accident."

They both froze for what seemed like an hour but what was actually five seconds. He closed his eyes tightly and his wife exploded into sobs as she buried her face in his shoulder. He held her and tenderly laid his forehead down on her head.

That's the hardest time of all notifications. You're powerless to do or say anything that will make them feel better. There is a tremendous temptation to say something, anything, because the sound of our own voice gives us a false sense of security when we feel helpless. That's why we sing or talk to ourselves when we're scared. The best rule to remember for times like this is to shut up and let them determine what you say next.

"How did it happen?", asked the father. Sam gave him a

brief summation of the accident.

"She graduated from high school two weeks ago." sobbed the father," and today was her first day of work at the drug store. She was on her way home from work. She . . ." He broke down and cried out loud. They held each other and shook with sobs for three or four minutes.

I stepped out of the room and asked the nurse at the desk to call the morgue and tell them we'd be coming over in a few minutes.

The Cardoza's were in control of themselves after a few more minutes. So I asked Mr. Cardoza if he was up to giving us a positive I.D. on his daughter. He felt like he was. Sam stayed with Mrs. Cardoza along with one of the nurses, while we walked through the hospital halls on our way to the Medical Examiner's secluded wing.

At this hospital they had a viewing window in a very private area. We walked up the plate glass window with white curtains on the inside of it. Mr. Cardoza was wringing his hands, hoping that there had been some terrible mistake and it wouldn't be his daughter Linda.

I pushed the buzzer on the right side of the window and waited. A minute later the curtain began to open, moving from right to left. Mr. Cardoza cried out, "That's her. It's my Linda," before I could even focus in on the body. White curtains were used as a back-drop around the stretcher and a white sheet covered the body from the neck down. They had taken another sheet and laid it over her forehead covering her from the eyebrows up. She was a pretty girl with black hair. Her lips, eyelids, and nose were purplish and the rest of her face was chalk white.

The curtain slowly closed in front of us. The father placed his hands on the glass and watched his Linda disappear behind the curtain. His head dropped down between his arms as his back jerked with lamenting sobs.

Back in the cubicle of grief, I asked them if they had a minister that I could call to help. They did, and in their presence I called him and told him what had happened. He said he'd meet them at their home.

Mr. Cardoza assured me that he was able to drive them home. I offered to drive them, follow them, or have them taken home in a cruiser, but they felt they could handle it alright alone. I wanted to do more for them but there was nothing more to do.

"Please call me later if I can do anything to help. Even two or three weeks from now. Don't hesitate to call me."

"We appreciate your help, Chaplain," said Mr. Cardoza. "We've got plenty of help from our family and our church. We'll be alright. Thank you. I will call if we need you." The Suburban drove off into the shadows of evening and out of my life. Driving home, instead of turning on the radio, I sang to myself. I sounded like Willie Nelson in a strangle hold, but it was better than crying.

The odd part about being depressed because of doing a death notification was that it drove me closer to the cops. Who else could I talk to about it? Who else would understand what it was like? Who else would be more appreciative of what I did than the cops? So any time I was involved in something like that, I made a point of riding with one of the guys as soon as I could. It became a therapeutic release for me because it gave me a chance to talk about what had happened. They'd understand, give me a few ego stokes, and to top it off, we'd be closer as a result.

Fortunately my wife understood, so she didn't mind when I went back out that night to ride with some lucky cop. This time the lot fell on Officer Walter "J.C." Graham.

CHAPTER EIGHT

Walt was a square-jawed, black haired young fellow just out of his rookie year as a cop. He was known as a ladies man and an expert at picking dump trucks that were overweight as they barrelled down the highways. Since the trucks were fined so much per pound over weight, catching one was considered a real plum. Walt got several each week.

Being a good looking, gung-hoe cop was not unusual, but being an ordained minister was. Walt had been a full-time minister for a few years before he walked away from it to be a cop. He explained it all to me one night by simply saying that his heart just hadn't been in it, so he quit. When he quit, he really quit. He hadn't been in a church building since. He made no pretense about being religious, yet he was clearly a man of strong morals and convictions. That, plus his last name, combined to allow him to be sacrilegiously tagged "J.C.". That was one nickname I never used. It didn't seem to bother him to be called "J.C." because most of the guys called him that, but I was a little too uncomfortable with it.

Walt was more cop than anything else. He had a coffee cup on his dash-board which had a picture of a masked burglar framed by a rifle scope. The cross-hairs were on his chest. Under the picture in bold black letters it read, "Cut Court Costs". He was a likable if some-what complex man. Intelligent, talkative, opinionated, and respectful to me. Next to Bud, he was my favorite cop to ride with.

The combination of being a slow night and having plenty of units on the street during the overlap, between 9 and 2 there are two squads out, we had plenty of time to converse. A quiet radio, a twelve ounce cup of Seven-Eleven coffee, and stimulating conversation soon had the earlier events of the day sufficiently white-washed for awhile.

Since religion wasn't Walt's choice for chatting, we covered a wide range of subjects. We talked politics, "I'd vote for Nixon if he'd run again." We talked international relations, "I'd like to shove a claymore up Khomeini's holy nose." We talked literature, "Have you read Wambaugh's new book?" We talked technology, "I think the Ruger's every bit as good as the Smith and Wesson, but the Python is better than either one." We talked shop, "Why should the Pin-heads at HQ care if I play my AM-FM at three in the morning when nothing is moving except Thunder's bowels."

The last tirade was interrupted by a call from EOC for him to take a larceny report. A bicycle had been stolen from a citizen's front porch and it was our duty to collect the facts, write the report, and satisfy the public. It was a tedious formality, but their property and their dignity had been violated, and it was our job to "collar the crooks". More than likely, the bike was repainted and sold before the family even knew it had been stolen. Just the same, we'd make paper on it.

Thirty minutes after arriving at the victim's house we climbed back into the cruiser. It doesn't take long to get all the necessary information on a bike theft. We had a description that fit only forty thousand bikes in the County, no serial number, and no suspects.

For thirty minutes we had severed ourselves from the rest of the County because our radios had been turned off. As soon as we switched on the cruiser radio we knew that something big had gone down and we missed it. There was a lot of radio traffic as units marked back in service "from the Signal 13". Signal 13 is 'officer needs help'. It's the call that causes every cop to drop whatever he's doing and haul tail to help a brother in need. It makes the Oklahoma Land Rush look like an egg rolling race. Lights, sirens, horns, screeching tires, and white-knuckled hands on steering wheels proclaim to all that they better move over or get run over, a cop's in trouble.

It's difficult to tell whether we were more upset because we'd missed all the action or because we didn't know what it was. We both fussed and speculated, and tried to decide what would be the quickest way to find out. We concluded the direct approach was best.

"Scout 95," said Walt to EOC.

"Scout 95," they acknowledged.

"We'll be 10-98 from the Signal 7. Do you need us to help with the Signal 13?"

"Scout 95. Isn't the Chaplain with you?"

"That's 10-4."

"You may want to transport him to the hospital. We have an officer being treated for minor injuries. It's Scout 520."

"Hold us in route."

"Isn't 520 Bud," I asked Walt.

"Yep. I wonder what he got into this time? He sure has a nose for finding action. I hope someone didn't try to take his nose off. Ole Bud can be a pretty wild character."

That was said with respect and concern. Walt and Bud were close friends. They had a constant bet on who would have the highest arrest stats each month. Bud always won, but Walt was right on his heels. Some of the older guys, particularly the burned-out ones, bad-mouthed Bud and Walt a little for being so gung-ho. But even they respected their abilities and record. Even though it made their own lack of results appear glaringly pitiful.

There are two hospitals in the County. The County hospital was the largest and therefore received the more serious cases. The other was a small privately-owned hospital with excellent emergency room staff and facilities, but nothing like the bigger

County hospital, especially for cardiac care. Bud was being tended to at the smaller, private facility.

There were two ambulances and three police cruisers parked by the Emergency Room doors. We added a fourth cruiser to the group.

The work area in the emergency room was a clean mixture of beige floor tile, mellow yellow walls, white muslin curtains, and plenty of stainless steel. The curtains divided the right wall into four cubicles each with its own bed. On the left was a polished pine counter with two nurses behind it wearing pale blue smocks. Only two of the cubicles were in use. The first had Bud, the Sergeant, and an attending physician. The fourth cubicle was closed with curtains, but I could see several sets of legs under the curtain and it sounded like a wrestling match was going on in there

"Hey Rev," said Bud with a smile that pointed to his rosy cheeks. He was fully dressed and only reclining on the bed. He had a 3x3 piece of gauze taped over his left temple.

"Hey big guy. What's broken? Your head?"

"Naw. Just a little goose-egg. They wanted me to stay laid down until they could check the x-rays and see if I had a concussion or if somethin' was leaking up here. I don't think there's anything hurt. I just got a headache. He's the one with problems," he said with a nod towards cubicle four.

"You should've been there Rev," he said with child-like glee. "I got some good stick time in."

"Well don't just lay there grinning. Tell me about it."

"I was coming down Rt. 30 when I noticed this black Olds Cutlass weaving all over the road. A sure DWI right? So I follow him and get plenty of driving pattern before I hit the lights and siren. Once I pull 'em over I find out that its my old buddy Jerry Cooper, the oldest of the Cooper boys."

"Good night! Only you could have that happen," I said, truly surprised.

"Yeah. Ain't it great! He wasn't none to happy to see me since I put him away once before. He almost didn't get out of the car when I told him to, but he did and I gave him a couple sobriety tests which he failed miserably. I couldn't smell any booze on him, but he was smashed on something. Probably PCP. Musta been celebrating a big drug sale.

"Anyway, I tried to kill some time waiting for a backup to get there before I placed him under arrest, but he wanted to get back in his car and leave. He was being his usual unpleasant self. Said he hadn't had a drop to drink and I had no right to hold him. So finally I told him he was under arrest for DWI and to place his hands on the hood of the cruiser. He went ape then. He jumped back and said he wasn't goin' nowhere. Well, he's a pretty good size Toad and I wasn't about to just grab him. So I pointed my mace at his face and told him he could come with me easy or hard.

"When he said, 'Up yours', I gave him a shot of gas right in the face. He grabbed his eyes, yelled and charged right for me. If I'd of stepped aside, he'd of gone right past me into the highway and been flattened by some semi. That probably would have been a blessing to mankind. Well, he got me in a bear hug and wouldn't let go for anything. I was able to get a leg up on the bumper of the cruiser and push us over into the ditch. We rolled all over the County before I was able to get an arm free and give him a couple of good punches in his head, which was hard as granite. Then he got his best lick in with his head. He caught me right here on the left side and really rattled my noggin for a minute.

"When I got my senses back he still had a hold on me like a boa. I reached down with my free arm and got hold of Boppin Betty, my night-stick, and started to run a test on the thickness of his head. It only took two good wallops before he decided to turn loose of this cop. I gave him a couple more for GP and by the time I had the cuffs on him forty thousand units showed up from all over the County. Some citizen had seen us fighting and called 911. They called a Signal 13. It was good to see the cavalry coming even though I didn't need 'em." He laughed at that and his chest expanded considerably. He was proud of himself and as giddy as a kid who has won his first football game.

"You're unbelievable Bud," I said with mock seriousness. "Don't you know that Jackleg could have been armed. He's already vowed to get back at you for the last time."

Ignoring my concern he continued, "I was hoping we'd find a concealed weapon or some drugs in his car when we impounded it, but it was clean. We'll have to settle for a DWI and assaulting a police officer. That should cost him a little after he pays his fines and pays for a lawyer and pays off the judges. I'm sure I'll get another crack at him soon."

The prospects of having another encounter with Jerry Cooper brought a gleam to his eyes. Still pumped up with adrenalin he felt like he could whip the world and he shared none of the concerns I had.

After we'd talked and laughed a while longer, I decided that I needed to get a look at the enemy in cubicle four. The curtain was open now as the doctor was putting sutures into Cooper's scalp. Cooper was strapped to the bed with leather straps on his arms, legs, and chest. An orderly stood at his feet, one cop was on each side, and the doctor was working on his head. He appeared to be unconscious.

Taking a closer look at the patient I had to laugh. He looked as if he had just stepped out of the Sci-fi movie. He was mountainous and mean looking. From his feet to his stitched-up head he appeared deadly. He had black leather bike boots that were well worn. Dirty black levis were covered at the top by a black leather motorcycle jacket with the sleeves cut off. Shiny chains hung down from his shoulder and across his chest. These were accented by a bevy of chrome studs scattered around the jacket. His arms were thick and muscular, with assorted sordid tattoos on them. Tattooed in large inch-square letters from his right shoulder point down his bicep were the words UP YOURS. A bullet head seemed to shoot out from a wider neck. The scars from chin to forehead were overshadowed by an oversized mohawk hair style. Dirty blond hair stood straight up four inches tall from the peak of his head down to the nape of his neck. It looked like something from a Three Stooges movie involving electricity, but the shine meant axle grease, not amperage.

My respect for Bud rose a few more notches. This guy, on a dark night, could cause anyone to need a change of underwear after just one look at him. I hoped Bud knew what he was doing.

CHAPTER NINE

Western Lexington County was in the throes of change. What used to be deep woods and farmlands was being gobbled up by developments, malls and office complexes. Roads were being straightened and widened, and many old white framed country homes were swallowed up by mammoth machinery. The police no longer were called upon to chase cows out of the roadway or herd horses back into their pens. Our station used to be called the Country Club Station, a place to send cops who were in the final stages of their pre-retirement days.

Now the western sector, our area, had as much crime as the other six stations. We actually had more B and E's and vandalism than the others. And, because of our older, deadlier roads, we had more accident fatalities too. Yet due to County easements and visual barrier requirements, everything was well concealed by large stands of woods and parks. It was deceptively high residential, but a casual ride down most roads gave one a real rural impression of the area.

One of the relics from the past, still well camouflaged from the eyes of the affluent citizens who fled from the big city to escape crime, was Camp 23. Camp 23 was a minimum security prison that handled the County's work-release inmates and those sentenced to a "chain gang". Every day, truck loads of prisoners left the camp, and 'spent the day working on road crews, under armed guards. Since the camp itself was minimum security, it had regular prison escapes the cops disgustedly called "walk aways".

About 7:30 one evening, at the tail-end of the evening rush-hour, the Signal 12 came over the radio. Bud grimaced and said, "Another stinking walk-away!"

Within moments though it became clear that this was not just another walk-away. There were two escapees and a third who'd been caught, and he was giving more information about the two who got away than we needed to hear.

"All units stand by for descriptions of the Signal 12's," said the dispatcher. "Subject one is Ervin Adam Hannah, white male, 5 feet 7 inches, brown hair, brown eyes, age 23. Last seen wearing blue jeans and a white T-shirt. The second subject is Lloyd William Elmore, 23, 5'5", brown hair and blue eyes. Last seen wearing blue jeans, no shirt, and a red bandana. Distinguishing marks include tatooes on both arms. On left forearm, a red heart with Mother across the middle. Both subjects were incarcerated for robbery and assault. Considered dangerous."

"Robbery and assault!", yelled Bud, "Can you believe that this screwy County had them in minimum security? At least they're not armed."

"Attention all units," answered EOC, "Be advised that the subjects are heading for a planted blue van. The van supposedly has weapons for them. They stated to an inmate that they would not be taken alive. Proceed with extreme caution."

"Anything else you'd like to ask for Bud?" I said in disbelief.

What followed in the next fifteen minutes was complete bedlam. Every cop in the county converged on our area. State Police poured in from all over. The prison called out all its off duty guards and a dozen K-9 units began sniffing through every bush. One county and two state choppers joined the search. Wester Lexington roads turned into a blur of cruisers scouring every nook and cranny.

The most surprised people in the County were the ones driving blue vans. Every blue van was not just pulled over, but pounced on by three or four cruisers and shotgun-wielding cops. Nothing is more intimidating than a shotgun being chambered with a shell. Kashunck! Eyes pop out and knees weaken.

We rushed from one traffic stop to another, usually backing up someone who'd spotted a blue van. We'd jump out, surround the van, check it thoroughly, and scare the mess out of folks who wished they'd bought red vans.

At one point Pretty-Boy and Thunder were pulling over a blue Ford van with two white males in it. We had it boxed in as it came to a stop. In the blink of an eye two things happened. We all bailed out of our cruiser and the van back-fired. Kashunck! Kashunck! Kashunck! I thought I'd have heart failure. The two men in the van saw their proverbial lives flash before their eyes. Everyone froze in place with shotguns poised and safety's clicking off. The two men raised their hands very slowly and paled quickly.

After being checked out they were sent on their way. Even though they laughed with relief when the guns were put away, it was clear that they were shaken. They'd have a difficult time getting to sleep that night.

Every time we'd start to relax some, additional information would be given over the radio concerning how imperiled the county was with these two on the loose and how careful the guys needed to be in apprehending them. And, periodically, there would be a sighting. A guard saw one here, a trooper spotted one there, a dog picked up a fresh trail, the chopper noticed movement in some woods. They were everywhere at once. These incidents served to get us jacked up and tense.

An hour after the first call had come out, a prison guard claimed to have shot at one in some woods three miles south of the camp. So everyone charged in that direction. We found a victim with four shotgun pellet holes. It was a "Give a Hoot Don't Pollute" trash can. The guards were not known for their competency.

By eleven o'clock most of the 'outsiders' had been called off the search. Those of us who were still looking had calmed down and were in fact tired of the whole thing. The radio returned to normal traffic and some of our squad were trying to clear for a 10-10, dinner.

Bud and I were patrolling an area where the County and City line meet. It was dark, quiet, and we casually rolled into the parking lot of a discount store which had closed at nine and was empty.

We checked out a couple of unoccupied cars on the lot and eased around to the back side of the store. As we turned the corner and started down the wide, partly-lit loading area, we saw a vehicle parked in a dark corner behind a platform.

We didn't think much about it until we were nearly ten yards away from it. It was a blue van. We both realized it at the same time. I gasped. Bud snatched the mike.

"Scout 530. 10-33. I'm on a blue Dodge van, Virginia, Frank-Henry-Lincoln 410. Behind the Super Discount Store. Send a back-up ASAP."

Without waiting for a response, he dropped the mike and reached behind his back. When his hand came out it was holding his back-up revolver, a small framed five shot 38. He dropped it on my lap and said, "We can't wait for a back-up. You cover the back and I'll take the front." And he was out the door.

As I stepped from the cruiser I held the small gun in the palm of my hand. It was cold and felt like a toy. My average-sized hand smothered the petite pistol grip. I naturally held it in my right hand and used my left hand as support. I felt strangely like Paul Bunyan using a steak knife in place of an ax.

The van was parked perpendicular to the store. We were facing the left or driver's side. Bud, with revolver drawn and held tightly in both hands, began slowly inching towards the driver's door. I moved laterally to my right, then straight towards the double rear doors. I was wound up like a jack-in-the-box ready to pop. I stopped breathing and began sweating. This couldn't be happening. Two minutes before, we were discussing the differences between subs, heros, and hoagies. Now I was prepared to shoot a prison escapee. Crazy!

A security light forty yards away and three miles high gave the entire scene a brownish, shadowy aura. Glass and crushed beer cans glittered from the pavement. Every step I took creaked and popped with grinding glass. I smelled garbage and dampness. What a terrible place to die, I thought. Die? Yes, it dawned on me then that I could be the one who died in the dark concrete mini ghetto. I gripped the tiny gun tighter.

The pressure in my chest was excruciating. Then I remembered to breathe and that helped considerably. But my breathing stopped again when I saw a movement in the rear window. With a hoarse strained whisper, I looked at bud and said "Movement!". He nodded his head, lowered his gun pointing it at the front door, and stepped closer. I did the same.

I stood four feet from the rear doors in a shooting position with arms fully extended, legs bent slightly, and my mind working overtime. I could imagine someone bursting out those doors with gun in hand and murder in their eyes. I was not going to be taken by surprise.

Just then a head popped up behind th window. A white male with humongous eyes stared at me. His mouth was gaping. I flinched and almost pulled the trigger. I started to take short breaths of air that sounded like hiccups. The gun started bobbing up and down. I was shaking like a junkie in withdrawal.

"It's O.K. Just some electricians taking a coffee break," said Bud as he walked back around the van towards me. His gun was holstered, and he was smiling like it was just another traffic stop.

It took all the strength I could draw on to act calm. "Great! I almost shot that guy when his head popped up in the window. That would definitely be bad for Department PR for the Chaplain to blow away an electrician. Here, take this before I shoot my foot with it. If you're going to hand me your back-up, next time carry a real gun. That one's too much like a toy." I couldn't shut up. I needed to talk and release the pent up nervousness inside me. I talked so much that Bud left there and drove straight to the station. I vented my anxiety on everyone in the station while he did his paper work. By the time he was done so was I. I went home and stared at the ceiling all night.

I re-lived the event a hundred times that night. There was a wild churning in my stomach and an undeclared war was taking place in my head. There seemed to be no way to control my feelings. I was torn between my conscience and my soaring spirit. Technically, doctrinally, I'd violated the principles I lived by. Yet, wow, what a high. There's nothing like danger to put some spice in your life. In thirty-two years there were few days that I'd never forget. This would be one of them. Not another routine day of work to be chewed up by time and spit out of the record books as insignificant. I'd experienced an event that every fiber in my body felt. A potential life and death situation had been faced, challenged, and walked away from. Life seemed sweeter, fuller, and energized because of it.

I'd taken up arms against a fellow man. That was wrong. Would I have shot someone if our lives had been threatened? It scared me to think about it, but I probably would have. That would have been terribly wrong. Yet, no matter how vociferous my conscience, I couldn't bring myself to feel guilty for what I'd done. It was a thrilling experience and I refused to feel bad about it. It was unthinkable to imagine my just sitting there while Bud endangered his life enforcing the law. Was I rationalizing? What would Jesus have done? Would He even have been in a police cruiser? Why not?

I did more than stare at the ceiling that night. I prayed a lot too.

CHAPTER TEN

A docile wisp of wind gave wee relief to the oppressive heat which had diminished little in the four hours the sun had been laid to rest. At midnight the black asphalt still radiated the August heat. Clothes stuck to our skin. The act of stepping out of the cruiser and leaving the air-conditioning became burdensome. The cotton camel-colored sports coat I wore had rings under the arms that were coffee-colored causing it to bind and chafe and give a malodorous announcement of my presence.

My face felt oily and gritty. My eyes hurt from straining to see traffic violations and I was ready to head home to my shower and my bed. As Walt headed towards the station I could already feel the shower massager beating the grime and salt off my prunish body.

When you are hunting deer, the best way to insure seeing one, is to put your gun down and respond to the call of nature. It never fails, one will come by and you won't have time to grab your gun. Things have a way of happening at the worst time.

It had been a slow, boring evening. Every time Walt asked me if I wanted to do anything in particular I said "no". Now I wanted very much to do something, go home and clean up. Then the deer came by. We got a call for a Signal 46 A and P, a suspicious auto and person, at Oakview Shopping Center.

The stores were all closed and the parking lot was empty. So the white Chevy Chevette was easy to see and find as it sat under a spotlight in a No Parking zone.

The driver of the car was a very nervous but polite black male. He looked to be about twenty one. His hair was short and his clothes were clean and neat. Even in that heat he had the top button of his plaid shirt buttoned. After Walt took his license and registration back to the cruiser to run a check on him and the car, I talked with him some. He was very articulate and intelligent. He said that he was just out riding around listening to some music and relaxing. I noticed that he had a radio-cassette player in the passenger's seat. The cops called them Ghetto Blasters, but I felt sure that this guy wouldn't appreciate that.

Walt came back to the car and returned his papers to him. Then the young guy got the standard sermonette about the dangers of being out alone and the probability of becoming a suspect if any of the stores were broken into. Plus, once the stores closed down, the parking lot was too. He smiled and thanked us politely, and promised not to do it again.

As he drove off Walt said, "Now there's a strange bird. He's got a D.C. drivers license, he's driving a rental car from Maryland, and he's cruising Virginia. I'd like to have gotten a look at what's in that paper bag in the back seat. Maybe he's just a clean cut burglar."

"You've become a suspicious cynic in your old age, Walt. That guy was so clean cut he squeaked. He probably suffers from insomnia and is just out taking a ride in the country. After all, it is Friday night and we all have different ways of getting our kicks."

"Just wait 'til you've been out here a little longer Rev," he said with a pessimistic sneer, "you'll find out that the only thing 'clean cut' is people's front yards. The worst kind of dirt is the kind that hides behind starched and pressed chic clothing.

"Spoken like a true cop. If you'd put a few scriptures with that it would preach in any church in the country. Are you sure you really left the ministry?" I said that laughingly, but I truly wondered.

"Naw, I just changed congregations. I now preach for the Church of the Street. The members maul and maim each other regularly. They worship the god called Big Bucks and are willing to sacrifice everyone else to get it. They're pretty much like any other church."

"Whoa! You really have gotten cynical."

"'Yeah, I guess I have."

On that somber note, he dropped me off at the station and continued his patrolling. He seemed to be troubled by the revelation that he'd truly become a misanthropic ex-minister.

During the drive home, the shower massage, and the thirty minutes I layed awake after going to bed, I was haunted by another "should have" in my life. The "should have's" of life seemed to attack me on a daily basis. I should have stayed with Walt a little longer and talked through what was troubling him. Instead I had let my tired and shower hungry body pull me away from a silent cry for help—my job. Well, hopefully, I'd have another chance to help Walt. The next day I was slapped with another "should have" that would stick in my gut for the rest of my life.

After doing some sermon preparation in my office the next morning, I swung by the station to see if I could catch somebody for lunch. I caught Merve the Perve.

Merve was a ten year veteran of the department. Before that he had been a Green Beret with two tours in Vietnam. His looks concealed the lethal training and experiences that he never talked about. He was only 5'9" with a healthy chunkiness and a happy countenance. He was laid back and felt none of the temptations others did to prove he was cut from Clint Eastwood's mold. He only wanted to get his twenty in and get out. So he didn't exactly burn-up the highways looking for Toads. When I'd ridden with Merve we did zero police work. But he was a good talker, and like me, a history buff. So I had a good time riding with him. We constantly exchanged books and recommended others to each other.

I never heard why he was called Merve the Perve. His name wasn't Merve but Marvin. Marvin Peters. Perve was short for pervert. I'm sure that it referred to some incident or case that he worked years ago. No one seemed to remember or at least they conveniently forgot.

Over a Big Mac and fries, we discussed the new book he'd just read about the Korean War. When we'd exhausted that subject he changed to shop talk.

"Did they call you out for that suicide last night?"

"No, they didn't," I said with disgusted surprise. I was miffed. I'd stressed to everybody that I was to be called out for every fatality, homicide and suicide. I had to make myself valuable to them and the way to do that was by doing the dirty work for them. But it's hard to change patterns and procedures overnight.

"Oh, well, it was a pretty simple one according to the read out. One of the guys, I think it was Lithlow, was trying to spot some deer in a field over on Simpson Road and saw a car back up in the woods. He followed a dirt road to the car and found it running with a hose going from the exhaust to the window. The guy inside was dead as a door nail. They called rescue anyways, but it was a waste of time."

Still perturbed about not being called I asked "Who was the victim and when was he found?"

"I can't remember his name, but it was a black male from D.C. Drove all the way out here to off himself. Strange. They found him about 1:30. He was driving a white Chevette."

The bells stated going off in my head like Big Ben. A black male in a white Chevette? Was that the 46 A and P from last night? I told Merve about the fellow Walt and I checked on at midnight. He raised his eyebrows, shrugged his shoulders and said, "Sounds like the same guy to me." He obviously didn't pick up on the same implications that I did.

I hurried back to the station and snatched the Daily Activity Board off the wall. The information on the computer print out confirmed my suspicions. It was the same polite, clean cut young guy that Walt and I had checked out. He must have had the hose and towels to stuff in the window in the paper sack that Walt wanted to see.

In frustration, I went over to the PCA at the desk and asked her, "Why wasn't I called out for that Signal 45 this morning? Who was the supervisor?"

Surprised she said, "I don't know. Let's see . . . . It was Sergeant Hinckley."

No wonder I wasn't called.

I should have talked to that guy more. I should have detected that something was wrong. We knew it was strange for him to be out alone riding around. I should have pryed the truth out of him.

The "should have's" ate me alive all day. I replayed the event at the shopping center over and over. I dissected his statements. There just was no hint at all that he was cruising around looking for a place to kill himself.

Then it hit me. I never even told him that I was a Chaplain, a minister. If he'd known maybe he'd have opened up to me. I might have been able to prevent his death. But he never knew I was a Chaplain. I SHOULD HAVE told him.

My tour of duty as a Police Chaplain almost ended that day. My job was to help and I failed. I had actually been proud of the fact that most people mistook me for a cop. I rationalized that as being good because then the Toads would think that the officer had a back-up with him and they'd be more cooperative. In truth I was playing cops. When the guy at the Pizza Hut told me, when I walked in with one of the guys, that I looked like Frank Furillo I nearly popped the buttons on my vest. I was in Flat-Foot fantasy land and I'd forgotten that my objective was to be Christ-like, not cop-like. I needed to chuck it all and get back to being an orthodox minister.

I sat in my office for several hours thinking and praying. I had pen and paper in front of me to write up my resignation letter. I'd concluded that God was telling me that Chaplain work wasn't for me. I picked up the pen and wrote on the top left side, To My Friends At Station 5. The phone rang.

"Hey Rev. This J.C.", he laughed, "I mean Walt. I've been thinking about what we talked about last night, and . . . well, could you ride with me awhile tonight so we could discuss it further? Just a couple hours is all, not the whole night."

It took a moment for his question to register. I started to say "Not tonight. I'm quitting this Chaplain junk." But then I realized what a difficult thing it must have been for him to call me and ask for help. Maybe God was trying to give me another sign before I did something that I shouldn't

"Sure thing man. Why don't you come by and pick me up here at the office at about eight?"

"O.K. I'll see ya in about forty-five minutes."

The "couple hours" turned into six. I'm not sure who counselled with whom. We talked about his cynicism and he announced that he wanted to come visit my church the next Sunday. I was floored. We talked about faith in God and our fellow man. He knew that he had been slipping into a deep depression because as he said, "I had no foundation in my life. I closed my mind to God because I didn't want to feel guilty about my loose life style. Yet all along I knew I was only kidding myself."

After we cleared up his depression we went to work on mine. If he had not been a former minister I would never have brought it up. But I felt like he would understand the conflict I felt. So I unloaded about the suicide.

"I know what you mean," he said, "that's why I never let a DWI off the hook. I always think about what would happen if I let him go and then he kills someone in a wreck because of his being drunk. I would go crazy blaming myself for it. But you had no way of knowing the guy was suicidal. Your feeling that you might have helped him if he'd known you were a Chaplain is just conjecture at best. He knew where to get help if he'd wanted it. If he'd made up his mind that he was going to end his life, nothing you or I could have done would change that.

"If you're going to stick with us Rev, you've got to learn to roll with the punches. It sounds trite, but you win some and you lose some. There are plenty of people who need your help now. It's to late to do anything about what happened last night. Just file it away as a lesson learned."

It's amazing what self pity does to the memory. I'd said those same things to scores of people for as many different reasons. It wasn't that I didn't know it, it was just temporarily lost in the soul searching. It took a cop to remind me.

Early the next day, a couple hours before church services, I tore up the sheet of paper addressed to My Friends At Station 5.

I pushed all the "should haves" into a tiny dark crevice at the back of my mind. For the moment I was reconvinced that I was doing what God wanted. How many more "should have's" could I endure? I had no idea. In fact, I couldn't decipher why it had all disturbed me so much. "Should have's" are an inseparable part of any minister's life. We incessantly pummel our consciences with "I should have visited so and so in the hospital," "I should have done that job myself", "I should have preached more on that subject", "I should have prayed about that", "I should have done a little more studying of this", "I should have . . . I should have . . . I should have". It was endless. So why had this one hit me so forcefully? Was it because it had been a life and death issue, or was it because I wanted so desperately to be Super Chaplain, the hero of every cop?

"Should have's" never brought me to the brink of resignation again. Nevertheless, it wasn't long until again I wondered what in the world I was doing being a Police Chaplain.

CHAPTER ELEVEN

One of the few men at our station who somehow escaped being tagged with a nom de guerre was Corporal Benjamin Trosko. Ben was one of the supervisors who was highly regarded by the men. Even though he went strictly by-the-book, he was understanding and very protective of his men. His average-sized frame appeared much taller due to his ramrod erect posture. He walked as if he'd come from West Point instead of the Police Academy. With a square jaw, short cropped hair, and slightly pock-marked face he had a no-nonsense cast which concealed his amiable nature. He was sharp, efficient, and destined to be upwardly mobile in the Department.

Each squad had two supervisors, a sergeant and a corporal. Their jobs were essentially the same, but of course when both were present, decisions were made by the higher ranking cop. The sergeant was Car 5 and the Corporal was Car 50. When there was an overlap of squads, the last squad to hit the street used it's squad designator after it's car number. Thus, when the midnight sergeant marked in service he was Car 5 Adam, or what ever letter distinguished his squad. They would maintain the letter designator until the evening squad marked out at 2 A.M.

This night I was riding with Car 50 Charlie, Corporal Ben. I enjoyed riding with supervisors. Since they had no assigned patrol area, they were free to go anywhere and roll on any call that came out. Whenever an officer had a problem or a question about procedure they would call for a supervisor. So they usually were on every crime scene of any significance.

They were not supposed to work traffic violations because that would tie them up too much when they might be needed for something more important. The only exception to that was DWI's and even then, if they could call an officer to make the stop and arrest they would. So when it was a slow night for the officers, it was real slow for the supervisors.

We'd barely left the station parking lot when Ben asked me about the church I preached for. That was like saying sic 'em to a dog. I was just beginning to wax eloquent, or "wax an elephant" as we used to say in college, when the radio interrupted my homily.

"Scout 520."

"Scout 520," he answered.

"Signal 21 at 4563 Cedarcrest Drive. Several youths are swimming in the Cedarcrest Community Pool. A representative from the Association will respond and they will press charges."

"10-4. In route."

"Scout 520 Charlie for back-up," added the dispatcher.

"Scout 520 Charlie direct."

"Scout 520 and 520 Charlie. 22:10."

Ben stepped on the gas and said, "We're just a few blocks away. Let's swing by and see if we can catch some teenie-bopper skinny dipping."

The three cruisers converged on the darkened parking lot of the pool at the same time. With flashlights in hand the four of us crept up to the clubhouse, which hid our approach from the pool area. We could hear whispers and giggles coming from the other side of the house.

The other two officers went to the left and we circled to the right. The six foot fence was easy to climb, especially since the pointed barbs on the top had been bent down.

As we rounded the house I had to cover my mouth to stifle the laugh that wanted to jump out. In the shallow end of the pool, just ten yards in front of us and the two cops approaching from the other side, were four rear ends sticking up from the water. We'd been mooned. I thought for a brief second that it had all been a set up, but when the four teenaged boys surfaced we scared a good three years off their lives. Our flashlights settled on faces that were as white as their backsides had been.

The guys were pretty rough on them. I thought for a moment that they were going to cuff them. As it was, the boys stood in the night air shivering, dripping, naked, embarrassed, and humiliated. These were not smart-aleck kids looking for trouble, but just some boys doing what boys occasionally do. Seeking adventure. I remembered the scores of times I snuck into the pool in the housing development next to ours. We didn't have one in our project, so we just borrowed theirs. Nothing was more exciting than those surreptitious dips in the neighbor's pool.

When the manager of the pool got there, the boys were finally told to put their cloths on. The manager chimed right in with the third degree.

"What if one of you'd drowned in there? Do you know what the penalty is for trespassing? I'm tired of you kids thinking you can use this pool any time you choose. You're gonna be sorry you ever climbed that fence."

On and on he went. I wanted to say "Ease up buddy. We got people killing and robbing each other and these kids just went for a swim. Cut'em some slack." But I didn't. He wanted an officer to go with him to each of their homes and let their folks know about their terrible crime. I thought to myself that if their mothers were like mine they'd laugh in the guys face. Boys will be boys, and jerks will be jerks.

Since we were not needed any longer, Ben and I returned to his cruiser and continued patrolling the neighborhood.

"The manager was a little overly dramatic wasn't he?", I offered. "They didn't seem to be nearly the criminals he was raving they were."

"Yeah, I guess. He's had so much trouble with kids sneaking

into his pool after hours that I guess he wants to make examples out of these."

"I can understand his being irked over it, but charging those kids with trespassing? That seems a little bit harsh. I would say that the embarrassment they just went through being caught was punishment enough."

"Being charged with trespassing is no big deal. It's more a matter of inconvenience. They'll have to go to Juvie Court with their parents, get their hands slapped by a judge, and sent home. Since they are only 15 or 16, their records will be destroyed when they're 18. So it's really not much more than a hassel for'em."

"I remember going to Juvenile Court when I was a kid. The Judge kept saying 'Next time you come bring your toothbrush with you because you're going to stay awhile'. Back then, when the authorities spoke you listened. He scared the mess out of me."

"Come on now Chaplain," said Ben with a skeptical tone, "you don't mean to tell me that you were a JD? Next thing you'll tell me is that you got 'born again' while in prison"

"Naw, nothing that dramatic. I just got in trouble for being in some gang fight as a kid in South East Washington, D.C. We had to be in a gang to survive back then. And I'm talking elementary school kids, not teenagers. Most of it was racially oriented too. Back then, most of the apartment complexes were segregated. So you had one block that was all whites and the next was all blacks. They had their gangs and we had ours. Without them it was hard to get home from school without making it a sprint. I never understood why it had to be that way. Some of my best friends at school were blacks. We'd sit together in class, play together at recess, and eat together at lunch. But when school was over it was go-for-the-jugular time. Everyone remembers the riots of '68, but that was Blacks hurting Blacks more than anything else. In the late fifties, at the beginning of the White Flight, it was down right dangerous to walk the streets alone or with a small group for that matter. It was a strange and dark time for our Nations Capitol."

"Now I am intrigued," said Ben, "how did you go from being a JD from Washington to a minister in Virginia? There are not many original Washingtonians around here anymore."

"Well . . ."

"Scout 510," EOC sure made it hard for a guy to tell his life story. "Start for a Signal 9-I on Wagon Trail Road."

"We'd better check on that one," said Ben, "that's a pretty ugly road and the accidents are usually bad. That 9 with injury might become a 9-F."

Wagon Trail Road was a narrow two laned sidewinder-shaped road that, due to increased population, had become a popular connector between two major thoroughfares. It was deadly. A series of sharp turns bordered on one side by woods and the other a white fence and pasture land, it infused many with a Grand Prix complex to 'go for it'. Unfortunately, ditches and oak trees are very unforgiving, and several would-be Al Unser's became statistics.

By the time we got to Wagon Trail Road, one of our guys was laying out flares and closing down the road at its beginning point and another was closing the other end. The wreck had made it impassable. Over the tops of the trees we could see the glow from flames. The accident appeared to be on about the second curve in the road. We left the cruiser so it could be used to help block off the road.

With orange traffic vests on and flashlights in hand, we hiked up the road to the scene of the accident. As we rounded the second turn, the pupils of our eyes were dilated by the light from an inferno which engulfed a Ford van. The van was on its side with its undercarriage against a large oak tree on the right side of the road. The van and the tree were ablaze. Two fire engines were trying to keep it from spreading. They were watering down the other trees around it as well as trying to extinguish the flames.

"If they didn't get out of that van there's no doubt about whether they're dead or alive. That sucker's really cooking," said Ben.

"Let's hope they got out in time. I can see an ambulance on the other side of the accident. Lets get over there and find out about the passengers of this oven." I had to yell over the noises from the flames and the fire engines.

We climbed the white fence and circled the scene from out in the pasture on the left side. As we walked up to the ambulance we were met by Thunder, who was Scout 510 that night.

"Hey Rev. Looks like Hell doesn't it?", he laughed at his own joke. "There was two guys in it when it wrecked and they were both walking away from it when it went up in flames. Hope they had insurance."

"They weren't hurt?" asked Ben, clearly surprised.

"Just a few cuts, scrapes, and bruises. They hit the ditch down there and it turned on its side and just slid into that tree. If it hadn't caught fire there wouldn't have been that much damage. I think it's safe to say it's totaled."

Turning to look back at the almost-extinguished flames, Ben said, "Yeah, I think that would be safe to say unless they're into cinder."

"Do you need any help with anything?", I asked.

"I guess not. It scared the Devil out of the two guys who were in the van, but they'll be O.K. I'll lay down the law and stroke 'em for a few violations. I think they'll learn their lesson."

"How old are they?"

Reaching into his right shirt pocket, he pulled out two drivers licenses and flashed his five-cell on them.

"The driver is . . . twenty, and the other guy is . . . nineteen. Old enough to know better than to exceed the speed limit on Wagon Trail Road."

"Looks like you got it covered." said Ben, "we're gonna hit the road."

"Oh, don't leave now," smiled Thunder, "I was just fixing to get out some marshmallows and do some roasting."

"Don't you dare get near that fire Thunder", said Ben, "cut one and you'd explode. And think of all the paper work I'd have to do. In fact, I'll have the fire engines stand by just in case you get near a hot ember while you're doing measurements."

Laughing, Thunder said, "If you see a bright flash on the skyline get your freaking paper work ready."

Amazing! Surrounded by fire engines and ambulances, men battling a blaze, and two more being bandaged up we're cracking jokes. Such is the nature of cops.

Just as we slid back into the cruiser we heard EOC advise Scout 530 that K-9 three was responding to his location. So with a "hum?" Ben snatched the mike.

"Car 50 Charlie. I'm 10-8 from the 9-I. What's going on in 530?"

"Car 50 Charlie. Scout 530 wants a K-9 unit to assist in tracking a Signal 21-34 suspect at 11253 Orrington Way."

"A trespassing mental case?", Ben said to me with a quizzical look on his face. Then, depressing the mike key, he informed EOC that we'd be heading in that direction to assist 530.

"Trespassing and mental case?", he said again with more emphasis and doubt. "It's got to be a domestic problem. A crazy neighbor who keeps walking into someone's house or a relative who keeps showing up when they're supposed to be confined somewhere. There's no telling. Orrington Way is a pretty ritzy part of the County. All the houses are on five or ten acre lots. Maybe it's a Howard Hughes type wondering around looking for someone to give a million dollars to?"

"Sure. Would you have someone arrested for trespassing if they were trying to give you a million dollars?", I said rolling my eyes to the ceiling of the car. "I have to give you credit for having a good imagination though. Just don't let it get out of hand or they'll be calling you a Signal 34."

Orrington Way is a country road. At this time of the year when the trees are all heavy with leaves, you'd almost think that it was a wilderness area instead of a residential development. The give-away was the natural wood mail boxes and the occasional split-rail fence set back from the road enough to allow people to ride their horses up and down the road at their leisure. All the homes were set back from the road, giving them privacy and distance from the common folks. At night, lights from the houses filtered through the foliage revealing their existence. It was the habitat of the well off. And in a County where a cave cost a mint, these folks were really well off.

Easing down a long gravel driveway, we came into a clearing lit with flood lights from a large two story colonial house. In front of the detached two car garage was an LTD stationwagon and an Audi. Parked behind them was two police cruisers. One belonged to Bud, 530, and the other had the distinctive cage of a K-9 car that divided the front seat from the rear.

We found Bud and K-9 three standing in the well lit back yard comparing notes from their 007's. K-9 three was of average build with the usual short cropped hair and neatly trimmed black mustache. He had a stern face but a twinkle in his eye that bespoke a mischievous streak.

They both turned towards us and I for the first time saw the huge German Shepherd sitting obediently at his master's feet. The dog barely gave us a glance and I found myself thinking, "That's right big fella, we're the good guys."

"Hey Corporal. Rev," said Bud. "Do you all know Max Riggins, K-9 three and his partner Skipper?"

Since Max's hands were occupied with a leash, flashlight, 007, and a coiled leather extension leash, we omitted the handshakes and settled for verbal greetings. I wasn't too keen on the idea of placing my hand any closer to the animal who looked capable of taking it along with my forearm in one bite. Max seemed to sense my reservations. He grinned and said, "Don't worry about ole Skipper here. He wouldn't hurt a flea unless I told him to. Or if someone tried to harm me. He does like to sink his teeth into Toads, but even then, it's only when I let him. Sometimes it's a better reward for him than a Doggie Snack."

"Just be sure and tell'em that Chaplains don't taste nearly as good as Toads," I said, trying to be friendly. Max smiled and said, "No problem. Skipper and I don't want to do anything to make the Man upstairs angry with us. We plan to patrol the Streets of Gold when we finish our tour on earth."

We all laughed at his little joke, but I think he was halfway serious about it. I wondered if he was a religious man or just using humor that was appropriate to my presence.

Bud gave us a brief run down on the case.

"The Hollings are the proud parents of a class A whacko. Their oldest son, Gary Hollings, age 19, got his brains fried by PCP. Probably supplied by the Cooper clan no doubt. Anyway, they had him institutionalized for a while and after he was released, they had him visiting a shrink regularly.

"To make a long story short, he stopped going to his shrink and started becoming a pain to the family. So for the sake of the rest of the family, they told him to hit-the-road and not come back until he was ready to get the help he needed. Well, instead of thumbing his way to California, like most guys his age would do, he took to living in the woods here behind the house. He hasn't really bothered anybody except his own family. Whenever the family leaves the house, he breaks in and takes some food and clothes and whatever else he needs then slithers back into the woods. That, of course, doesn't do much for the family's sense of security. They think he has even slipped into the house a few times at night after they're all asleep."

"Just another All-American family," chimed in Max.

"Yeah, well the family isn't nasty or hateful about him. They just wanted to force him into getting help and it's kinda backfired on 'em. So they talked to the magistrate and he issued a warrant for trespassing. It's just an excuse to get him and hold him until they can get a mental petition.

"When they came home about an hour ago, they caught him in the house. He ran out the kitchen door there and presumably into the woods back here." Bud pointed his 007 at the darkness just past the manicured back yard.

"We should be able to get a good track," said Max, "the heat and humidity will help hold the scent on the ground. You all stay about twenty feet behind me so that the trail isn't messed up and ole Skipper will find this guy in no time."

He fastened the extension leash to the smaller leash on the dog. This allowed the dog to work the trail about twenty feet in front of him. Skipper seemed to immediately pick up a trail. Off they went, with the dog leading Max and the three of us ten yards behind.

Once my eyes adjusted to the darkness, I could see that we were following a well-worn trail. We didn't talk and we only moved when the dog moved. At times he stopped for several seconds, running his nose back and forth across the trail. Then he'd plunge ahead quickly for twenty or thirty yards. I felt like we were playing a game of Simon Says with the dog being Simon. Yet it was fascinating to watch Max and Skipper work. It was obvious that they'd been together for a long time. Max would mumble something that only the dog could hear and he seemed to attack the trail with renewed vigor.

Except for the occasional cackle of our portable radios, the only sounds were sniffing and the creaking of the leather gear Bud and Ben wore. Excitement was building. Would we find him up a tree? Maybe he's built himself a shelter or a cave somewhere. I even wondered if he'd be wearing a loin cloth and speak without verbs.

As we came up on a dark thicket, Max held up his hand for

us to stop. We did and he didn't. Max and his dog disappeared into the thicket. We could hear them tromping around and see the temporary streak of Max's flashlight as he shined it on spots in the thicket.

Skipper came out first and snorted twice as if to protest something he'd found noxious. Max came out right behind him, taking up the slack in the leash until Skipper was only three feet in front of him.

"That's where he's been staying," he said, "There's blankets, clothes, stove, and trash everywhere. I think we've been back-tracking him. Skipper hasn't been too excited about the trail. So, this must have been the way he went to the house. Let's go back and see if we can pick up a different trail."

Once we were back at the Hollings house, Bud, Ben, and I stood in the driveway as Max and his partner circled the house trying to pick up a fresh trail. Having no success, Max explained that either we'd really messed up the scent or the guy was still inside. Since either one was entirely possible, we attacked the one we could do something about. We searched the house.

Actually it wasn't "we" that searched the house, but "them". I talked with Mr. and Mrs. Hollings while the others, including Skipper, went through the house.

It's hard to avoid the trap of pre-judging people. Usually you just make a fool out of yourself jumping conclusions that you're not trained to jump. The Hollings were not the snobby rich aristocrats I'd expected. I don't know why I'd expected affluence to create arrogance, but these folks were warm, open, and deeply concerned about their son. They felt awful about calling the police in to get their son, but they'd swallowed their pride because he desperately needed help. They felt they had to do something, even if it incurred recriminations from the neighbors.

"Unless he fits in a ten inch by four inch air-conditioning vent," said Bud, as they all entered the living room where I sat with the Hollings, "he's not anywhere in this house."

"Skipper would have smelled him if he were," bragged Max.

"Maybe you should check the garage," suggested Mr. Hollings. I could see the proverbial "idea" light flash on in the three officers eyes. It was like "Why didn't we think of that? We walked all around it."

The garage was dwarfed by the house. It was small, about 20x30 feet, and had been turned into a shop. It was so clean and tidy that it clearly hadn't had a car in it for a long time. With studs exposed, it had ladders, tools, and yard implements hanging on one wall, a work bench on another, and snow tires leaning on the third. Nothing was blocking the two sliding garage doors. It looked like it could have been the model for garages across the country. At least they seemed to have the same interior decorator as most folks, Hap Hazard and Associates.

There was nothing to hide in. In fact, with Skipper laying down in the middle of the floor surrounded by three cops, two parents, and one Chaplain, there was barely room to turn around. Ben got down a ladder and checked out the attic above the garage. We waited breathlessly as he scanned the attic with his flashlight.

"Nothing up there," said Ben coming down the ladder. As he returned it to its place on the wall he added, "That's amazing that he left no trail for Skipper. I guess we must have trampled all over the scent, although we really didn't do much walking around."

"Well, he'll be back," said Bud as he turned to leave.

Bud was followed out the door by the Hollings, and then Ben. Just as I started for the door Max slapped me on the left arm. When I looked at him he had his index finger up across his lips giving me the universal sign for "quiet".

I followed his finger as it pointed from his lips to the workbench just eight feet away. What was he pointing at? A bench? Skipper was still laying down facing that direction and he seemed to be bored with the whole thing. What was it? A bench made of 2x6's covered with tools and with a pile of newspapers under it, and a pair of tennis shoes sticking out from under the papers.

Those tennis shoes had feet in them! Like I'd been hit with a bolt of lightning it all came into focus. It wasn't a pile of newspapers it was two or three papers opened and spread over someone sitting curled up in a ball. It or rather he, was so completely out in the open that a cold shiver raced up my spine. We'd walked all around him. The dog, a trained tracking police dog, had been laying just a few feet away and never noticed him. The cover he'd used was so pitifully insufficient that he should have been the very first thing we saw when we came in the room. There was nothing else under or beside the bench to hide behind. The place was well lighted and uncluttered. How in the world had we managed to miss him? It was scary. Especially when I considered what could happened if he had had a gun or a knife. Wasn't there some saying about "If it had been a snake . . ."

Bud came back into the garage to see what was holding us up and he instantly saw the focus of our attention.

Max got a tight grip on Skipper's collar and stepped closer to the workbench. The dog instantly became aware of the concealed fugitive and strained at his master's restraining grip. Allowing the dog to get within eighteen inches of the guy, Max leaned closer and said, "If you don't crawl out from under that table and spread-eagle on the floor in five seconds, I'm gonna turn this dog loose. Move! Now!"

Immediately the papers separated and I could see a pair of eyes staring at the growling Skipper. I half expected him to say "Who me?", but he slowly let the papers fall to the ground and, as Max pulled the dog back some, he began to stretch out on the floor, stomach down, arms and legs spread out. Bud quickly cuffed him and checked him for weapons.

He was a good looking kid. A little grubby, but more like a beach bum instead of a crazed hermit. He had sandy blond hair that fell across his forehead and barely covered his ears. A handsome child-like face with no whiskers and bright blue eyes gave him the appearance of being as dangerous as Peter Pan. He smiled and shrugged his shoulders as if to say, "I gave it my best shot and lost". It took a minute, but then I recognized why he looked familiar to me.

As Bud and Ben led the boy from the garage, I said to Max, "Don't you think he looks just like the guy who played the part of Luke Skywalker in Star Wars?"

Raising his eyebrows in recognition he answered, "Yeah, I guess he really is a Space Cadet."

We both laughed at the pun. Space Cadet is the unofficial police label for any Signal 34, mental case.

Even though Max was laughing, I could tell that he was uneasy. It had genuinely disturbed him that he and Skipper had been so completely deceived by their spoor. Cops don't like to be vulnerable. They like to always be one up on the "bad guys", but this time they had nearly been made a laughing stock by a guy who was supposed to be a few slices short of having a full loaf.

Later, as Ben, Bud, and I talked about it, they both tried to be blase about the whole thing, but they were clearly rattled.

Bud said, "Imagine, being completely suckered by a fugitive from the Funny Farm. If he'd had a gun and flipped out, he could have iced every one of us before we ever knew he was there."

Ben was more philosophical. "That's just the nature of the job. You never know when you stop a car or walk up to a house whether or not it's hiding a whacko or an Arab terrorist. You just have to be alert all the time."

"Yeah, but that Jack-leg was five feet away from us hiding in plain sight," protested Bud. "The freaking dog didn't even know he was there and he was looking right at him. We all looked right past him because it was a totally illogical place to hide. It makes you wonder how many times we've searched houses and other buildings after a B and E and walked right past the Toad sitting on a coffee table or laying on the couch."

"Well, look at it this way," I chimed in, "the next time you'll examine everything a lot closer and you'll see the Toad before he sees you. This experience might very well save your life the next time."

"No, the next time," said Bud straightening his shoulders and swelling up his chest, "I'm gonna chunk a grenade in the freaking room and then sort through the pieces."

A perceived loss of control will always produce at least one thing, stress. An affliction that goes with police work as surely as the badge does.

CHAPTER TWELVE

The Saturday morning sunshine burst into my bedroom, saturating the walls with a buttercup yellow hue. It was one of those mornings when you leap from the bed and shout to the world that it's great to be alive. I looked in the mirror and rubbed the sleep from my eyes and I didn't even care that I looked like Phyllis Diller after a bad night.

Bounding into the bathroom I thrust back the shower curtain, cleared my throat, spread my arms like a bird, and gave my best Robert Schuller impersonation of, "This is the day the Lord hath given, let us rejoice and be glad therein." I showered singing How Great Thou Art and my favorite oldie, Duke of Earl. I'm sure there's some Freudian insight there somewhere, but I felt to good to care.

I always feel good on Saturday when I've got both of my sermons finished for Sunday. I've spent many Saturday nights finishing up a lesson. It tends to get me uptight on Saturday to have that hanging over my head, especially when the day is full of other obligations. But not this Saturday. I was loose and ready for fun. No one from my congregation was in the hospital. No one was lined up for counseling. No one in particular needed to be visited. Of course, all that could change with one phone call, but for awhile at least I was free to spend some time with my wife and kids.

From 8:30 in the morning until 3:00 in the afternoon we watched cartoons, played games, and straightened up the house. At 3 the kids settled down to watch a movie on T.V. and my wife started sewing a new dress. I felt an uncontrollable urge to attend Roll Call.

When I left the house, I told my wife that I'd be back in about an hour. I never ride on Saturday evening because of study needs or church events. I fully intended to visit the guys awhile, attend the 3:45 Roll Call, and go home. I stayed out until 1:30 Sunday morning.

The moment I walked into the station I knew it was going to be a good visit. Everyone greeted me in a friendly, warm manner. They all seemed genuinely glad that I came by. I was further encouraged when I sat down in the roll call room and realized that I had ridden with every person on that squad at least once. They were all in my circle.

Leather creaked, shoes shuffled, and desks rattled. The reading of the boards was interrupted by the usual cursing, swearing and laughter. The guys were all in a good mood and seemed primed for something special.

That "something special" was Captain Chicken. I had to laugh at that name. It was the name given to Patrolman Second Class (P-2) Chuck Irving. As the P-2 of the squad, it was his responsibility once a week to spend a few minutes of a roll call in training the rest of the group. Chuck was a traffic man. That means that he got most, if not all, of his stats from doing traffic violations as opposed to criminal cases. The County really likes for an officer to do both, but since it's easier to catch someone speeding than breaking into a house, the majority of cops are heavier on traffic than criminal. Chuck was ALL traffic. He had a reputation for writing tickets for charges that most guys would never write. These charges were called "Chicken" charges by everyone. Charges like having a head-light out, to loud exhaust, or unauthorized exhaust equipment. There was even a charge for improper beeping of your horn. In fact, there are hundreds of "Chicken" charges that go virtually ignored by the cops. Most cops. Not Chuck, "Captain Chicken," Irving.

In reality, Chuck's reputation far exceeded the facts. He had written a couple questionable charges way back when, been labeled, and because of his comedic disposition, he fanned the fire and played the part all the way. His roll call trainings became popular due to his wit and dramatics as he'd pull out the State Code book and read some obscure law. His embellishments usually had everyone rolling on the floor laughing.

The sergeant tossed the Daily Report Boards aside, leaned back in the rusted gray swivel chair and said, "And now it's time for da-da-da-da Captain Chicken! Take it away, Captain."

Raucous applause caused the Captain to take a brief bow.

Chuck was one of the "older guys" at the station. He was about thirty-six, a fifteen-year veteran of the force who came in after a tour in the navy and before the County required a college degree. He was sharp. In spite of the ribbing, he was respected for his knowledge of both the State and County codes, and was regarded as one of the experts in the County on accident investigation. At six feet with broad shoulders and a James Dean hair style, he exuded confidence and professionalism. He was the only guy at the station who ever noticed that my suits were not made of polyester. I liked him.

With an exaggerated flair, he pulled the State Code book from under his chair. Stretching his arms and flexing his fingers in preparation of opening the book in his lap, he had every eye riveted on him. In a very reverent manner, he lifted the book up level with his chin.

"Ladies and gentlemen, boys and girls, perverts and queers. Please brace yourself for another thrilling insight into our legal code. Contained in the pages of this book are codes guaranteed to ruin the day for upstanding citizens and at the same time up your stats. And if you don't like it, well, UP YOUR STATS."

Laughter and applause.

"Hush, ye wearers of leather who do strange things with your nightsticks. I am about to open THE BOOK and empower

93

you with The Law."

Silence gripped the group as he began to open the book to a pre-selected spot. He was still holding it at chin level.

When the book was opened to a forty-five degree split, he blew into it and a cloud of small chicken feathers flew into the air and seemed to hang suspended in the ever-present smoke.

The place fell apart. It caught every one of us off guard. A couple of the guys literally slid to the floor laughing. Others roared back with heads looking at the ceiling. Some, like me, laughed in our hands until tears came. It was so unexpected and so appropriate that it hurt. He had always followed the same pattern, using the same words, and that lulled us into the perfect set-up.

It took several minutes to restore order to the roll call room. Chuck had enjoyed it more than anyone else. His face was red with laughter. It was all he could do to pull himself together and continue with the training. With feathers scattered around the floor and chairs squeaking from officers who were still shaking with laughter, Chuck continued.

"What I am about to lay on you is the ultimate Chicken law. It should make you swell with pride, which in Thunder's case is a preferable element to swell up with." He had to stop and laugh some. So did everyone else. I could tell this was going to take awhile. Once our funny bone has been stimulated everything is funny.

"I'm referring, of course, to State code eighteen-point two-dash three-two-two. The terror of tobacco chewers and the rage of red-necks everywhere. This code was enacted to clean up our fair county. It reads as follows, the title is 'Expectorating in public places'." We all lost it again.

"I realize that this is an emotional issue," he said, barely able to hold his composure. "and I know you are filled with righteous indignation over the shocking discovery that a person would actually do such a disgusting thing, but . . ." He had to stop and giggle. Everyone else was too, including the two guys who were spitting their tobacco juice into empty Coke cans.

"Now listen up. You'll need to know this stuff. Take notes:

No person shall spit, expectorate, or deposit any sputum, saliva, mucus, or any form of saliva or sputum upon the floor, stairways, or upon any public building or place where the public assemble, or upon the floor of any part of any public conveyance, or upon any sidewalk abutting on any public street, alley or lane of any town or city.

Any person violating any provision of this section shall be guilty of a Class 4 misdemeanor. And as you know, a Class 4 misdemeanor carried a fine of twenty-five dollars. The moment someone spits they join the ranks of the criminal element of the county. They must be made to recognize that mucus is money.

Or, to put it in terms they can understand, 'you spit on us we'll dump on you'. Captain Chicken has spoken."

Amid laughter and scattered applause, one officer raised his hand and shook it like a third grader wanting to answer a question.

"Yes Officer Smith," said Chuck in a professional tone.

"Ah, Captain Chicken, sir, does the fine for this gosh-awful crime vary depending on whether it's sputum, saliva, mucus, or spit that is deposited?"

"Absolutely not. Each and every offense is punishable by a twenty-five dollar fine. There are rumors floating about that the legislature is considering increasing the fine on sputum, but they think that may require our having to take lab samples to be held for the court hearings, so it's been canned, so to speak, until a later date."

Holding up his 007 book and feigning a lick of his pencil tip, one of the guys said, "And how do you spell sputum, sir?"

"Come on Jake. Get with the program. That's Sam-Paul-Union-Tom-Union-Mary. Write that on the front of your book so you'll stay on the look-out for violations."

"With all due respect," said one of the tobacco chewing cops as he paused to unload a copious deposit into his Coke can, "I'll start enforcing that Chicken law the day they tell cigarette smokers to stop blowing their stinking smoke in public where it gets in my lungs and smells up my clothes."

Several followed up with a chorus of "Yeah's" and "Amens". Smoke-filled roll call rooms were always a source of irritation to those officers who didn't smoke. Some squads had even outlawed smoking during the roll calls. Usually that was only when the sergeants didn't like the smoke.

"Ah-ha," said Captain Chicken as he pointed a finger in the air, "that will never happen in our lifetime because most of our legislators are smokers. The same holds true for the Department. Most of the White Shirts in the Ivory Tower suck butts as well as kiss them."

"Here, here!"

"Amen!"

"Right on!"

After roll call and amidst the bedlam of lockers slamming and officers shouting, Chuck asked me who I was going to ride with. That's the way cops let you know they're available to ride with. Just coming out and asking you to ride would mean risking rejection.

"How about you?" I asked.

"No thanks. I have my own cruiser."

It took a second for me to catch the joke. "No, Officer Irving. I meant why don't I ride with you."

"Oh O.K. Glad to have you," he said feigning ignorance. He

95

was still giddy from his performance in roll call.

"We need to discuss the refining of your vocabulary. A man of your obvious intellect should not stoop to such blatant crudeness."

"Sweet Jesus deliver me!" he said walking towards the parking lot.

"Alright! I knew I'd get you interested in religion."

We had a good time together that evening. He was always interesting to talk to, but that night he was primed and ready. Between analyzing the stock market and debating international relations, we wrote traffic tickets like they were on sale. His nickname proved to be spurious and groundless. All the tickets we wrote were legitimate and deserving. I was amazed at his ability to spot violations while completely engrossed in a conversation with me. He'd mark 10-31 on the radio and I'd have no idea who or why he was stopping someone until he told me.

It was after 9:00 before we could get clearance to stop for dinner. Chuck took me to a little Italian cafe just out of our jurisdiction. It was quaint, and the owner doted over us so much that I found it hard to relax. Chuck loved it. Especially when the owner, in broken English, insisted that we not pay for it. I knew that was against Department regs but it happened all the time. I felt like one of the gritty cops in a Wambaugh book, who makes up for poor pay by accepting graft. The free fettucini gave me indigestion.

"Let's do a security check on the stores over in Willibby. I like to make sure that all the merchants remembered to lock up their businesses." said Chuck as we pulled out of the cafe parking lot.

Willibby was a small crossroads on the edge of the County that consisted of a tiny branch bank, a Post Office, and two gas stations. They all closed at 10:00 and their parking lots became a favorite roosting place for carloads of young people who had nothing to do. So it was a favorite past time for cops to go by and chase them away. Occasionally, they even got a drug bust or a DIP for their efforts.

As we came up to the stop light in Willibby, we could see several vehicles in the parking lot of the bank diagonally across from us. A maroon van with a yellow lightning streak on it side immediately pulled away from the others, entered the street, and slowly drove away in the opposite direction from us.

"Boy, I wish he'd squeal his tires or fishtailed a little. I'd love to stop that sucker and see what's in that van. You know who that is don't you?" asked Chuck.

"Oh, yes. That's one of the famous Cooper boys. I believe that belongs to Brian doesn't it?"

"Yeah. And you can guess what that pusher was doing over in the parking lot. A little business."

Before we even turned into the lot, the rest of the vehicles were started and moving. Some of the people looked at us with a hatred I could almost feel. Others waved and gave us that "not-this-time" grin, which is just a more mature version of sticking your tongue out at someone.

"That's right. Get out of here you pus-sucking Toads.", yelled Chuck out his window. Then he turned to me and said, "Did you see that pink Monte Carlo. The one that looked like a bottle of Pepto Bismol? Well, that's Jerry Cooper's girl friend or I should say sow friend. She's a real pig. Not bad looking, but ruthless. She used to be part of a biker gang and was used by everybody. But now she belongs to Cooper."

"He sure won't win any beauty or personality contests either. I saw him at the hospital the night Bud had to stick him and he's one ugly dude."

"You better believe it. I wouldn't doubt it if he's not responsible for half the unsolved murders in the County. Remember that guy down on Route 3 in Area one who was shot in the head at a traffic light."

"Yeah. The one they said was the result of a traffic argument? Wasn't that a shotgun to the back of the head number?"

"That's the one. Someone pulled up behind him, got out of their car, shot him in the back of the head through the rear windshield, and drove away. Well, our good buddy Jerry Cooper use to have a sawed-off pump shotgun and we used to try to catch him with it in his car. The homicide guys, after that murder, searched his house and car, and found nothing. Because of rumors about his shotgun he was a prime suspect. But you can bet that it's somewhere where he can easily get it. It's what he uses to instill fear in all his drug competition."

"He's threatened to get revenge on Bud. Does Bud know about the shotgun?"

"Sure, but Bud thinks he's faster on the draw than Cooper."

"I think he's been watching too many John Wayne westerns."

Pulling up to the front door of the bank, Chuck told me to sit tight while he checked the doors. He gave each door a hard jerk, flashed his light around inside, and returned to the cruiser. He did the same thing at the Post Office, and the Texaco station. As we pulled up to the Shell station, the last business we were going to check, we drove in with my door facing the door of the station.

"Step over there and give that door a jerk so we can get on down the road," said Chuck.

Happy to stretch my legs, I hopped out of the cruiser, and walked over to the station door. Through the posters on the windows I could see orderly pyramids of oil cans and the shiny, black rubber of new tires on display.

I placed my hand on the metal door handle and looked through the glass door. After seeing nothing unusual, I took a step back and gave the door a sharp jerk to make sure it was locked.

The instant I tugged the door, I was blinded by an interior security light and my ears were deafened by a piercing alarm which echoed through the dark night. My heart didn't leap, it stopped. It scared ten years off my life. The dark sleepy calmness of a Saturday night was shattered by a bright light and a burglar alarm. And I had been the burglar. Or rather the sucker.

Slowly I turned and glared at my dinner partner. The sight of him doubled over in the cruiser convinced me that his nickname was appropriate after all. I caught myself saying, "Sweet Jesus deliver ME," but I was serious.

The alarm cut off and reset itself after five minutes. It took much longer for my pump to reset itself. How many nights had I awaken in a cold sweat after a nightmare about having a shoot-out with Toads? Why was I worried about that? The cops, my buddies, were gong to kill me with a heart attack long before any Toad took a shot at me.

As expected, within minutes every employee in the County knew that the Chaplain had fallen for the old Shell station trick. For several days after that, along with the Security Check assignments on the roll call black-board, someone wrote Willibby Shell-Chaplain Five. It stayed up there until Hardnose got fed up with me getting so much attention and he erased it.

CHAPTER THIRTEEN

The crosshairs of the .308 came to rest on the forehead of my target. At a hundred yards the powerful scope caused the head to fill up my field of vision. It was no problem to hold the well-balanced rifle steady. The Remington had been customized to meet the specifications of the County Special Operations Team. Most departments had a SWAT team. We have a SOT team, and they are very good at what they do.

Gently I squeezed the trigger. The pressure needed was borderline hair trigger, but enough to keep a freak twitch from causing a hostage to lose their head. The recoil was nearly nonexistent and the report was muffled by the ear protectors I wore. This was one beautiful piece of weaponry. I owned a Remington .30-06 that was similar in style, but a flintlock by comparison in terms of smoothness and precision. Still, I'd hit every deer I'd ever shot at.

"Bulls-eye, or should I say between-the-eyes," said the SOT sergeant, Bill Colombi, the paternal leader of the team as well as its sharpshooter.

Looking at the silhouette target through the scope, I could clearly see the dime sized hole about three-quarters of an inch above the eye line. A chill coursed through my body and I shivered with the realization that that gun was customized to shoot people, not silhouettes.

"I can see it now," laughed Colombi, "the SOT team needs a shooter so they call the Chaplain. Wouldn't the papers have a field day with that. POLICE CHAPLAIN OFFS CRAZED SNIPER. Wouldn't that be somethin' to write home about."

"That's quite all right, Bill," I said while getting up from behind the shooting table and handing him the rifle. "Remember that old cliche', Don't call us we'll call you? That's the way I feel. This is one job I don't envy even a little bit."

"Aw, Rev. It's a great way to relieve your anxieties."

"Well, I'm afraid it would greatly increase mine."

"Actually, in the eight years I've been with the team, I've had to pull the trigger only twice, and won't be upset if I never had to do it again. But, if I have to, I will."

I was amazed at how quickly he had gone from silly to serious. I could imagine the mental battles that must have taken place behind those clear brown eyes that were set off by laugh wrinkles.

"You just keep practicing. The next life you save might be mine. I'd be very upset if you missed," I said jovially.

"Don't worry, Rev. They probably won't even call us out if it was just you."

"Thanks a lot. You better not stay out here in the open much longer. It looks like lightning might be coming to this very spot.

Some people say God is their co-pilot. I like to think of Him as my sharpshooter. Watch yourself."

With hands raised in pretend penitence Bill said, "All right, I take it back. We'll protect you from the vermin of the world. You make sure it doesn't rain when we go fishing."

"Sorry. I'm in P.R. not management. Instead I'll spot you one free wedding or funeral, which ever comes first."

"Gee, thanks a lot, Rev." He chuckled and started to dismantle his rifle.

"Catch ya later, Bill." I gave him a pat on the back.

"Take it easy, Rev. Breathe easier knowing I'm on duty."

"Lord help us!"

I had caught a ride with Merve the Perve who had some gun trading business with one of the SOT members. So for the past hour I had been wandering around the range meeting some of the SOT guys and trading war stories with them. It was good therapy for me, because I was still down over a death notification I'd had to do the day before. For some reason, the cops were more sympathetic with my burden than anyone else. They truly appreciated what I did because it meant they didn't have to do it.

I'd received the call within minutes after having preached my Sunday morning sermon. One of our Deacons whispered to me that there was a call for me from the Police Department. It turned out to be from the station PCA and she informed me that there had been a fatality on Digby Glenn Road at Tulip Road and the officers would meet me at the hospital. When I stepped out of my office, I could see the closing announcements were being made to the congregation. Even though the service would be over in a minute, I decided that by the time I shook hands with everyone I'd be late getting to the hospital. So I took off to do my OTHER job and hoped my brethren would understand.

Nineteen year old Doug Feldman had worked all night stocking the shelves at the Safeway where he worked. Putting in a few hours of OT, he left the store at a little past 9 A.M. in the pouring rain. Anxious to get home and get some sleep, he drove faster than he should on the always dangerous Digby Glenn Road. Approaching a sharp curve to the left, his Toyota Celica began to hydro-plane causing him to lose control of the car, cross into the oncoming traffic and be struck head on by a large Dodge Power Wagon. Doug was killed instantly as his car folded up like a stepped on beer can. The Dodge was barely dented and its occupant was unscathed physically, but well scratched emotionally.

Doug's father was a tall, lanky man with sharp facial features and short hair. When I dropped the bomb on him in the hospital consultation room he froze. His eyes bore into mine with a penetrating denial of what he'd just heard. Then his jaw muscles began flexing, rippling on the sides of his face like puppy dogs playing under a blanket. His face became flushed with anger, so intense, I half expected him to take a swing at me.

Seconds seemed like hours as we remained visually locked on each other. Then his purple tight lips began to quiver and his bloodshot brown eyes became pools of tears. Just as the first drops overflowed from his eyes he buried his head in his hands. There was no wailing or heaving of his body with sobs. Just a silent, almost meditative hiding of his face.

When I took him into the emergency room to have him ID his son, he very stoically looked at the body and said, "That's my son Doug." This was the time that I fully expected him to fall apart, but instead he calmly asked me if we could go for a walk. He knew how important it was for him to walk off part of his anxiety before he went home to the rest of his family.

As we walked circles around the hospital at a fast clip, I was thankful that the rain had ended. As it was, large perspiration crescents were forming on my favorite light blue suit. It was the third lap before he started talking and it was like the dam broke loose. What he said caused my eyes to tear up and change my Adam's apple into a watermelon. He clearly had lost more than his son. He lost his best friend. He talked about the hiking trips they'd taken and the football games they'd gone too, and the special jokes that had inside meanings to them. He talked about how his son wanted to work on his own for a while before he entered into a partnership in his father's business. Dreams. Plans. Grandchildren. Hopes. The future.

On the eighth lap he came to an abrupt stop, took a deep breath, exhaled with a sigh, and said, "Now I've got to get home and help my wife and daughter get through this. Doug would want me to be concerned about them and not worry about him. He was a very special boy. I'm going to miss him a lot. But now, it's time to get on with helping the living. Thanks for your help."

After shaking hands and offering further assistance I watched him drive off, and like the others, out of my life. I was filled with a mixture of hurt and admiration. Somewhere Doug was telling angels about how special his dad was.

That father and son team weighed heavy on my mind the rest of that day, and when I couldn't shake it off the next day I decided to visit the cops, which in turn gave me the opportunity to place a bullet in the forehead of the range silhouette. The therapy worked. I felt much better.

Marvin took me back to the station and within minutes I was back on the road with Corporal Ben Trosko. We immediately became wrapped up in "stroking citizens" with traffic tickets and the Feldman fatality became a distant memory.

Ben was jacked-up and ready for some action. I think he knew that I needed the diversion so he kept us hopping from one

101

complaint to another with a liberal dose of traffic stops in between. We joked and laughed about everything we saw. One of the rookies got his cruiser stuck in mud while he was scavenging around the county dump. He was so embarrassed, and the axle-deep cruiser looked so ridiculous that Ben just laughed and told him to dig it out himself. If we called a wrecker to pull him out Ben would have to write up a report about it. If he could get it out on his own, Ben said he'd pretend that it never happened. We drove off with the evening sun setting behind the trash heaps and the lone cop leaning on his immovable chariot. We knew that his only alternative was to walk to a service station and have them pull him out at his own expense. A rough way to learn a lesson, but then trash sifting was unbecoming of an officer. From that day on Glen Jones was known as Junk Yard Jones. That hurt worse than the towing bill.

It was 9:30 before we could stop for a Double Beef Whopper with a side order of indigestion. Since we were on duty they only charged us half price for the Whopper and nothing for the indigestion. Actually the food was good but it was intended to be chewed not inhaled. Ben didn't like being off the street when things were so busy so I had to eat it in two bites. One pattie at a time. I didn't even notice that the paper was still on it.

Walking back to the car Bud's voice came over our portable radio.

"Scout 530. Hold me out with a citizen at the old Amoco Station on Concorde Road."

"10-4 Scout 530. 21:43."

"Come on Rev," said Ben, "let's go see what Bud's gettin' himself into this time."

"Just as long as it doesn't involve the Cooper Toads. I think that boy has a death wish or something.", I said more seriously than I intended.

The street lights on Concorde Road did little to flatter the dilapidated white block gas station with the boarded up windows. At one time it was a major thoroughfare with a thriving Amoco Station hopping with business. Now it was a backroad with an eye-sore on it.

We pulled in behind Bud's cruiser which was nose-to-nose with a gray Buick Skylark. As I walked around to the driver's side of Bud's car, I saw a sight that stopped me in my tracks. Ben was also frozen in place by the unexpected spectacle. Big burly Bud was standing there with rosy cheeks and smiles, as a cute young blond had her head buried in his chest crying. More comical than the geewhiz grin on Bud's face was the ungainly way he held his arms out from his sides as if he had no idea what to do with them.

"Hey Corporal, Chaplain," said Bud sheepishly.

The young girl immediately straightened up and turned

towards us and we in turn stepped a little closer to them. She was pretty. Even with puffy eyes and running mascara she was attractive. Natural blond hair and the expected blue eyes only highlighted her petite frame which was well proportioned and unhid by the pale blue shorts and knit shirt she wore. Yet her innocent face and school-girl figure caused me to see her as someone's little sister rather than as alluring. I don't know whether that was because of chivalry or my age, but Bud was clearly taken with her.

Bud cleared his throat and spoke up. "This is Sheri White. Sheri, this is Corporal Trosko and our station Chaplain Mark Temple. Miss White says that as she came through the intersection back at Graham and Route 3, a pink Monte Carlo ran the red light and almost broadsided her. The driver of the Monte Carlo got out of her car and started to verbally abuse Miss White. When Miss White got out of her car the woman slapped her twice, jumped back into her car and drove away."

I noticed for the first time that the young girl's left cheek was bright red. She continued to sob and even seemed to increase it as she heard the story again.

"That's right," she said between sobs, "she scared me to death. She was a big lady and mean looking. I think she was drunk too."

Her dainty voice was barely audible as she tried to stifle her crying. With her fingers interlocked and held just under her chin as if praying, she was visibly shaking with fright. All three of us were becoming irate to think that someone had mistreated this cute little damsel. I felt like someone had abused The Flying Nun. In fact, she even looked a lot like Sally Fields.

Surprisingly, Bud found out what to do with his arms. He walked up from behind Sheri and put his arm around her. She instantly put her head back on his chest and cried. Bud was not embarrassed in the least. He was genuinely trying to be considerate. I was glad that there was not any other cops there except for Ben and I. He knew that we wouldn't ridicule his motives.

The old complaint "there's never a cop when you need one", has a flip side to it. There's never a Toad when you need one. However, occasionally the fickle finger of fate points at the cops and drops a freebie in their laps. As we stood there filled with indignation and primed for retribution, our combined attention was captured by the squealing of tires from down the street.

A pink Monte Carlo was pulling onto Concorde Road from a side road and traveling away from us at a high rate of speed.

"That's her," shouted Sheri as she pointed at the disappearing pink vehicle. Without a word, Bud released the girl, sprang in his cruiser, and pealed out after the culprit.

Ben and I stood there looking at each other for a few

moments. We wanted to follow Bud but we didn't want to leave Sheri standing there. Before we could decide what to do with her, we heard Bud mark 10-31 over the radio. Evidently, the gal didn't get very far down the road.

After we determined that Sheri was up to driving her car, we had her follow us down to where Bud had made the traffic stop. Ben told her to stay in her car until we asked her to get out of it.

I knew it was wrong to pre-judge people. I'd preached several sermons against that very sin. But, it's difficult not to have pre-conceived ideas about anyone who drives a hot pink twelve year old car. Especially when the driver's boy friend was Jerry Cooper, who looked like he was invented by Stephen King. That was enough to cause any imagination to work overtime.

Bud had her between her car and his cruiser talking to her as we walked up. She was leaning against her trunk with her arms folded and her eyes glaring.

She was an enigma. One could describe her as ugly or pretty depending on the angle of their head. She almost defied description. At one moment you saw shimmering light brown hair that fell straight to her shoulders and on to her back. Then you saw ice cold gray eyes that smoked with virulence. Her cheek bones were high and aristocratic, but the lines of her jaw and chin were harsh and dictatorial. Her nose was as perfectly proportioned as a statue of a Greek goddess, but her full lips were tight and venomous. The white T-shirt with a Harley-Davidson insignia on it did little to conceal her bra-lessness.

She wore a pair of nasty looking cut-off blue jeans. Most of the jeans had been cut off. In fact, the frayed fringe, which was a good two inches long, was more on her hips than her legs. Her legs were muscular and dotted with bruises. Her bare feet, except for the bright red toe nails, were black with dirt.

With a little soap, make-up, and a pretty dress, she could have been Cinderella. However, she could just as easily have been the Wicked Step Mother.

As Bud talked with her and gave her the sobriety tests, it was obvious that she'd been through this before. In fact, she gave the impression that she'd experienced a great deal. She had the "let's get this over with, I'm bored" attitude down pat. One second she'd squint her eyes and tighten her lips and look ruthlessly mean. Then the next second she'd give one of those "this is ridiculous" smiles and look almost captivating. Remembering some of the stories I'd heard about bikers and their girls, and thinking about Jerry Cooper, I was confident that she was one tough Toad.

I saw something move in the back seat of her car. When I walked around and looked into the window I was dumbfounded with what I saw. Sitting curled up in the corner of the back seat was a beautiful little girl. She must have been three or four. She had huge brown eyes and pixie cut brown hair. She was tightly squeezing a brown Teddy bear that was nearly as big as she was. Her smile could have captured Scrooge's heart in his pre-ghost days. Looking at me from around the shoulder of her bear, she brought her hand up and gave me a wave. I smiled and returned her wave. I felt like I'd found a pearl in a trash dump. The innocent smiling child was a sparkle of goodness in this dingy drama. I wondered what kind of childhood memories she'd have. Memories like the night her mom assaulted a girl and then got arrested for it plus DWI.

When I went back to where they were talking, Bud had already put the woman in cuffs and Ben was bringing Sheri over to get a positive ID. When she saw Sheri holding on to Ben's arm and frightened to death, she smirked with disdain. I half expected to see her bark at her just to see if she'd jump.

"Yes. That's the woman who stuck me.", said Sheri softly. She immediately started to back up towards her car.

"That's right sweetie," growled Cooper's girl, "you're lucky I didn't rip your arm off and beat you with the bloody end."

Sheri squealed and ran back to her car. The woman laughed heartily. She was pleased with the reaction her taunting got. We're talking mean. I could see nothing to indicate that it was contrived. She wasn't the slightest bit inhibited by our presence or the prospects of being arrested. I'd never seen such hardcore indifference.

"In addition to placing you under arrest for Driving While Intoxicated, when we get to the Magistrates office, we will obtain a warrant for assault." Bud said that while his face was just five inches from hers. His jaw was sticking out and his tone was threatening. He was daring her to add to the list, but she just looked him in the eye and said, "Who's gonna take care of my daughter?"

Bud and Ben looked surprised. They hadn't seen her.

"She's in the back seat. Cute as a button too." I said. "Do you have someone we can call to come and get her?" She did and Bud had EOC call them.

Bud placed her in the back of his cruiser. Ben went back to talk with Sheri. I leaned in the window of the pink car and talked with the charming little girl. Charming doesn't do her justice. She was enchanting. She was sweet, vivacious, and cheerful. How could she be related to the woman in cuffs in Bud's cruiser? She talked about her Teddy bear, her friends, and her mommy.

"Where is my mommy going?" she finally asked.

I was speechless for a couple seconds. "She's going with the Policeman to see a Magistrate or judge. Someone is coming to take you home and then your mommy will be home in a few hours. She'll be there when you wake up in the morning."

She smiled and said "O.K.!"

To her the woman in the cruiser wasn't a crook, a Toad, a drug dealer, a Biker groupie, or even Cooper's girl. She was Mom. I felt strangely guilty about our hauling her Mom away. I had no doubt about her deserving it, but for the sake of the precious little girl I wished we could let her loose and forget the whole thing.

Five minutes later Ben and I were cruising the streets again. A woman dressed just like Cooper's girl came and picked up the little girl. I heard her say as she left, "Wait 'til Jerry hears about this". Bud had Sheri follow him to ADC (Adult Detention Center) where he charged the woman with DWI, Assault, and refusal to take a Blood Alcohol Test. If convicted, that last charge carried an automatic suspension of the driver's license.

Because of the woman's daughter I felt miserable about the whole thing. I had visions of the sweet, innocent angel growing up to be like her mother. I wondered if anyone had ever looked at her mother when she was a child and envisioned the same thing. The worst Toads that ever lived were at one time, somebody's sweet little boy or girl. I remembered the words of "The Duke" in The Alamo when he saw a little girl who belonged to one of the defenders, "It's a shame that they have to grow up."

One week later, after I'd had the worst week of my life, I thought it a shame that I'd had to grow up.

CHAPTER FOURTEEN

In hushed tones and suppressed giggles, the two "experimenters" quickly tied the soldier to a stake which had been embedded into the ground. Satisfied that he was securely bound, they stepped back to plan their next course of action. The decision was made. One had the lighter fluid, and the other had the matches. With glee the soldier was thoroughly drenched by the stream that squirted from the lighter-fluid can.

The moment they had planned for had arrived. Deep in the woods where no one could see their destructive deed, the two were ecstatic with anticipation. Giving themselves a buffer zone from the expected explosion, and tensing themselves to jump in case they miscalculated, the match was struck and tossed at the silent soldier. The whoosh of the ignited fluid and the accompanying billow of flames were all the two had hoped for. A spontaneous cheer of delight came from their throats as they watched the conflagration swell then diminish to a slow burning fire.

The thrill was short lived. It doesn't take long for a three inch toy soldier, tied to a popsickle stick, to melt down and burn up. A cowboy and one of the Knights of the Round Table met a similar fate that night before the two little boys got bored and decided to go home and trade baseball cards.

One doesn't have to be a criminal psychologist to diagnose those two boys as future mass murderers. I can only speak for one of them and he's a Police Chaplain.

Death was so simple back then. You either purchased some new soldiers or you laid still until you counted to ten. Then you were alive again and available to be shot by Roy Rogers, Matt Dillon, Zorro, or a dozen other assorted good guys.

I was thirteen when I saw my first dead body. It was my favorite uncle, Uncle Bob. I saw him at the funeral home in a spacious wood paneled chapel. He was in a beautiful mahogany coffin that, at the time, I thought would have made a great coffee table. He looked like he'd got ready for church but then fell asleep. His suite was wrinkle free, his hair was combed, his glasses were on, and he even had make-up on his face that made him look warm and alive. But there was something fishy about his eyes and lips. They were closed unnaturally tight. I watched his eye-lids closely, and sure enough, there was no movement underneath them. I sighed deeply and said out loud, "See you in heaven Uncle Bob." Then I promptly forgot about the whole thing as I went outside to check out the cars in the parking lot. Especially the small fast ones.

The older I get, the more complicated Death gets. It's hard to settle all our feelings about Death. When friends and relatives have died through the years, I've reacted in every way from complete shock to envy. There have been times when it seemed cold, scary, and mysterious. Other times I viewed it as warm, inviting, and a Five Star vacation. I guess that's the difference between seeing it as a grave or a Gate.

For most of us, the hardest part about witnessing death is that it reminds us of our own inevitable appointment with the Grim Reaper. Most of our lives we have managed to transfer any consideration of it to "the other guy". It's always someone else who is facing death, not me. After many years of developing a strong faith in God, I was able to resolve most of my apprehensions concerning my own mortality. There was, however, one aspect of death that remained to be settled. One element that, prior to being a Police Chaplain, cried to be satisfied. Some call it morbid curiosity. The fascination we all have with seeing death before the morticians clean it up.

For intellectual reasons and, more accurately, social reasons, we like people to think that we are above that. I've had discussions with groups of people who all piously raise their noses and declare their total disinterest in seeing blood and guts. Then they are the ones who hold up traffic as they crawl past an automobile accident because they didn't want to miss any gruesome details. Anyone who is half way aware of what the public wants to see on the nightly news must concur that we all have a certain curiosity about tragic death. In fact, at any death scene, regardless of the circumstances, it takes four times the officers to control the crowds as it does to investigate the crime. Books and video tapes that show gory death pictures sell like crazy. We have a fascination with death that stays with us from children who burn tory soldiers at the stake to adults who buy Time Magazine just for the pictures.

Many of the men who came back home after World War II, Korea, and Vietnam no longer had any morbid curiosity. They were sick of death. Men who went off to war with visions of glory came back with nightmares of gore. For reasons of conscience, I didn't go to Vietnam and I felt cheated. For the same reason my brother went and he felt raped. Morbid curiosity is a thirst that is easily quenched. If one drinks too deeply of the morbid experiences of life, they can develop a sickness that taints life and gives it a permanent gray cast.

By this time in my career as a Police Chaplain I had seen several traffic fatalities. It was almost enjoyable to be able to tell people about all the ugly things I'd seen. They'd listen with intense fascination. Mouths hung open and eyes widened. Rarely could anyone get one up on me in terms of true-life stories. I wasn't bragging or prideful about it. They were my war stories. My experiences. Those experiences just happened to concern death, which everybody wants to know about.

One week I lost my morbid curiosity. One week I'd seen

enough. One week nearly caused me to turn my badge in and run back to the cloistered walls of traditional pastorhood.

It started on the Lord's Day. To most people Sunday is the first day of the week. To me, it may be technically the first, but I think of it as the last. Everything I do all week long is pointing to and preparing for Sunday. It is the climax of the week for me. So by the time I finish my sermon at the Sunday evening service, I am ready to relax for awhile. Monday is my day off, fortunately, which makes it my Saturday. So day seven for me is day two and day one is day seven. And you wondered why preachers are a strange breed?

I went to the 9:00 roll call that evening for two reasons. I wanted to relax and take my mind off preacher work for awhile and I wanted to talk to my favorite Corporal, Ben. I'd heard a rumor that he was considering quitting the force so I though I'd better intervene and see what the problem was.

Roll call was uneventful. I think everyone was tired because it was their first night on Mid's. The only laugh came when Ben asked me if I had any thing to say to the troops. I cleared my throat, held up my hands with palms facing out, and extolled, "Bless you my sons. May you triumph over temptations and Toads, whichever causes you the most problems."

That stirred a few cracks about Holy Water and kicking Habits. At least I knew they were awake.

After getting a large coffee from 7-11, I had an excellent talk with Ben. As we cruised up and down one of the main highways, he told me about why he was considering resigning. His father-in-law had a successful cabinet making and installation business and he wanted Ben to come to work for him. It wasn't as exciting work as being a cop, but the pay was better and some day the whole business would be his. Future-wise and salary-wise it was the best thing to do, but Ben loved his job. He felt, and I agreed, that he would move right up through the ranks in the Department and could have a very satisfying career.

I didn't try to advise him, but I did try to help him consider all the pros and cons of each. In my heart I didn't want him to leave the Department, but at the same time I wanted him to do what was best for himself and his family.

Our conversation came to an abrupt halt as we heard two units dispatched to a secluded reservoir on the western edge of the County to look for a missing boy. We immediately started in that direction to see if we could help in the search.

By the time we arrived, one of the officers had taken the report from the parents and was ready to fill us in on the particulars. A fifteen year old boy named Jimmie Branch had left home at three that afternoon to fish in the reservoir a half mile from his home. He was supposed to have come home at 5:30 but he did not, and it was nearly ten now.

109

He was described as being 5'4", brown hair and eyes, and wearing a white T-shirt with blue jeans.

I didn't even know there was a body of water anywhere around there. The reservoir was well hidden by a large stand of trees, which surrounded three sides of it. The other side was hidden from view by houses and yards. I'd driven around the entire place dozens of times and never noticed the water.

The four of us spread out with our flashlights and radios to search for the boy. We all expected that he would turn up at a friend's house and wonder why everyone was so uptight. That's the way these cases usually ended. We would much rather leave the scene fuming about a thoughtless teenager than leave with our worst fears realized.

The woods were thick and the darkness was intense. I couldn't imagine anyone being out there if they didn't have to be there. Yet as my light reflected off discarded beer cans I realized that I was not in uncharted territory.

"Car 50." came the voice of Ben over my portable.

"I have found a fishing pole, a carton of bait, some shoes and socks, and . . ." his pause was painful. ". . . I found a wallet that belongs to the boy. Have rescue respond and bring their boat and divers."

As I made my way to where Ben was, my brain was working overtime trying to conjure up scenarios that would explain why Jimmie would have gone off and left his shoes and his wallet. Only one explanation fit. He had gone swimming.

The next two hours were frustrating and anxious. The divers tried to search the water but it was just too dark. They covered a large area with the boat, dragging their grappling hooks behind them, but again with no luck. It was clear that we'd have to wait until daylight. And maybe, just maybe, Jimmie was at some friends house, but that was not very likely.

The Branch house was somewhat dilapidated. The screens were ripped and the paint was peeling. The small front porch was filled with so much clutter that we had to zigzag through it to get to the front door.

Jimmie was the youngest of four children. Harry and June had Jimmie when they were in their mid forties. One of those accidents, but the kind that tends to be extra special. As we sat with them in their living room on furniture that was covered with bed spreads to hid their worn condition, they looked even older than the sixty years they'd lived.

We couldn't give them much hope. When we showed them the shoes and the wallet, they both identified them with shrieks of bereavement. With the older three daughters hanging on their parent's necks', they were a mass of sobs and screams. We sat in helpless silence until things calmed down enough for us to try and comfort them what little we could.

When I crawled into bed at 1 A.M. I felt guilty. I knew the Branchs wouldn't be doing any sleeping and somehow I thought I should stay awake and worry with them.

I had been in my office working for an hour and a-half when they called me the next morning. They had just found Jimmie's body in the reservoir. I had them send an officer by to transport me to the scene.

The ambulance and other County vehicles were parked about a hundred yards behind one of the houses that concealed the reservoir. As soon as I arrived, I met with the Homicide Investigator who was handling the case. They investigate every death no matter how it happened.

Investigator Jim Bowen was not his usual jovial self. Usually he managed to stay amusingly removed from the gut wrenching emotionalism of tragedy, but this was a kid. There would be no jokes or macho humor today.

"Good to see ya Rev," said the big Irish cop. Then he arched his right eye brow and in hushed tones asked. "Say, explain to me in twenty-five words or less, how God could allow something like this to happen to a good-looking fifteen year old kid?"

Everyone wants simple answers to ageless questions. If the boy had been ten years older or not so good-looking, he probably wouldn't have asked the question. But when it's children, we feel a terrible injustice has happened.

"There is no easy answer to that Jim. Believe me, God didn't want this boy to die. That's why we call it an accident and not an act of God. He hurts too. Remember, He knows what it's like to see a relative die."

He stood there staring at me for a few seconds. With a wink of his eye he turned away and started for the ambulance.

"Come on Rev. Help me put the toe tag on him."

As I hustled along to keep up with his massive strides he continued, "I didn't mean to put you on the spot Rev. I know you're right. My Catholic upbringing taught me all that, but, well, these kinds of case are harder to deal with. Most of the time there is a clean-cut bad guy. A drunk, a murderer, or some kind of low-life. But this, well, there's no one to blame or to be mad at. It's a heck of a lot better to be angry than to have to deal with it as it is."

"I know exactly what you mean Jim. But listen, don't be afraid or ashamed of hurting. Just accept the fact that you're upset, cope with it, and get on with your job. If you ever get to where something like this doesn't bother you, then you need to cart yourself over th the County shrink. Personally, I like cops who are humans not Vulcans."

"What's a Vulcan?"

"Haven't you ever seen Star Trek?" I asked with genuine

surprise.

"No. I'm not into astronomy."

"ASTRONOMY!" I yelled.

"Ease up Rev. I'm joking. I've been a Trekkie for years."

"So much for deep counseling," I said with a sigh.

After we exchanged subdued greetings with the other officers and rescue personnel, Jim and I went by ourselves around to the back of the ambulance. When we opened the double rear doors, we both stood there and stared at the oddly shaped green body bag laying on the floor. I say "oddly shaped" because the bag had an unusually large raised area about where the bodies chest should be.

Jim climbed up into the ambulance. I stood in the opened doors. Straddling the bag, Jim began unzipping it from the head, which was near me, to the feet. When he pulled the sides of the bag back off and away from the body, I had another picture burned indelible into my mind.

Framed by the body bag, Jimmie's brown hair and white T-shirt seemed to take on a greenish tint. His hair was plastered to his head, still wet, yet loosely covering his forehead, like my son's hair looks on a hot summer night as he sleeps. His closed eyes added to the illusion, but his bluish white skin destroyed that in a flash.

Jimmie's arms had caused the odd shape of the body bag. They were locked in a strange hug position. As if he had reached out to give his mother a farewell hug and froze forever in that configuration. It was eerie. Almost like he had been holding a beach ball. Jim explained that it was from the way he had floated in the water for so many hours. He probably had floated feet down and his arms, in death, had simply floated up to a forty-five degree angle from his body.

His baby face was marred by a copious foam that had eased out his nostrils. It was a mixture of blood, mucus, and reservoir water. It covered his lips, chin, and cheeks, removing any possibility of seeing him as sleeping peacefully.

Jim did his obligatory check of the body and then attached the toe tag. Toe tags were required to be attached at the scene to prevent any mix-ups at the Medical Examiner's office.

I was considerably relieved when Jim finally zipped up the bag. Though the "odd shape" was a glaring reminder of what was hidden inside.

I went with Jim back to the Branch house. Since he was the investigating officer, there were several questions that he had to ask the family before he could complete his report. Fortunately, they had already been told about Jimmie's body being found. The worst of the shock had already passed by the time we sat down with them in their debris-strewn living room.

We sat on chairs that had been dragged in from the kitchen

table. Both cracked vinyl chairs looked to be coated with some unknown substance that gave me a brief shudder as I eased down on it and realized my pant legs were sticking to it. The Branches, parents and three adult daughters, surrounded us, sitting in and on various indescribable shrouded appendages. They were red-eyed and drained from loss of sleep and emotionalism. With one hand holding Kleenex and the other a cigarette, they chair-smoked and wiped. My normally strong stomach was getting somewhat queasy because of the combination of anxiety, thick smoke, and unsanitary conditions. I wasn't sure at that point whether it was bad or good that I hadn't eaten breakfast.

While Jim did his duty, I got the name of their church and minister from one of the daughters. I peeled myself, like adhesive tape, off the seat and made use of their phone. Their minister was expecting the call and said he'd be there in ten minutes. Within minutes other family members and friends arrived. I felt confident that they had a good support system available to help them through their grief.

By the time their minister arrived, I'd talked to all five Branches and had a prayer with the entire group. Yet, even though I was in a good position to exit, the hardest part remained to be accomplished. A positive ID of the body. Due to the way Jimmie looked in the body bag, it was felt that the ID should be done at the hospital after he'd been cleaned up some.

It seemed cruel and unnecessary to force a member of the family to go through that terrible ordeal. Especially when there was no doubt in anyones mind about who it was. It was classic CYA. There had been several horrifying situations when a youngster was mis-identified because they didn't have identification on them. Families were notified, people went into shock, relatives were called, entire neighborhoods were disrupted. Then the deceased teen walked in the room and asked what the problem was. It started all over again with another family. The media ate it up and the lawyers got rich. Now there was a policy that was enforced no matter what the circumstances. Every corpse must be positively identified by an unimpeachable witness. In most cases that meant family.

Only one person in the family could handle it. The daughters were emotional basket cases and the father had heart trouble. Mom had to do it. ID the child of her old age—her only son.

Mrs. Branch, riding with a neighbor, followed us to the county hospital. Jim hated it as much as I did, and he fussed and fumed all the way there. I just listened and Amened.

Nothing about it was good. When we got the hospital the neighbor wanted to wait in the car. We barely got Mrs. Branch into the hospital door when her knees buckled and we had to put her in a wheelchair. I held her hand and told her that there was no hurry. We prayed. We waited. After fifteen minutes she felt up to doing it but we all felt we should take her down to the infamous window in the wheelchair. A nurse accompanied us.

As we pulled the wheelchair up to the window, I pushed the buzzer to let them know that we were ready. With Jim on one side of Mrs. Branch and I on the other, we helped her to stand up. The window was too high for her to see into it from the chair. We held her arms. She cupped her hands over her mouth and held her breath.

I was thinking to myself, "I hate this. This poor woman has lived through a night of absolute terror and now to top it off she gets to see her child laid out in a morgue." I was in agony for her—and for me. Most people prayed to be spared from pain. I had volunteered for it. A biblical phrase kept popping in my mind. "Be wretched and mourn." It's hard to mourn and not be wretched. I felt wretched. I was intruding on someone else's grief and adopted their anguish. I didn't need this. I was supposed to be in the Never Never Land of weddings, baptisms, and church fellowships. I needed . . . well, that didn't really matter. What mattered was that she needed me.

Jimmie looked considerably better than he had in the ambulance. Under the white sheets with only his head and shoulders showing and his face cleaned off he was strikingly good looking. He looked peaceful. I wondered what they had done to keep his arms down close to his body. They probably tied them down.

For a long moment Mrs. Branch just stared at him. Her hands still covered her mouth. Then she cocked her head to the right and I heard her say, "My baby" just before she fainted. Jim and I caught her as she collapsed and we eased her down into the wheelchair. The curtains of the window were closed and we wheeled her down the hall a short ways. The nurse quickly checked her pulse, then broke open an ammonia capsule and waved it under her nose a few times. She woke right up and immediately came to the realization that it all wasn't just a horrible dream. Quietly she began weeping in her hands.

It was thirty minutes before she got herself under control and back into her neighbor's car. I watched the car disappear around the corner, taking her back to her hovel of broken furniture and spirits. As usual, I felt guilty. Like I'd just ripped off their social security checks. I felt guilty about not being able to do more for them. I felt guilty because I'd had to bring them bad news. I felt guilty about being able to go home and forget about the entire incident. I felt guilty about wanting to never do this sort of thing again.

My self flagellation was interrupted by Jim who slapped me on the back and said, "Chaplain, don't tell anyone I said this, but I'm sure glad that you were with me today. I've been doing this for more years that I care to count and this was one of the toughest. That kid was the spittin' image of my boy. All I could think about was how I'd feel if it had happened to him. I was having a difficult time coping with the whole thing. You made it a lot easier and you did a terrific job talking with the family."

"Well Jim, I appreciate that. This kind of case is tough on everybody. I feel absolutely drained."

"Me too. Let's get some grub in the hospital cafeteria. It'll make you feel better. Besides, since it's half price for us it will be my treat. Come on."

And with that the subject was ended. We didn't talk about it any further. Yet clearly there was a new sense of respect that Jim had for me. It was like I'd all of a sudden become a special friend of his. All the doubts and reservations I had had earlier, the temptation to get away from Chaplain work, vanished with the knowledge that I was valuable and needed. What's more is that I was accepted and respected. That led to the most important essentials in the job. Trust and confidence.

My sense of euphoria lasted just eighteen hours. At 7:30 the next morning I was called to cover for a Chaplain who was out of town. So not only was it a new case and a new experience, but it was with a group of cops that I didn't know in an area I was unfamiliar with. The worst part of the news was that it involved another youngster.

CHAPTER FIFTEEN

A good night's sleep and the crisp brightness of a new day would normally do wonders for purging the soul of all it's dark memories. Yet this morning, as I drove across the County, the shimmering glare of the early morning sunlight failed to heal the wounds from the day before. I had managed to keep them from my mind until I received the phone call from EOC which sent me on this disturbing mission to an unfamiliar area.

"Chaplain, we have a Signal 45 in station six's area," said the tired voice from the bowels of the Ivory Tower, "and we need you to respond. The victim was a sixteen year old male who was discovered by his younger brother. The address is 1691 Cider Ridge Dr. in the Cider Ridge development off Rt. 602."

The houses in Cider Ridge were not mansions, but they didn't miss it by much. The houses were on spacious lots and were colored variations on about five themes. All were two story and had immaculately manicured yards. The 8 to 10 foot trees that lined the streets bespoke a new neighborhood. These were the homes of governments GS 15's and the Pentagon's Colonels. Even then, most homes had to have two wage earners to pay the hefty mortgages they had. Everything about the shiny new development said success, peace, and material happiness. Unfortunately, while the houses had the Good Housekeeping Seal of Approval, the homes were not all so idyllic. At least one that I knew of anyway.

1691 looked like all the other houses. The pale blue aluminum siding with red shutters and trim set off the colonial style of the house. The two bikes on the front porch and the basketball in the front yard screamed life where death now resided. A patrol cruiser and two unmarked were parked in the driveway.

Since the front door was partially opened, I walked on into the early American living room. The house was strangely quiet. Usually crime scenes were bubbling with activity, but then I'd never been to a suicide scene before. I walked through to the hallway, stopped, listened, and still heard nothing. I started to walk up the stairs that were in front of me when a movement caught my eye from down the hall to my left.

"Hello," I said for lack of a better idea.

"Yo," came a voice from behind the door at the end of the hall. It looked like he was in some kind of utility room.

"I'm Chaplain 5. You guys called for me?"

"Yeah, good to see ya Chaplain." he said jovially. Then he opened the door a few inches more and signaled me to come into the room. "Come here and take a look at what happened."

As I stepped around the partially opened door and into the room, he moved back away from me a few paces. Looking to my right I saw a cluttered utility room. Boxes, toys, and hundreds of things that should have been thrown out, but like most families were stored, were stacked up around ducts and various pipes that crisscrossed the walls.

As my eyes came back around to the left I jumped back in horror at what I saw barely one foot away from where I stood. A body was hanging from the ceiling.

I did my best to try not to appear to be too shocked. After all, I was an experienced, battle-hardened veteran now. I was as tough as any cop and nothing could disturb me. Yet I'd never seen anything like this. I was disturbed.

Disturbed but not devastated. The whole scene was so unreal that it was difficult to be too emotionally upset. The young boy, unlike Jimmie from the day before, looked to be peacefully asleep. His handsome face was not distorted in pain. His head tilted towards his right shoulder and his blond hair hung down straight across his forehead. The only unnatural looking thing was the bright yellow nylon rope that went from just behind his jaws to a pipe in the rafters just ten inches above his head. His neck was barely distended. His shoulders were slouched and his arms extended straight down beside him. He wore a gray and rust colored plaid short sleeved shirt with the tails hanging out. His blue jeans were clean and unfaded. His bare feet were purple with lividity.

"What would make a sixteen year old boy do something like this?", said the investigator, interrupting my thoughts. "I can't imagine anyone's life being so miserable that they'd rather be dead. I've been on scores of suicides and I'll never understand them."

"According to the experts," I said, "in their twisted minds the victims have made what they consider the best decision. They feel alone, helpless, and with no hope of improvement. The only alternative is to end it all. It takes a lot for anyone to overrule their basic desire to survive."

"Yeah I guess so. Oh! Sorry Chaplain, I'm Skip Dimmer. I've heard some good things about you. 'ppreciate ya coming over."

We shook hands and I added, "Good to meet ya Skip. What have you figured out about this and where are the rest of the family?"

"They're all next door. The parents are in the process of getting a divorce so the father doesn't live here. In fact he arrived just before you did. You know, I think every teenage suicide that I've ever had involved families with marital problems. At least most of 'em. I wonder if there's connection there somewhere.

"Anyways, the two boys, Sonny, the deceased, and his younger brother Tony, went to the movies last night. They saw some animated science fiction movie that evidently was pretty explicit, but the younger boy Tony couldn't remember the title of it. They got home about 11:30. Mom was already in bed. Tony went to bed at midnight and said the last time he saw Sonny, he was reading a magazine in his room upstairs. The mom got up and went to work without checking on them or coming into the utility room. Fifteen minutes after she left, Tony came in here and found his brother like this. That should be a great memory for him to carry the rest of his life."

"That's right, in fact he's probably the biggest victim in this whole thing," I added.

"He's at the next door neighbor's house. He's got a couple of friends with him."

"Any possibility of foul play?"

"No, I don't think so. I can clearly see evidence that he did it himself. Why he did it we may never know. His brother said that Sonny had experimented with different drugs but he wasn't addicted to any. The autopsy will show it if he was. He left no suicide note and he wasn't having girlfriend problems. The guys are checking his room upstairs for drugs or pornography."

"Pornography?" That was a new twist for me.

"Yeah. A lot of these cases involve pornography. Not just a Playboy but excessive, hardcore stuff. Usually it involves auto-sex too."

"Auto-sex?" I was really showing my ignorance now.

"Masturbation. It's amazing how many people die each year from hanging while they masturbate. I don't completely understand it, but for some reason they masturbate while cutting their wind and blood flow off. A lot of the time they never intended to kill themselves it happened by accident. And of course we never tell the family about it, and especially not the news media. But it's amazing how often it happens."

"We had one awhile back where this guy had a pulley built into the roof of his closet. With the noose around his neck and the other end of the rope in his left hand, he'd masturbate. The combination of blocked air and blood, and the orgasm would cause him to faint. But the last time he did it, the rope jumped off the pulley and got caught. We found him hanging with his knees three inches off the floor and his pants around his ankles."

All through this inglorious discussion I was staring at Sonny. The entire scene seemed outlandish. We were in a junk-filled utility room, telling war stories, with a young boy's body hanging from the rafters three feet in front of us. There should be weeping and wailing. Dramatic music with violins and organs. We should be crushed with sorrow.

A voice deep inside me told me to cool it. If I was going to deal in the world of dolor and death I had to develop a thicker skin. I had to learn to sympathize not empathize. The name of the game was service but the number one rule was survival.

Survive to serve again and again. The homicide investigators and the ID team did it, I could too.

I left Skip and his informative insights into suicide, and went to the neighbor's house to do what I'd been called for.

I introduced myself to the parents who were sitting arm-in-arm on a couch in the living room of the spacious house. I must have been around the cops to long. I found myself thinking that if they'd been arm-in-arm a little more before last night this might never have happened. That was unfair and cynical, but I didn't feel terribly gracious at the moment.

We talked and prayed. I made a few phone calls for them including one to their minister who said he'd be right over. After a few more words of comfort and advice, I excused myself to go find Tony.

I found him in one of the bedrooms with two other boys his age, which I assumed to be about twelve. They all sat with their chins resting on their hands which were propped up on their knees. They each shook my hand and displayed confused, bewildered faces.

Tony was handsome, like his brother, except he had dark brown hair. T-shirt, jeans, and name-brand tennis shoes gave him the credentials to be classified 'an All American Boy'. At first he only grunted agreement to my comments, but within minutes he was talking openly with me. I was impressed with him as a sharp, stable kid. I felt like I could be up front with him.

"Tony, the biggest temptation you're going to have now is the temptation to blame yourself for what Sonny did. More than likely he had planned it for along time, and he waited for a time when no one would be there to stop him. All you will do by thinking 'If only I'd woke up . . . or . . . If only I'd seen the signs . . . If only this . . . If only that . . .' will be to drive yourself crazy. 'If only's' are guilt carriers. Don't waste time thinking about it. You need to help your folks to get through this. O.K.?"

He understood and even smiled by the time I left. I really liked him and felt sorry for him. If it had been feasible I'd have taken him with me. He needed positive reinforcement and lots of love. Somehow I didn't feel like he'd get it at home.

I stayed with them until the body was removed from the house and the ID team was finished. By the time I walked them back to their house they had an army of friends and relatives with them. Also their minister had arrived. He seemed to be somewhat experienced with this sort of thing, so I felt comfortable leaving them in his hands.

When I drove out of Cider Ridge I wasn't thinking about the blond young boy hanging in the utility room. I worried about the smaller brown hair boy sitting in a bedroom, hurting and not

119

knowing what to do next. I had left him my business card. I usually gave it to adults, but for some reason I only wanted him to have it and use it. I hoped he would call me and let me help him.

It was ten in the morning by then and it dawned on me that I was hungry. After the way things had been going the last two days, I decided I'd better eat while I had the chance. Just to be on the safe side, I turned off my portable radio and my pager before I went into the restaurant. I was going to get at least one undisturbed meal.

Somehow I managed to keep Jimmie, Sonny, and Tony on the back burners of my mind for the next few hours. I spent those hours in my office at church doing the work I got paid to do. Maybe it was because I needed the escape, but I got so engrossed in my work and studying that it was time to go home for supper before I knew it.

Around the dinner table that night we laughed and enjoyed being together. I was keenly aware of the value of small things. The way my children squeezed my hand during the dinner prayer. The peck on the cheek my wife gave me as she refilled my tea. The smiling faces of a family that was happy, together, and in love.

I had mixed feelings about being a Chaplain. My family had no idea that my stomach ached with sorrow for people who had lost a loved one. Why was I complicating my life? I had a very stable, happy family, and keeping one's own family contented was job enough for anyone. Why borrow someone else's ponderous problems? Because I could help? Surely there were other ministers who could do the job. Probably better than me and could handle it. So why was I doing it? The reasons were starting to blur a bit. Maybe the job wasn't for me.

As I always did when I needed reassurances, I went to the Station for the 9 o'clock roll call. I promised my wife that I wasn't going to ride with anyone, and I was determined to not break that promise. I just needed to talk to a few of the guys and remind myself that they needed me, whether they knew it or not.

One of the side benefits of having been called to a major crime scene was that I was the only one who knew all the gory details. And cops like to know all the gory details. So I was the center of attention at roll call as they fired a barrage of questions at me about the two cases I'd been on. Contrary to popular perceptions, it's not unusual for a cop to go through his entire career and never have a suicide case. For the average cop, suicides, homicides and even traffic fatalities are few and far between. As Chaplain, I'd already seen more dead bodies than many cops did in a twenty year career.

Since Hardnose was running roll call, he soon called a halt to the Chaplain-centered discussion, and began reading the boards. He didn't do much to contribute to the reassurance I was looking for. I wondered if he's ever come around and be on my side. Maybe not.

After roll call I ran into Thunder in the report room. He was really glad to see me and he invited me to ride with him. It took an extreme measure of self control to say "No thanks, I've got to get home."

"Did you hear about Bud's latest run in with Jerry Cooper?" He asked excitedly.

"No, what happened?"

"Well, he arrested his girl friend for DWI down on Concorde Road, and . . ."

"I know about that. I was there when it happened. I was riding with Trosko."

"O.K. When he got her locked up at ADC he stayed around there for a few minutes talking to some pretty little thing. Before he left the lobby at ADC, in walked Cooper. He was there to see if he could get his Hog released. Anyway, they stood there facing each other for several minutes. Then Cooper says, 'This ain't my territory Pig, but the next time I see you on my ground, you better watch your back.'"

"I'll bet Bud loved that."

"Yeah well he just looks 'em in the eye and says, 'You want to make an appointment?' and Cooper just snorted and walked over to the Magistrate's window. I ain't kiddin' ya man, them two are gonna have it out one of these days. I just hope that Bud has a back up. If for nothing else than to be a witness and prove that Bud didn't kill him in cold blood."

"You have to remember that we're not talking about a fair fight. Cooper doesn't know what that is. I'm more worried about him bushwacking Bud some dark night." I almost added, "When I'm with him;"

Pulling out of the station parking lot I tried to decide whether or not I'd been reassured about being needed. Hardnose didn't want me, and Bud might get me killed. I decided that I had not been reassured.

The Lord must have known that I was reaching the limits of my ability to cope with calamities because on Wednesday he gave me a day of rest. It was a quiet day of study and the performance of other pastoral pursuits. I had a Bible class to teach that night and I was able to immerse myself in the preparation of it. I had to resist the temptation to use the stories of Jimmie or Sonny to illustrate a point. I had learned earlier to use Chaplain stories sparingly. They were simply too overpowering to use. People tended to react one of two ways to my narratives. They'd either be so overwhelmed by it that they missed everything else I said, or they'd immediately assume that I was spending more time with the Police then I was being their minister. It wasn't worth the distraction or them misunderstanding.

The next morning was another radiant sun-drenched day. I had my morning coffee in one hand and the door knob in the other, on my way to the office, when the phone rang. It was for me from EOC.

"Chaplain Temple. Officer Hicks is working a 9-I possible 9-F on Route 3 at Bainebridge Rd. He would like for you to respond to the hospital to be with the family. He will meet you there in a few minutes."

"Was the victim an adult or a teenager?" I think I was getting a little punchy about kids dying.

"The injured was a white adult female. She's being transported to County Hospital but will probably be Medivaced to the Trauma Center."

"Did I understand you to say that the family had been notified?"

There was an unnatural pause. "Ah. The family had just been let out of the car. They saw the accident."

"How many are we talking about?"

"The victim's husband and five year old daughter."

"Please advise Officer Hicks that I am enroute to the hospital."

I had a jumble of different feelings as I hung up the phone and headed for my car. I felt sorrow for the woman, but I was relieved that it wasn't another youngster. And yet, there was a five year old little girl who had just seen her mom seriously injured in a car wreck. Injuries that could prove fatal. I'd seen it before. A serious head injury but they are able to keep the victim alive for a good while. Then they get them down to the trauma center and discover that they are brain dead.

The first person I saw at the hospital was one of my favorite nurses, Isaac. Isaac was a huge head nurse that I met early in my Chaplain career. He ran a tight ship in the emergency room and was well liked by all. But he was big. 6'5" and about 300 lbs of compassion. He was called Humpty-Dumpty by the cops. The only nurse in the county who rated a nickname from them.

I asked him about the woman who had been brought in from the accident.

"It don't look good Rev. The chopper will be here any minute to take her downtown, but between you and me, it's a waste of time. She'll never breath again on her own. I'm almost sure that she's brain dead."

"Are the relatives in the consultation room across the hall?"

"Yep." He shook his head. "Just wait 'till you see that precious little girl in there. It's a crying shame that her mommy has been taken from her. I'd hate to have your job Rev, but I'm glad it's you and not some others I've seen."

"Thanks Isaac. But right now I'd give this job to just about anybody who'd take it. See ya later."

I was one step away from the room the family was in when I heard, "Hey Rev.". I turned around and was relieved to see Sam coming in the door. Since I hadn't been to the scene of the accident, I was anxious to talk to him. I didn't like going into see the family without having as many facts about it as possible. It can damage your credibility to not have answers to the questions they might ask.

With a somber look on his face he said, "I really appreciate you coming down and helping with this Rev. This is a tough one."

"I haven't talked to the family yet. Why don't you fill me in on what happened."

"Sure. Mrs. Tidwell, the victim, dropped her husband and daughter off at the bus stop there on Route 3 in front of the 7-11. She traveled one block east and signaled a left turn onto Bainbridge Road. For some reason that we may never figure out, she turned left, right in front of an oncoming dump truck that was barreling down the highway to catch the green light. He caught her broadside and just flattened her little Chevy Chevette. Company 14, which is only a block away, was there in seconds, but it took several minutes to get her freed from the wreck. I got there within seconds too and helped pull her out. I couldn't believe that she was still alive. Her husband and little girl were there and saw everything."

"According to Humpty," I added, "there's not much chance that she'll make it. They're going to fly her to the trauma center anyway and hope for the best. I'd better get in there and see the family. Coming?"

When we entered the room Mr. Tidwell was sitting in a folding chair with his daughter on his lap. The hospital social worker was sitting next to them and she stood up as we came in. She seemed glad to see me and excused herself from the room. Most hospital social workers are very caring and helpful people, but are usually more than willing to turn tragedies over to the Police Chaplains.

I introduced Sam and myself and then sat down in the seat next to them. We began talking.

Mr. Tidwell was rather distinguished looking. His handsome latin features were set off by a crop of black hair with touches of gray on the temples. He wore an open collar white shirt and navy blue dress slacks. His tight lipped smile and humble demeanor were only made more genuine by his reddened eyes. And then there was the little cherub perched on his knee.

Her name was Tabitha. She was Shirley Temple reincarnated. Black curly locks cascaded down the sides of her face and across her forehead. Her big bright hazel eyes were shaded by eyelashes that would be the envy of Mary Kay. She had a pudgy, slightly upturned nose that belonged to royalty, and a smile that could bring about nuclear disarmament if only the right people could see it. She seemed to be oblivious to the seriousness of the situation as she played with a small Raggedy Ann doll and batted her big eyes at me.

Her dad was completely aware of the seriousness of the situation. He calmly asked some very pertinent questions and seemed satisfied that everyone was doing what they could for his wife. He had seen her while the medics worked on her at the scene, and I gathered that he concurred with Isaac's assessment. We were all emphasizing hope, but he was expecting none.

I was soon in a quandary about what to do for them. They were new to the area so they had no friends or neighbors who could help. Also, there was no minister, priest, or rabbi to contact. All they had was an aunt who lived with them and she had already been called. She didn't have transportation, so there was no one who could be with them and comfort them except Sam and I.

Just then Isaac came into the room and told us that Mrs. Tidwell was being taken out to the helicopter. Since two doctors were needed with her, there was no room for Mr. Tidwell in the helicopter.

"Is there anyone who can take me to the other hospital," asked Mr. Tidwell, "I don't have a car anymore and I don't have anyone I can call."

Sam stood, and reaching for the phone said, "I can take you down there, but I'll need to clear it with my supervisor first. I'm sure we can work it out."

I put my hand on Mr. Tidwell's shoulder and said, "It's probably going to be a pretty rough experience down there. Is there some place that we can take your daughter for you?"

"If someone could take her to our home, my aunt will be there and she can take care of her."

"Why don't I take her home while Sam takes you down to the Trauma Center."

Before he and Sam left, he gave me his address. I grasped his hand and told him to call me later if I could help. I told him I'd be praying for them. He gave me a kind smile and said thanks. Then he gave his daughter a huge hug and whispered something into her ear that made her nod her head yes. Then he and Sam rushed out the door.

Before I left with the little princess that had been entrusted to me, I called the Chaplain at the Trauma Center and advised him what to expect. He said he would be waiting for them.

I had been saying for a long time that Police Chaplains had to do a little bit of everything and now I could add baby sitting to the list. Yet, this wasn't a chore but a delight. I actually considered taking her home with me and letting her play with my kids for awhile. Why not give her a few hours of happiness before she is thrust into trying to understand why mommy's not coming home. But I knew that wouldn't be smart. Her dad was expecting her to be at home and there were probably some legal ramifications too.

She sat quietly in the passenger's seat playing with her doll as we drove to her home. Every time I'd glance at her I couldn't help but smile. Then a surge of remorse would stab into my heart as I remembered the loss that she wasn't even aware of yet. I'm not sure about ignorance, but innocence is bliss. I envied her. It might be nice, for a change, to think of pain only in terms of skinned knees and missed ice cream cones.

Just before we arrived at her house she finally spoke to me. She softly said, "Can I have some gum?". Her head was slightly bowed causing her to look up at me with arched brow and wide eyes. Like she might be doing something wrong.

I rarely chewed gum, so I didn't have any with me. I solved that problem by pulling into a convenience store and buying some. I bought the kind that came in big cubes and took extraordinary stamina to chew. She was ecstatic. I'd picked her favorite kind. It looked like she had an inner tube in her mouth but she loved it.

The Tidwells lived in an apartment complex that was government subsidized. The grass was worn down all around the buildings but the apartments themselves seemed well maintained.

The door to their apartment was opened by a petite Mexican woman who must have been the aunt since the little girl ran to her and hid behind her apron. I told her I was the police chaplain but she just stared at me and smiled. Then Tabitha peeked around the apron and shyly said, "She only speaks Spanish."

Since the only Spanish I knew was how to count to ten, our communication was severely limited. I smiled and showed her my badge. She smiled back and nodded. I knelt down to Tabitha's level and said, "What am I going to do with the rest of these pieces of gum?"

She peeked around at me again.

"I know. Why don't you keep them for me?" I held out my hand which had the remainder of the pack of gum. She eased over and gently took it.

"Thank you," I said. "I'll see you later."

With that I waved bye to them both and left. I knew then that those big eyes and that precious smile would forever be part of my memories.

That evening when I plopped down in my easy chair in our den, I said to my wife in exasperation, "Boy, what a week this has been so far." After I spent a moment meditating about that statement, I had to laugh at the mental comparison it generated. How many times in the past had I made that statement and truly thought I'd had a tough week? Why had it been tough? Hospital visits to folks who'd had minor surgery; problems with broken office equipment, paper work; counselling; extra studying; and discussions with brethren who didn't like the new carpet color, wall paper, or my new tie.

I don't mean to say that those things are meaningless or even petty, but in terms of "tough", well, everything is a matter of perspective. I've learned that principle if nothing else. Those burdens, compared to a fifteen year old drowning, a sixteen year old committing suicide, and a mother being crushed in front of her husband and daughter, looked terribly lightweight in retrospect. It had never crossed my mind that preaching was so difficult that I might quit. Yet there I was, a Police Chaplain with a whopping four months of experience, and I was seriously considering chunking the whole thing. I hadn't bargained for this much grief. Three heart rending tragedies In less than five days.

The week wasn't over yet.

CHAPTER SIXTEEN

The phone rang causing me to jump out of my skin. I had dozed off in the easy chair in the middle of an introspective debate on the pro's and con's of remaining a Police Chaplain. The voice on the phone belonged to Nick Ellenburg, the Captain of my station, the man who first introduced me to the troops. He had been friendly and helpful, but so far he'd reserved any comments on my job performance.

Nick was a good Captain. The men at the station rarely made any of the usual derogatory remarks about him that were directed at most in the Command staff. He was one of the few who worked his way from blue shirt to white shirt but never forgot what it was like to be a blue shirt, a street cop. His salt and pepper hair and his Rod Steiger looks gave him a commanding presence. He was one of those rare men who you could tell was a born leader. He was a man whose respect I would like to have had, but in the twenty years he'd been on the force, he had never worked with a Chaplain, so he obviously had a "wait and see" attitude about me.

After the expected exchange of meaningless greetings he said, "You've had a busy week. People are beginning to wonder what we did around here before we had Chaplains."

"Good!", I said with a laugh, "I was thinking about asking for a raise."

"No problem Rev. From this moment on your salary from the County is doubled. We'll send you a W-2 form that has two zeroes on it instead of one."

"Gee thanks Captain. Such generosity is inspiring."

"Actually, while it may not be as good as a pay-check, I called to pass on a couple of 'at-a-boys. Sergeant Skip Dimmer at homicide was bragging on what a good job you did for them at the teenage suicide yesterday. He said you really made their job a lot easier and the victim's family was very appreciative.

"Also, Sam Hanks told me how helpful you were to him this morning at the 9-F. He mentioned that you drove the victim's daughter across the county to her home. He wanted to know if we couldn't at least reimburse you for your gasoline expenses."

I was pleasantly surprised. I said, "I truly appreciate you telling me that Captain. They were both pretty gut-wrenching tragedies and it's good to know that I was helpful.

"As far as gas reimbursements go, it's really not that much money, but it would be nice to get some kind of recognition from the County. Something that says we're valuable to them."

"Well, we have a Command Staff Meeting at HQ first thing tomorrow morning, and I will recommend to the Chief that we cover your gas expenses. It's the least the County can do after all the free work you do for us. It's not right to expect you to run all over the world doing work for us and making you foot the bill." He sounded very indignant.

"That would be great. If nothing else, at least it will make them think about us a little. At least one person will be in there fighting for us. Thanks."

"Glad to. And I want you to know Rev, that I personally appreciate all the things you've done for us. The men have really grown to like and trust you a lot. That speaks highly of you. If you ever need anything or have any problems here at the station, come see me. I'll take care of it."

By the time I hung the phone up I was sitting on the edge of my seat. I was enthralled with the vote of support and confidence I'd just received. I'd come a long ways from the outsider who wandered into roll call one day and announced "I'm yours". The acceptance had been slow but sure. The circle got larger and larger every day as they saw me jump into battle, whether it was restraining a drunk or comforting a grief-stricken relative. I'd proven myself and with the singular exception of Hardnose Hinckley, I was considered an insider now.

The melancholia from moments earlier had vanished like a sock in a washing machine. I don't know where it went but it wasn't available to wear anymore. I'd been praised and that was enough to take me from the pits to the pinnacle of self-satisfaction. It reaffirmed what I knew in my heart. The work I was doing as a Police Chaplain was important and meaningful. I was needed. I performed a service that few wanted to do or could do. That made me feel special. The cops appreciated it and soon I'd receive acknowledgment from the County.

I shot up from my chair and suddenly the words of Paul came to mind; "Forgetting what lies behind, I press on . . ." I always liked that verse. I thought about it some more as I pressed on to bed.

I awoke Friday morning to the sound of rain rumbling on my roof top. Everything was a deep shade of gray that whispered suggestions to me concerning the length of time I should stay in bed. There's an eeriness about waking up to rain that makes you refuse to accept the existence of that day. The bed is abnormally comfortable and the motivation is uncharacteristically weak. You know that if you keep your eyes closed long enough the options will be improved.

It got worse. Both the weather and my disposition. Even after my morning shower and coffee, I had the feeling that if I ventured out of the house someone would ask me if I got the name of that truck . . . And I might slug 'em.

I was suffering from an emotional hangover. It showed in the bags under my eyes and the growl in my throat. It was an experience that I would come to recognize as "part of the job". It was the result of the wear and tear of being emotionally uptight. When the body runs on adrenalin for long periods of time, it leaves the body drained and feelings frayed. The rain was just icing.

Fortunately, it was a quiet day at the office. I studied my sermons, prepared the bulletin, and took a few calls. I purposely finished up by three in the afternoon so that I could drop in on the Captain and see how the Command Staff Meeting went. Especially the part about the Chaplains.

The station was unusually tranquil as I sloshed in and set my umbrella off to the side in the foyer. I made the rounds of all the little cubicles in the station. The PCA, the Crime Prevention Officer, the station secretary, and the on duty investigator. The last office at the end of the hall was the Captain's. When I peeked in and saw that he was alone, I gave the door a light rap and walked in.

"Hi Captain. How ya doing today?"

Bringing his hands up over his head and stretching in his seat, he said, "Doing O.K. Rev, but I have had better days."

"Hey, I know the feeling. I felt like a walking zombie all day today. I think the last few days wore me out a lot more than I thought they did."

"Well, have a seat and I'll tell you something that will get your blood moving." He said that with a touch of irritation in his voice.

Sitting down I said, "Let me guess. The staff meeting wasn't a vote of confidence in the Chaplains?"

He leaned forward and rested on his desk. "I couldn't believe it. When I suggested that you all be reimbursed for your gas expenses, only one other station commander spoke up in favor. Others argued that they never called their chaplain and when they did they had an officer drive him. I was furious. Then the Chief spoke up and made some comment to the effect that most of you were required by your churches to do so much civic work and that gas expenses were just part of the job."

"I wish." I interrupted. "Some of my folks feel like they shouldn't be paying me to work for the county. I'm their preacher and no one else's."

"Yeah, well I did my best, but the whole atmosphere was negative to the idea. I'm really sorry about it, but there's nothing I can do about it when the Chief says 'No'. In fact, we'd have been better off to have never brought it up. I should have just done it. Now there's a command directive that says don't give the chaplains gas."

"Don't worry about it Captain. It's not that big of a deal. The important thing to me is that you thought I was worth the effort. I really appreciate that too. I don't have a County perspective towards being a Chaplain. I see myself as a chaplain for this station. My station, with my men. And that's not going to change no matter what the County does."

"As far as I'm concerned Rev, you can get gas from our pump anytime you want it and just have one of the guys put it on their account."

" I appreciate that Captain, but it's not worth the risk of getting you in trouble."

We sat in silence a moment then I added, "If it gets to tight for me I'll just pass the hat at roll call."

He laughed and said, "That might just get you some cigarette butts and empty coke cans."

We talked for a few minutes longer and I did my best to let him know it was a dead issue with me. I convinced him but not myself. I was demoralized.

I left the station before the 4 to 2 roll call. I wasn't in the mood to be the happy, back slapping, Chaplain everyone was use to. I knew the County's insensitivity to the chaplains had no bearing on my relations with my men. Still, it was deflating to think they saw us as men just doing our jobs and not as men who were doing far more than our jobs required. I didn't have to do this. I wasn't getting paid to witness human catastrophes, but I was paying to get there. I guess it was a question of who was doing a favor for whom. It looked to me like the chaplains were the only ones giving out favors.

Giving the chaplains a little gasoline wasn't the issue. It would have been a very inexpensive way for the county to show a little appreciation. The loss of gasoline would have been a drop in the barrel, but the encouragement and recognition would have paid great dividends.

I guess my peak experience from the night before was on fragile footing. The small slap on the hand from the county knocked the wind out of me and I was on a subjective roller-coaster ride that went only one direction, down.

I stayed away from the station and police work all weekend. My attempts to not think about the chaplaincy failed dreadfully. Throughout the weekend my mind was constantly evaluating the amalgamation of feelings which sprang to the surface in the last few months and especially the last few days. Many things troubled me greatly and the easiest solution was radical surgery—quit. But I was experienced enough to know that most of my ill feelings were a reaction to the stress from the recent calamities I had been called to. So I wanted to give myself time to get beyond that before I made any decisions.

I came to the Police Chaplain job with several serious apprehensions. Could I handle the dramatic increase of pain and suffering that I'd see? Would I do the right thing in a crisis situation? Would the cops accept me? What might happen if they discovered my conscientious objector beliefs? How far would I go in defending and protecting someone's life? Would I violate my conscience and shoot to kill? What if I failed miserably as a Chaplain?

These were all 'stay-awake' questions when I started and so far, I'd settled only a few of them and added some new ones. Why didn't Hinckley accept me? Was it me personally, or just his distrustful nature? Could I keep on seeing death, injury, and disaster, and be able to walk away form it without being haunted? Was I being the right spiritual influence on the cops? Some had come to church, Bud regularly, yet in my attempts to be accepted, had I diluted my influence? If I truly felt that it would be wrong for me to ever take another person's life under any circumstances, why was I putting myself in places where that might happen? Was it because my CO feelings were based more on intellectual conclusions than heart-felt feelings? Bud already had me wielding a gun when the prisoners escaped that time, and he was determined to have a shoot-out with Cooper. What if it happened when I was with him? And then there was the County's shameful lack of support. If they didn't appreciate what I had been doing, maybe I was fighting a losing battle.

And yet, the guys did like me. Most of them were good friends already. And they, if not the Ivory Tower crowd, truly saw me as valuable. The captain had said as much, and I was good at what I did. At a death scene or afterwards with the family, I knew what to say and do. I knew my limitations and my responsibilities. Not many folks could do the tough things I'd already done several times. I came in with little support and few allies. Now I was 'one of the guys'. And, most everything else I did was a blast. It fulfilled all the childhood fantasies I'd had. I got to be a cop, complete with badge and equipment. I loved it when some Toad thought I was a plainclothes detective. It was a kick to direct traffic. With stern face I roared with glee inside when I made some teenager pour their can of beer out on the ground.

And yet . . . It went like that all weekend.

CHAPTER SEVENTEEN

Anytime you want to discover how opinionated a cop is, just bring up the subject of department hiring practices. Most will get wild-eyed and fill your ear with fiery rhetoric faster than you can say "expletive deleted". Emotions will surface that you may never have suspected. With very few exceptions, cops stay perpetually resentful of their employer's hiring practices.

"If you want to work for this Department," they'd say with disgust, "you've got to be either Black or a female. If you're a Black female you might make Chief in two years."

It wasn't always a matter of being prejudiced either. Though that is the case in some circumstances. Most of the men I'd spent time with were educated and enlightened men who saw bigotry as a malady from ages past. The real sore spot was the qualified white males who were being turned down because they were the wrong color and sex. They felt that reverse discrimination was a poor way to make up for mistakes of the past.

I tried not to get myself in a position where I had to voice my opinions about the issue. As a citizen, it was my county and my department. I wanted them to hire the best person for the job regardless of their color or gender. As a Chaplain, who rode with every officer, I could see no evidence proving that the female or Black cops were inferior in performance to the Wasp cops. In many cases they tried harder because they felt a need to prove themselves equal to all.

I found this to be particularly true with the woman officers I rode with. I always had an active night of police work when I was with them. That was the reason why I didn't feel cheated when, after being an emotional yo-yo all weekend, I caught a ride with Kathy Meyers on Monday evening.

Kathy had just finished her probationary rookie year with high evaluations and respectable stats. Unlike some female cops, who tried to not only perform as well as the men but look like them too, Kathy was able to present herself as a professional no-nonsense police officer, and still maintain her femininity. She was very attractive in a natural, down-on-the-farm sort of way. She could have made commercials for cereal that tasted like bales of hay. Or she could have been a back-up singer for John Denver.

Kathy had an alluring figure that was not diminished by her broad shoulders or the bullet proof vest, which did little to hide her often commented on assets. Her healthy complexion and pretty face needed little if any make-up. Her turned-up nose pointed to green eyes and auburn hair, which usually was pulled tightly back behind her head. She was pretty, but not stunning. Her greatest feature was a beaming smile and a pleasant outlook on life.

Even though she had proven to be capable and able to take care of herself, the moment I slipped into her cruiser I took on a father-protector attitude. I am sure if I'd been anything but a minister she would have quickly squelched that attitude or demanded my immediate removal from her car. Most people expect ministers to be somewhat fatherly, so she was not offended, thinking I was being spiritual and not chauvinistic. In truth, she gave me more credit than I deserved. I was being more John Wayne than Jesus. "I need to protect this sweet little thing from the villians of this world," I unconsciously thought. I didn't take time to consider that she could probably do a better job of protecting me than vice versa.

After spending three days being tangled in indecision and personal assessment, I desperately needed an escape, a reprieve. Though Monday nights are notoriously slow nights for police activities, this one was a churning torrent of calls, complaints, and crime. A perfect night for getting my mind to shift gears and recharge my enthusiasm for law enforcement.

It started with a short high speed pursuit down route 14. It was just a young guy who'd ran a red light and thought he would play Miami Vice for awhile. It only lasted for a couple minutes, but nothing gets the pumper pounding like screaming Code 3 down a highway, zig-zagging through traffic and watching your life flash before your eyes. Most citizens didn't know how inconsequential it was, legally speaking, to attempt to flee from the police. I'd always assumed that it led to a much more serious charge, but in most jurisdictions, the captured speedster was merely charged with speeding or speeding to allude, which was practically the same thing. Occasionally, an officer was able to stick them with reckless driving, but that was harder to prove if they went to court.

Following that, we worked an accident without injury at one of the major intersections in Kathy's area. It was no fun for her because she had to do all the paperwork. I, however, was in my element again. I donned my luminous striped orange traffic vest, fastened my badge to it, and started igniting flares and directing traffic. For cops who direct traffic on a daily basis, it was the arm pit of the job. But for fair weather cops like me, it was our chance to be Caesar. For a brief moment in time I was in complete control. The glowing flares were my Praetorian guards and the cars were subjects poised to obey my every whim. Some were forced to wait a respectful amount of time before they paraded past me. Others, because of their position or beauty, received my immediate attention. Occasionally I smiled condescendingly at a passing lord of European origin. Then I'd frown at a peasant who came coughing and clanging into my court. Periodically I'd laugh at a jester, who tumbled and jerked in his outlandish decor. And, even though I was supposedly above it, I would stare wantonly at the sleek ladies of the court who glided by.

Alas, the time for fantasy ended and we moved on to a new challenge; trying to receive clearance for a dinner break. Things were so busy that we could only get permission to eat with our portables left on. That way they could call us if we were needed. It's difficult to relax and enjoy a meal when you're expecting to be called over the radio any moment.

I decided to live dangerously. I asked Kathy to let me speak to EOC.

"Chaplain 5," I said in my most authoritative voice.

"Chaplain 5," answered the female dispatcher with something of a question in her tone. They were not accustomed to us using the radios and they had no idea about our official position in the department. They didn't know what their authority over us was, if any at all. It put us in a good position to bluff our way through anything.

"Be advised that I'm with Scout 51. We'd like to take a 10-10 without our portables being on. If it's 10-4 with you, just make a note that we will be at the Rustler's Steak House on Donner Road. You can call us land-line if you need us. 10-4?"

"10-4, Chaplain 5 and Scout 51. I'll hold you 10-10."

Feeling mischievous I answered, "Bless you my child," and was followed by a chorus of clicks.

Kathy was easy to talk to. A college graduate, she was articulate and opinionated, but also a polite listener. Our thirty minutes of uninterrupted conversation went by in a heart beat. I don't even remember what I had for dinner.

Once we were back on the street, we both commented how unusually active it was for a Monday night. When she marked us in service we were the only unit on the street, including the supervisors, who were usually free to patrol. Everyone else was tied up with accidents, complaints, or getting drunks booked at the jail. We knew our freedom was only momentary. It was just a matter of time until a call came in and we were the only ones available to take it.

When it came, we were cruising through one of the many housing developments in Kathy's area.

As Kathy grabbed the mike to answer EOC's call, she groaned, "Since everyone's tied up, you watch, it will be clear across the county."

"Scout 51," she answered.

"Scout 51, Signal 271 at Comanche Trail Court. The number is 724. Be advised that I have no units available for back-up. Proceed with caution."

"10-4, enroute."

A 271 was a Break and Enter in progress. The realization of what that meant impacted me at the same moment I was jerked back against the seat from the cruiser's acceleration. When I'd thought about us being the only unit available I grumbled because I assumed we'd get some namby-pamby call like a larceny report or an abandoned car. I hadn't considered heavy action. We were rolling on a call that most cops lived for. A chance to catch a crook in the act. A chance to dust off the hardware and approach with caution. And, then it came into focus for the first time. "My stars, I'm the back-up!"

"We are only a few blocks away so I'm not gonna use the siren," shouted Kathy over the roaring motor.

I could see that she was wild eyed with anticipation. I wondered if she was aware of the fact that no other unit would be able to back us up.

As if on cue she yelled, "I'm going to hit the release on the shotgun. Pull it out of the holder."

While she pressed the release button, I flipped the clamp off the shotgun and pulled it up and out of its holder. It felt cold in my hands. Not uncomfortable but unnerving. It was just like the one I owned except it was loaded with double-0 magnums, which were bigger than anything I ever used. Also, it held seven shells while mine, by law, could only hold three. I knew it was loaded because checking the shotgun was one of the mandatory pre-check items every cop performed before leaving the police parking lot. I'd wait until I was outside of the cruiser before I chambered a shell

It was oddly exhilarating to be headed for a potentially dangerous encounter, at warp speed, and holding a powerful weapon. I forced all of the 'what if's' out of my mind and just concentrated on what had to be done.

"When we get there, I'll cover the back of the house while you take the front. Maybe we can catch him sneaking out of a window or something." I yelled. Then I decided that I'd better attach my badge to a visible spot on my body to identify whose side I was on. I had a brief memory flash across my mind of someone saying that badges gave crooks a good target. What a time to have a good memory.

We came to a slow, quiet stop in front, and slightly to the left of, a two-story red brick colonial. Immediately we leaped from the car and crossed paths as she ran to the front and I circled to the back. Standing at the back corner of the house in a shadow that the street lights couldn't penetrate, I tried to quietly chamber a shotgun shell. Even with great care, it still made a muffled metallic Kershunck.

I could feel the perspiration dripping down my back. I held the shotgun tightly to prevent it from sliding in my hands. As I eased around the corner of the house, I could clearly see the entire back of the house and the yard. With slow steps, holding the gun poised for action, like I did when I hunted quail, I moved to the first of two windows between me and the back door of the house. Cautiously I checked them both and found them to be locked and with curtains closed.

The silence of the late evening was dramatic. With my senses keenly tensed, expecting the worst, I was a spring that had been wound to its maximum, poised for release. Placing each foot carefully, I stalked the back door. Once I was next to it, I squatted down enough to allow me to peek into the door window at about waist level. I surmised that if someone was standing there waiting with a gun, they wouldn't expect a head to appear that low. I stole a quick look. Nothing.

Next, I slowly reached over with my left hand and checked the door knob. It was locked. I expelled the breath of air I'd been holding since I left the cruiser. Just one more window in the back to check. It was smaller and higher than the others. Like it belonged to a bathroom or a utility room.

Stalk. Peek. Check locks. Breath. This was exciting.

As I approached the far corner of the house, moving with a stealthiness that would have impressed Rambo, I heard a twig pop around the corner. I froze and listened. I heard the faint sound of crunching dirt as someone took a slow step. Someone was sneaking up on that corner. I instantly went down on my right knee and brought the shot gun up to my shoulder. Who ever it was would look around that corner and look out not down. Then I'd have'em.

I definitely wasn't out there alone. Then like a bolt of lightening it hit me. Of course I wasn't out there alone, Kathy was with me. Quickly, before I made a terrible mistake, I whispered "Kathy?", and received an immediate "It's me" from around the corner.

In one move I jumped back up to a standing position and pointed the gun at the ground. When she rounded the corner, I was leaning against the house and had the shotgun resting in the crook of my left arm with the barrel aimed downward.

"You look like you're off on a pheasant hunting excursion. See anything?" she said.

"Not one pheasant on this entire place," I pretended to be terribly distressed.

"Give me a break."

"Everything locked and secure. No sign of forced entry. Did you have any luck?"

"Likewise, everything secure. I'd better find out who called it in."

Taking her portable out of its holder she contacted EOC. "This is Scout 51. Everything seems to be secure here. Do you have a Signal 4 for this?"

A Signal 4 was the person to be contacted upon arrival at a complaint. In this case, EOC said it was one of the neighbors.

Kathy wrote down their house number and advised EOC that she'd be talking to the complainant, to see why they called us.

As we started toward the next door neighbor's house, I realized that I was still carrying the 870.

"I'll tell you what," I said to Kathy as I stopped in mid-step, "you talk to the neighbor, I'll go put this thing back in its cage. It's probably not a good idea to walk up to someone's door with a shotgun in your hands. I'll meet you back at the cruiser."

Ten minutes later Kathy was back at her car. The neighbor had seen shadows around the house next door, and since those neighbors were in Canada on vacation, she assumed they were being robbed. So she called in a B and E instead of a Suspicious Person or Event. Classic. Most potentially dangerous calls that police roll on turn out to be flukes. Yet they can never afford to expect it to be a fluke. The day they do, that is the day they walk into an ambush.

It was two hours later, when I was home and in bed, before the implications of that evening sank in on me. Oddly enough, I had mixed feelings about the entire incident. Each time I'd think "What if someone had come charging out of that house? What would I have done?", I'd shiver with regrets. But then I'd remember the spectacular thrill of danger, the challenge of survival, the adrenalin high, it was addicting. It was scarry, but I had to admit that I'd enjoyed it. What about my convictions? Was I simply trying to impress a female officer with my courage? Was it because I had felt so good that I just got caught up with the events of the evening, forgetting who I was and who I represented?

I couldn't figure it out. Actually I didn't want to figure it out. It felt good to enjoy being a Chaplain. Especially after the depressing events of the previous week. I decided to postpone any self-examination of the evening for as long as I could. For the moment, I was keyed up and happy. I wanted to bask in the sunlight of self-satisfaction for awhile.

CHAPTER EIGHTEEN

The crisp September breeze was like a glass of cool water to the parched lips of a desert wanderer. It was fresh and keen. It was blessed respite from the sweltering scintillation of August. After being kiln dried for three months, the hint of autumn was balm to a burned spirit. The refreshing wind whispered anticipatory rumors of holidays, hunting, and harvest time. Of course, there was very little harvesting taking place in our area now. Not much grows on asphalt.

Our first frost of the year was still a few weeks away, but it was cool enough to put some zip in my step and swing in my arms as I walked into the old red brick Police Station. Station 5, my home away from home. Due to some serious demands at church, I hadn't been by the station in three days. In fact, I hadn't even talked to a cop for three days. I was anxious to see everyone and make sure that I hadn't missed anything "Big".

The first person I saw when I stepped in the door was Nat Kawalski, my favorite New Yorker. His large frame was placing a tremendous burden on the reception counter he leaned against.

"Hey Rev," he said in his booming Bronx, "where you been. Hadn't seen you around here in the last few days?" His "you" came out sounding more like "use".

"You noticed? I'm touched. Those folks over at church think that just because they pay my salary I should work for them occasionally. So that's what I've been doing. It sure puts a crimp in my Police Chaplain activities."

Since I was being overtly facetious, it was tit-for-tat time.

"What you need to do Rev, is chunk all that and join the Department. We'll get you in blue and you'll have a field day hasseling Toads. You'll be able to put in forty plus hours every week fighting crime and busting heads. Of course, you wouldn't be making the Big bucks like you are now, but, what the hay, you're not in it for the money anyways right?"

"I'm sorry Nat, but I enjoy all the time I spend at the bank counting my money. I couldn'd leave that to become a cop. One of these days I'll have my own T.V. show." I slipped into my best impersonation of a well known T.V. preacher. "Reach down into that purse. Dig into that wallet. Open up that check book. Send your money to me now. Keep this ministry alive. Keep this great work going. Keep your favorite preacher rich."

Slapping his leg Nat laughed and said, "I'm the one who's in the wrong line of work. What do I need to do to become a preacher?"

I scratched my head a second then answered, "Four years of college, two or three more years of post-grad work, loads of natural ability, training in twenty different side areas like counselling and running a vacuum, and a desire to serve. Or, you could have some business cards printed up that say you're a preacher. Take your pick."

We continued our banter for a few more minutes and then he abruptly changed the subject and the tone with an interesting piece of information.

"Did you hear about the Cooper boy getting iced?"

"No kidding? Which one?"

"I think it was the middle one, Ralph."

"He's the only one I haven't seen yet. I've seen Brian and Jerry. How did it happen?"

"I haven't heard all the info yet. I'm sure we'll hear about it at roll call, it's on the board. From what I've heard, one of his drug pals wasted him with a shot in the back of the head. They're not sure what the weapon was yet."

With a grimace I asked, "Bud didn't have anything to do with it did he?"

"No. Of course everyone's joking with him about it, saying he did it or paid someone to do it just to make Jerry irritated. No, it was over in Station 7's area. Let's get on down stairs to roll call and see what's up."

We both lumbered down the wooden stairs, sounding more like horses than men. We joined the others who were merging on the roll call room. After the appropriate salutations and seat selections, we settled down to hear the scoop on the Cooper killing.

When Sergeant Scott began reading off the routine transgressions on the Daily Activity board, I noticed that someone had taped a large brown manila envelope to the front of the ugly government issue desk. On it, in green magic marker, were the words "Flowers for Ralph Cooper".

I had to laugh at the cruel humor of cops. The envelop was not there as an act of sympathy for the Cooper family. It was their way of cheering the removal of another piece of trash from the street. The only remorse felt in that room was due to the fact that a cop hadn't been the one to blow him away. In this case, they'd come nearer sending flowers to the killer than to a family as sleazy as the Coopers. There would be no money put in that envelope.

Never missing an opportunity to impose guilt upon myself, it struck me as being odd that we could be so devastated by one person's death and then rejoice over the death of another. I am sure it stemmed from our innate willingness to ascribe justice to our mortality. Death isn't accepted as a part of life. It must be assigned a rightness or a wrongness. If it's deserved then it's not so bad, but if it's undeserved, unjustified, or unexplainable, it becomes a terrible mysterious enemy. A dark sinister robber of innocence and happiness. It was cause for jubilation when the Indians were mowed down on T.V., after all they were the bad guys. Yet when the hero's life became imperiled, we sat on the front inch of our chairs and chewed our fingernails off. Many of us to this day, hate to see a movie where the good guys die. If you're good, you're supposed to live 'happily ever after'.

"All right, listen up, gentlemen," commanded Scott, "unless you had your head in the clouds, you know that Ralph Cooper, one of our Top Ten Toads, got wasted last night. Here's the info on the Poop Sheet.

"Signal 36 in Station 7's area at approximately 21:30 hours, last night. The victim was Ralph J. Cooper of 1503 Sutter Road. White male, 5'11", 182 pounds, brown hair, brown eyes, and a D.O.B. of 3-16-60. The perp is unknown . . ." He paused for effect. "But, he is believed to have rosy cheeks and wearing a blue shirt."

"Let's hear it for Bud!" shouted Thunder.

A few claps and hoots followed.

"I told Bud to use some camo on his cheeks," said Pretty Boy, "but did he listen to me? No!"

Bud, who was sitting next to him, gave him a back hand across the shoulder then said, "Listen you turkeys. If I had been the one who ended Cooper's miserable life, I would have done it to his face and I would have left a note for his big brother that he was next."

"Ladies," said Scott, "since we're needed on the street let's finish this up and you can continue your debate out there."

He cleared his throat and continued the reading.

"Rescue received a call from a citizen regarding an injured man lying in the parking lot at 11473 Rogers Place. The caller refused to leave their name. Upon arrival at the scene, rescue found Cooper face down in the parking lot. He had sustained a blow or a shot to the back of his head and was pronounced dead at the scene. PD was contacted and Investigator Bowen has been assigned to the case."

Looking up from the clip board, Scott added, "Since this came out early this morning, the boys at homicide have determined that the murder weapon was a high powered gun fired at close range. Possibly a .357 or a .44 magnum. At first they thought it had been a big club of some kind because the head was caved in from the back. They still have no suspects, but they feel confident that it was drug related."

"He probably was making a sale and got ripped off. I hear that they didn't find any drugs or money on him," said one of the officers.

"I'll bet it was a case of pay back," said Nat Kawalski. "The Coopers, especially Jerry, have iced so many competitors that one of'em decided it was time to even up the score. They know better than to go for Jerry himself, so they went after the next best thing, his brother."

That gave everyone something to mull over as they left roll call and started loading up their cruisers with gear. Nat was probably correct. He had a lot of street savvy after several years with the NYPD and several more with us. Yet like many cases, knowing and proving were two different categories. And like most drug murders, this one had a slim chance of being solved. That thought didn't disturb the cops too much this time. Nat put it in perspective when he said, "We may not catch the gigger but we got the Toad."

"New York" Nat truly had a way with words. Riding with him that evening I remained in a constant state of amusement because of his colorful metaphors and Brooklyn bromides. At times, I felt a need for an interpreter, but rather than ask for clarification I simply laughed and said, "Right on". I didn't want to tarnish his image of me as being "worth my weight in gold".

After two hours of cruising the neighborhoods without a single "job related" interruption, Nat was ready to open up and tell me what was on his heart. It had taken two hours to melt away the facades of Eastwoodism, and "Boy have I got my act together" before we could get to the pain buried underneath. Some of the guys, I'd discovered, had fire-proof facades. Fortunately, Nat was not one of them.

"Chaplain," he said with his eyes on the road, but using automatic pilot, "this is just between you and me now, right. I mean, this is confidential and, well, I mean, well, I know you won't be sticking no ice pick in my back, but no one else knows about this and I want to keep it that way."

I thought about saying something like "My lips are sealed" or "You can trust me", but everything I thought of sounded trite and demeaning. So I said nothing. He knew he could trust me or he wouldn't even be talking to me.

"Ya see, we just found out last month that my wife has lymphatic cancer. And, well, it doesn't look good. She's taking radiation therapy and all sorts of medicines, and she's lost all her hair, and she's, well, she's having a hard time dealing with it all. She won't talk about it. She cries herself to sleep every night and I feel like, well, like she's given up and just wants to die."

Nat said that with such deep emotion that it cut me to the heart. I had to think for a moment and clear the walnut from my throat before I spoke.

"Nat, it's obvious how your wife has reacted to all this, but how do you feel about it?"

That opened a flood-gate of feelings for Nat. He painted a portrait of pain, helplessness, and love. It took more courage for this cop to bare his soul than it did for him to pull the three teenagers from a burning overturned car, for which he had received the Silver Medal of Valor. Even with all his friends in blue and all the support systems the County liked to brag about,

Nat had no one to talk to. But now he had me.

I prayed for a quiet radio as we talked, and my request was accepted. After we got all the problems and worries out in the open, we began to construct a course of action. I outlined an approach to improving his communication with his wife. We set up a time during the morning when he and his wife could come talk to me at my office. He rejected outright any suggestion that they talk to the County's psychologist. We discussed ways for him to cope with his feelings and ways that he could help his wife with hers. It was a simple strategy of positive communication, confrontation, and cooperation. I could see his entire outlook change as he discovered that he could do something to change the situation. He couldn't change the cancer, but he could improve their relationship.

Later, as we took our 10-10 at one of the fast food joints in our area, Nat said, "Ya know Rev, if it could be done, I'd have that cancer transferred to me in a heart beat. I can handle dying, but I can't handle my wife suffering."

"I don't know your wife, Nat, but I'm sure that if she knew how much you loved her, it would make the suffering a lot easier to endure. And she probably knows, but she needs to hear it."

"Yeah, it's hard to stop being a cop when I get home," he said with great sadness.

"Well, Nat, it's all right for cops to be in love and show it."

Within minutes of marking back in service we received our first call of the evening. Actually, it was a call for me, not us. One of our men was on the scene of an attempted suicide and he wanted me to respond. On several occasions I had counselled with people who had attempted suicide, but usually it had been at the hospital where they were being sewn up or having their stomach pumped.

It was easy to determine at which townhouse we were to stop. The one with three police cruisers and an ambulance in front of it. Nat's cruiser had to be parked a block away because of lack of spaces available. It was odd to see the rescue team waiting in the ambulance. At the risk of besmirching an honorable profession, they reminded me of vultures waiting for someone to die.

Walking into the living room of the townhouse I found Sergeant Scott and two other officers standing in a wide semi-circle, as if giving a wide berth to a rattle snake. Looking past them, I saw a young girl, perhaps twenty years old, sitting on the floor against the wall. She was nearly hidden by the window curtains that hung down the wall to her left and the couch that was on her right. The frail blond girl held a six inch kitchen knife in both hands with the point directed at her stomach. She was plain, not pretty. With her head bowed and her shoulders shaking from sobs, she was a pathetic sight.

Scott directed me back to the front door where in whispered tones he filled me in on the situation.

"The young lady over there," he said with a nod of his head, "came over here to talk to her estranged husband. When she got here she found him having a party with three girls and another guy. They're all down stairs in the basement. Anyway, they got into a shouting match and she grabbed the knife from the kitchen and threatened to kill herself. She's been over there ever since.

"It's my judgment that she really doesn't want to kill herself, but every time we start getting close to her she freaks out and starts to stab herself. I had rescue standby just in case she does. Her name is Jennifer Tune."

I pondered that a few moments and said, "Let me go over and introduce myself to her. If it looks like I can talk to her, I'll need you guys to leave the room. I know that's not PD policy, but I really don't think I'll be in any danger. Alright?"

"Sure Rev. I agree, she's not much of a threat. If she had a gun instead of a knife we'd have to stay put, but I think it's O.K. for you to be here with her alone."

When I started walking towards her, she stiffened up and became wild-eyed. But before she could say anything, I announced, "Jennifer, my name is Mark Temple. I'm a Police Chaplain. Do you know what a chaplain is?"

Her face was blank. So I continued, "I'm a minister, Jennifer. I want to help you get out of this mess, O.K.?"

Her eyes filled with tears and she visibly relaxed.

I took a few steps closer and sat down on the couch about four feet from her.

"Jennifer, I'll have the Policemen leave the room if you will talk to me. Will you?"

Without looking up she nodded her head yes. Scott signaled the other two officers and they went out the front door leaving me alone with the troubled girl.

I eased off the couch and sat on the floor just a yard away from her. Now we could talk on the same level. There would be no hint of her being talked-down to.

"Things really have a way of getting out of hand don't they?"

She responded with a muted laugh and more affirmative nodding.

In a sympathetic but firm voice I asked, "Jennifer, tell me why you want to die?"

In a voice thick and raspy from weeping she answered, "I don't want to die I—I just wanted someone to listen to me."

I had never heard a statement that more appropriately described the torment of loneliness. How many attempted suicides and even completed suicides were simply lonely people screaming for someone to listen to them.

She continued with her story. It was an old familiar story of heartache, abandonment, and helplessness. She married young, had a baby, her husband left her, she was living on family charity, saw no hope of improvement, and she was weary of worrying about it all.

"I can't even buy food for my little baby," she cried, "let alone the pretty clothes I'd love to buy for her. I wanted her father to help out a little bit, but all he wants to do is chase girls, drink, and get high."

It took nearly a half hour for her to get it all off her chest. I'd listened, but there was very little I could do to change things. I offered to take her to the County Counselling Center, but she'd have to want to go and she'd have to give me the knife. Strangely enough, she'd forgotten that she was even holding a knife. With a shy smile, she handed it to me handle first.

I thought about going down to the basement and talking to her husband, but I knew I'd have a difficult time controlling the urge to horse whip him. She would have to settle for a ride to the Center with Nat and I.

At the center, I took her in and introduced her to one of the counsellors. When I stepped out of the room and left her there, I felt like I was 'bailing out'. Even though there was nothing else I could do, I was uncomfortable about leaving her alone. But I had to.

Nat made me feel much better about things when he pointed out how important my efforts had been. I had been able to talk to her and defuse a life threatening situation when no one else could. As he said, "There's no telling how it would have ended had it been left up to cops."

Within minutes I was able to put the entire incident behind me. I had a long way to go still before I could walk away from every case and not let it affect me personally, but I was getting there. So I thought.

CHAPTER NINETEEN

Every county has an area which reeks of opulence. Areas whose names conjure up images of Mercedes, minks, and millions. Names like Bel-Aire, Waterford, and Georgetown. Places that normal people visit on Sunday afternoon drives and then dream of someday living there. Where houses sat so far off the road you had to have binoculars to really get a good look at them. Communities where homes were judged by the number of magazines they'd appeared in and where the yards were so perfect they looked like molded plastic. The exclusive domain of the rich and powerful. People we say we pity because they couldn't possibly be happy with all their wealth. Yet people we desperately wanted to emulate

Greenhaven was almost that kind of area. I say almost because the houses were not monstrous mansions but were nevertheless exorbitant. They were build on Lake Greenhaven, a small but picturesque lake surrounded by a lush green forest that protected it from the highways. This gave the homeowners the envious advantage of having both privacy and quick access to their offices downtown. It was an old established community that had escaped the ravages of urbanization. Most of the homeowners were long time residents, who protected Greenhaven's privacy with a tenacity matched only by the Red Guard at the Kremlin. The police were rarely called into Greenhaven and for the most part, they avoided even patrolling it. Even though it was in the middle of Lexington County, most residents weren't aware of it's existence because it was so completely concealed and secluded.

I never had any particular desire to visit Greenhaven. Yet the one time I did was an experience unparalleled in my career as a Chaplain. I should have been more callused about death by then, after what I'd seen. But, in Greenhaven I saw a scene which caused me to be more soul-sick than I'd ever been before, and I never even saw a body.

I was expecting the worst when I arrived at the orange brick rambler at 13667 Green Apple Lane. I had spent the last hour at the station consoling the three officers who first arrived on the scene. The hour before that had been spent with the men of the ambulance team who had removed the bodies from the house. They had all witnessed a scene so gruesome, so tragic, and so heart-rending that they would never be completely able to shake it from their memories.

Sometime during the early morning hours of that day, a crime was committed in the peaceful environs of Greenhaven that would forever mar its image as heaven on earth. No longer would County residents think of its posh elegance or its lovely lakeside grandeur. Greenhaven's beauty had been eclipsed by the dark cloud of death. Horrible, unthinkable death.

Who knows why, but for some reason, Roger Crutchfield slipped out of bed without waking his wife, and took his .38 caliber revolver from its hiding place in the closet. Sandwiching it in his pillow to muffle the report, he fired one shot into the right temple of his wife. He crossed the hall to the room where his two daughters slept undisturbed by the noise. The little girls were four years old and six years old respectively. They slept in identical twin beds across the room from each other. They each died from one shot to the head.

Leaving their room, Mr. Crutchfield went down the stairs to the basement to the room his ten year old son slept in. After killing his son, he returned to the master bedroom crawled in bed beside his wife's body, and fired one round through his open mouth.

This was the scene the cops and medics found after breaking in the garage door to the house. Not one of them, even the most experienced, had ever seen such a sight. In the process of checking the bodies to see if any might possibly be alive, two officers and three medics got sick and had to run from the house. Later at the fire house, one of the men I talked to broke down and cried like a baby as he described carrying the children's bodies from the house. He had children of his own and now he had a desire to find a new occupation.

I had been called to help the police and fire personnel who'd been at the scene. That in itself was unusual, but then, there were no survivors to help. Only men who were supposed to do a job without being personally affected. Obviously, in this case, that was impossible. The cops on TV may be made of unbending steel, but the cops on the street are made of flesh and blood, and more importantly, feelings. No one could leave a sight like that and immediately go back to writing traffic tickets. They had to cope with the despair and grief that gripped each of them. And it was my job to help them.

Captain Ellenburg called me out of the room that I'd been using to meet with the downcast men. He had a melancholy expression on his face reminding me that within hours the entire Department would be demoralized as the terrible story traversed the grapevine.

"How's it going, Rev?"

"Captain, these guys are pretty shaken. I think you should request that each of them have a session with the County's shrink. She can give them some guidance that will help them not only get over this, but not let it affect their families and their jobs. This isn't something that they can sleep on tonight then get up tomorrow and act like it never happened."

Raising his brow in agreement he said, "I'll arrange that right now so that she can see everyone today."

Thinking out loud I said, "I can't imagine what would cause

146

a man to do the things that Crutchfield did. He must have been completely crazy."

"It's hard to say. Obviously he wasn't thinking rationally, but more than likely there was a terrible logic to what he did."

That shocked me. "What could possibly be logical about killing one's family?"

"Well I'm no psychiatrist, but I had a criminology class once that covered this kind of mess. What may have happened was that he decided to commit suicide. After he thought about it awhile, he probably decided that he needed to spare his family the grief and shame of having a husband and father who killed himself. The only way to do that, in his twisted mind, was to take them with him. He may have truly thought that he was doing them a favor. By all reports he was good and loving father, so he didn't do it out of hate. We'll never know of course. It's a shame that he didn't get professional help. That would have been a lot easier on the rest of the family."

"It's so hard to imagine someone thinking like that," I said. "There is no urge in me that is stronger than the urge to protect my children. I can't even bear the thought of any harm coming to them, let alone their death."

He cleared his throat to signal that he was changing the subject. "Listen, the reason I called you out here is because I need you to do a favor."

"Sure, just name it." I shouldn't have been so willing.

"We finally managed to contact some relatives of the Crutchfields in Boston. They're on the way down here and should be here by tonight. The problem is that I hate for them to find the house in the state it's in. We need to get someone to clean it up before they arrive. Could you go over there and see if any of the neighbors would clean up the mess? Surely someone would help get it presentable."

" Sure." I said without a second thought, "there's bound to be a Good Samaritan over there somewhere."

But there wasn't, or if there was I couldn't find him.

Parking my car in the Crutchfield driveway, I walked to the neighbor's house on the right. An eighty year old woman answered the door. Rather than ask her what I had intended to, I asked her who in the neighborhood might be able to assist in cleaning up her neighbor's house. She had no suggestions at all. She said most of the people were at work and I probably wouldn't find anyone at home.

She was right. I went to six houses and the people either weren't home or they weren't answering their doors. By then, because of the size of the lots, I was a half mile from my car. So I returned to the Crutchfield driveway and stared at the house for awhile.

The cop shows on TV never tell you who cleans up the gory

murder scene that they so casually contaminate by walking all over. It's not the job of the police to clean up the mess. They just investigate and try to solve the case, hopefully with an arrest. Many a relative has had to get down and scrub up a pool of blood that once coursed through the veins of a loved one. Sometimes the rescue team or the police will bundle up sheets, throw rugs, and cloths and cart them to the dump, but that was the exception, not the rule.

Enter the Chaplain. One of the responsibilities that chaplains had accepted was the job of getting someone to do the clean up. Most of the time there were people around who were more than willing to help, but sometimes due to weak stomachs or overactive imaginations and superstitions, the only person available to do the work was the chaplain. That was a rather disparaging thought as I stood there scrutinizing the house.

The one-story house was much smaller and older than the other houses I could see. Actually, it was rather plain considering it's location. But one look around the corner of the house at the serene lake down below it and I was reminded of its worth. The rest of us, who wanted to live on some water, had to drive two hours to the ocean or two to three hours to some other lake or stream. Greenhaven was twenty-five minutes from downtown.

The covered double carport could have been in any housing development in the county. It was a jumble of domestic peculiarities. Unmatching trash cans, lawn mower, tools, work bench, and bicycles. A one year old white Olds occupied one side of the carport.

"Well, I might as well get in there and see what needs to be done," I thought.

Expecting it to be tough, I adopted a steely frame of mind. I walked directly to the side door in the carport and pushed it open with the authority of a man who was ready to give the boss a piece of his mind. It was manufactured bravado.

The door opened up into the dining room of the house. The kitchen was on the other side of the dining room. Before my eyes could focus on anything, my nose was attacked by the powerful odor of stale cigarette smoke. That plus the full ash trays scattered around confirmed that Mr. and Mrs. Crutchfield were heavy smokers. I had a strong desire to open some windows. The smell was almost nauseating.

The Crutchfields's hadn't expected company. The house wasn't dirty, just cluttered. Maybe lived-in would be a better description. Signs of family life were everywhere. Toys, school papers, aspirin bottle, full trash cans, family pictures, kid's shoes by the door, dishes in the sink, sofa pillows on the floor, plants, magazines, and a stereo with a record on the turn-table, all were signs of a family that went to bed expecting to get up the next morning.

As I walked into the living room my eyes were drawn to a large portrait on the fireplace mantel. It was the Crutchfields. My eyes rested on each face for a moment. The bright eyes and wide smiles of the three children seemed like flashing neon signs blinking Why?—Why?—Why?. I had to look away and remind myself that I had a job to do.

There was a light on in a room down the hall on the right, just past the stairs to the basement. It was the master bedroom.

It was a spacious room with plush carpet and elegant hardwood furniture. At the foot of the king-sized bed the bedspread had been bundled up with the corner of a pillow poking out of the top. I felt sure that it was the pillow Mrs. Crutchfield had died on. The other pillow, the one used as a silencer, had been taken by the investigators. As I stood at the lower corner of the bed, it was easy to see who had lain where. On the right side of the bed, where her head had been, was a large red stain on the sheet. It was actually a rusty brown color due to drying and soaking into the mattress.

On the left side of the bed, most of the stain was mixed with yellow bed stuffings. The investigators had dug into the mattress to retrieve the spent bullet. There was enough of a stain to tell that Mr. Crutchfield didn't bleed from his wound nearly as much as his wife had. Stepping over a couple feet, I could see were they had retrieved from the floor the bullet which had killed her. There was a small slice in the carpet dissecting the bullet hole. A faint chalk mark encircled it.

The night stand on Mr. Crutchfield's side was adorned with a lamp, a radio/clock, and a pair of glasses resting on the latest issue of GOOD HOUSEKEEPING. The other stand had several bottles of prescription medicine on it and a worn King James translation of the Bible. I shivered to think of a religious fanatic running through the house killing his family because he thought God told him to. Even the best of medicines can be abused.

The room across the hall showed more evidence of the medics attempts to find life. The beds had been pulled away from the walls to allow medics to work on the little girls from both sides. It wasn't a large room but it was adequate for the two twin beds, two dresser drawers, toy chest, and desk that was in it.

It was a typical girl's room. Care Bears and Cabbage Patch Kids watched me with innocent grins. The walls had posters of the Muppets and Sesame Street characters. There was even a poster of Bugs Bunny. On the desk, which separated the beds, was an assortment of school supplies, crayons, coloring books, and small toys. On the wall above the desk hung a small framed mirror. A small sheet of paper was wedged into the frame. It was crayon drawing of a heart with a caption reading "I love you Mommy".

I stood transfixed, seeing nothing, but aware that tears were streaming down my face.

The bed to my left had the expected stain on it that covered the pillow and sheet. Laying against the wall was a brown-haired, blue-eyed doll dressed in a pink jogging suit. It had speckles of blood on it.

The other bed had been pulled completely away from the wall about a foot and a half. The blood stain was on the wall side of the bed. Looking closer, I saw with horror that the dark panel was splattered with blood and brain matter. It had dripped down the wall and made a considerable puddle on the floor. At the foot of the bed, wadded up in the sheet and blanket, was a small stuffed Big Bird.

I stepped back and grabbed my forehead with both hands. A scenario crashed into my head with the subtlety of an atomic bomb. There was no way in the world he could have killed them both at the same time. One had to wake up when the first one was shot. The implications of that were beyond contemplation. Too heartbreaking to consider. Yet I couldn't stop my imagination from launching into the unthinkable.

I left the room and started down the basement stairs. Each step gave off a dull thud of gloom as I descended to the final scene of this unbelievable tragedy.

At the bottom of the stairs I faced sliding glass doors which looked out on a beautifully terraced yard. The yard sloped down to the blue, still waters of Lake Greenhaven. The basement was paneled with tongue-in-groove cedar panels. At one end there was a family room and a wet bar. The other end of the basement held an office and a bedroom. A little boy's bedroom.

The room was a museum of childhood memorabilia. Model airplanes lined the shelves, baseball bats and fishing rods leaned in the corner, and comic books covered the desk. The rumpled and stained bed was similar to the others. What was different was the line of Match Box cars on the edge of the bed. A couple had been knocked to the floor by the medics, but it was obvious that he had gone to sleep playing with his toy cars. Just like my son did.

I left the room and sat on the basement steps for awhile. I prayed for the strength I needed to keep from leaving the cleaning, the house, and even the Chaplaincy as fast as I could.

Using advice I'd given many others, I determined to turn my despair into physical energy. I attacked the cleaning with a vengeance. All the blood stained pillows, sheets, and bedspreads were dumped into one of the unmatching trash cans. Rather than try to do something to clean the mattresses, I simply hauled them out to the carport and leaned them against the wall with the stained side hidden. Someone would have to take them to the county dump. The stain and the stigma of death made them good fodder for the incinerator.

Using an old plastic pail from the carport and towels from their bathrooms, I cleaned up the worst mess in the girls room. I had to sing a song out loud to distract my mind as I wiped blood and indescribable gore off the wall and floor. It wasn't spotless when I finished, but at least it was not grisly any more. I did more removing and hiding than scrubbing and cleaning. The pail and towels went in the same can as the bedding. What did get thoroughly scrubbed was my hands. I washed them three times just to be sure they were clean.

Without a last check or a backwards glance I closed the door behind me and walked around to the side of the house. I took several lung-stretching breaths of air as if to cleanse them of the ghastly aroma of death. A slight breeze caused ripples to dance across the lake top like giant water-bugs. The loosening leaves on the oaks and hickory trees clattered a song of tranquillity. A song I couldn't harmonize with at all.

Later that night, after my children were fast asleep, I slipped into their rooms. With each one I laid down beside them on their dainty twin beds, and held them for awhile. I kissed their foreheads, and said a little prayer for each one. I also said a prayer for three children who were in the arms of Jesus. Children whose father came to them one night, but not to give them a kiss.

Before I succumbed to the blessed escape of sleep, I made an important decision. I didn't need this much turmoil in my life. It was time to rethink and resign, but I didn't want to do anything until I'd laid it all on the table for one of the officers. It was important that someone see the entire picture, and that someone was my favorite cop, Bud "Cowboy" Cabot.

CHAPTER TWENTY

I knew that Bud would be a settling influence on me. His rosy cheeks mirrored his outlook on life. He had an almost childlike enthusiasm for his job, that never failed to recharge my disconsolate post-tragedy attitude. In the two days since the Greenhaven disaster, several doldrum periods had come to an end with the thought, "When I get with Bud I'll feel better." It was ironic that I felt my cure would come from the people I'd set out to heal. I longed to feel excited about being a chaplain like an addict longs for a fix.

It had been my plan to go to the station in time to catch the afternoon roll call, but when I discovered that Bud's squad was on midnights, I waited until the 9 o'clock roll call before I came to the station.

One evening on each midnight shift, the Sergeants arranged to have some Roll Call Training. That night, the training was from an investigator on the Sexual Crimes team. They were unsympathetically called the Sex Squad by the men in blue. They had to work in the despicable world of child abuse, rape, kiddie porn, and other areas of vice and depravity.

Our teacher was a dark complexioned Italian named Anthony Sparangetti. He was short and stocky, with asphalt black hair and mustache. His small, almost non-existent chin, and piercing cool blue eyes gave him a look of ruggedness one would assume he'd need for the job of catching perverts and sadists.

He launched into his presentation with surprising wit, and not so surprising vulgarity. In making his points and using graphic examples to illustrate them, he displayed a rare ability to shock even the cops. Many of the guys stole quick looks at me to see if his coarseness was affecting me. He had no way of knowing who or what I was, since I was wearing a suit and tie. Like most people, he probably thought I was one of the cops.

As the obscenities increased, so did the furtive glances at me. I wasn't offended. It seemed to me that Sparangetti was using the uncivil language to conceal the obvious compassion he had for the victims of sex crimes. He wanted his fellow officers to view him as a hard-as-nails investigator who was unaffected by the gross criminal abuses he saw. It's sad that he couldn't let his "cop face" down and share some real heartfelt lessons with us.

He suddenly stopped in midsentence and stared at me. The air was heavy with anticipation as his blue eyes glared.

"What the heck's going on here? Why does everybody keep looking over at you?" He had a slight uneasy grin.

Sergeant Scott, who was filling in for Hardnose, was sitting next to him with his arms folded across his chest. He leaned over as if to whisper to Sparangetti, but said loud enough for everyone to hear, "That's our Chaplain. Reverend Mark Temple.

152

We call him Rev for short."

The look of shock on Sparangetti's face could have been used in an Alfred Hitchcock movie. The roar of laughter from the guys in roll call would have made any comedian proud. He slapped his forehead with both hands, blasphemed briefly, and started to literally crawl under the table. That raised the ruckus to a new fever pitch.

I was laughing as much as everyone else. It was encouraging to see someone who truly was ashamed of the language they had used. Most of the time the guys seemed determined to be unaffected by the possibility that they might have offended me with their vulgarity. It was a constant source of jesting for them. One would say to the other, "How dare you use such language? And in the presence of the Chaplain, too." To which I'd reply, "My presence never changed anything before, why should it now?"

One time, when I was playing basketball with several of the cops, one of them came up to me and said, "Rev, I sure would feel a whole lot better if you used just one dirty word. That's all, just one dirty word." I was so surprised that all I could say was, "Sorry".

I'd never preached to them or even hinted to them that I didn't approve of vulgar language. I did joke with a couple of them about it, but never in a judgmental tone, and not in the presence of others. Yet somehow they were sensitive about it. It was a non-issue to me. Most swearing and cussing involved the use of meaningless phrases that were intended to cause a response to the tone or attitude behind it. It was verbal toughness, not a denotative message.

Sparangetti apologized profusely before, during, and after the remainder of his presentation. I felt sorry for him because he was seriously embarrassed by his indiscretion. While I hadn't been offended, I didn't want to belittle his penance by saying, "Forget it, it was no big deal, I can swear with the best of 'em." His sense of guilt came from a sensitivity that needed to be cultivated, not calloused.

The second time that he apologized to me after roll call, I said, "Anthony, I appreciate your sensitivity, and your respect for me. Next time, before you start, ask if there are any chaplains present. It might save you some embarrassment." We laughed and became friends. I had an uneasy feeling that he'd need a chaplain some day and when that day came, I wanted him to call me.

By the time I jumped into Bud's cruiser, I was primed and ready, not for action, but for discussion. I knew the chances were excellent since Bud had been assigned area 540, Siberia. Located in the southwestern corner of the County, area 540 was called Siberia for obvious reasons. It was out in the boonies, the

153

country, the horizon. Because of the distance between the houses or farms in that area, there were few calls and loads of patrolling. In fact, it was so far out that in some spots the car radios didn't transmit. The standard line for any unit heading out to patrol 540 was, "Be sure and pack a lunch." It was a fifteen to twenty minute drive just to get to where 540 began. That plays havoc on the response time.

It was a peaceful night in Siberia. Floating over the rolling hills on unlit and unmarked two lane country roads was conducive to serious conversation. There was very little to distract and interrupt. Checking dead end roads for parkers and trying to be as visible to the taxpayers as possible, could be accomplished with a minimum of brain power. It was a good area to relax the normal paranoid instincts that are second nature to most cops.

We spent an hour talking hunting, guns, and sports before I broached the subject that I'd wanted to discuss with him.

"Bud, I need you to help me with a problem. I'm really having second thoughts about being a Chaplain. I'm not sure that I'm cut out to be one. Maybe the place to begin is for you to give me an evaluation of my performance. You're the only one I'd ask that because we're pretty close friends and you know that I'm not reaching for compliments. I really want to know if I'm effective or not."

Bud seemed somewhat surprised. He said, "Are you sure that you're not just a little burned out after that 36-45 in Greenhaven the other day? I heard that was pretty rough."

A Signal 36 was murder and a Signal 45 was a suicide.

"No, I've had a bunch of concerns from the very beginning. I never dreamed that I'd be so affected by the death and, well, heartbreak that I'd see. I don't know if I'll ever be able to be detached from the tragedy and pain of the people I have to counsel and comfort."

"Maybe you're not supposed to be detached," said Bud. "Those folks need someone who cares and shares their hurt. Investigators need to be detached because they can't let their thinking get clouded up by personal feelings. Besides, they're not there to comfort, they're there to close out a case. I don't see how you can ever be detached. You'll just have to learn to cope quickly."

Amazed at his insight, I answered, "Yeah, Bud, but that's a lot to require. A while back, when I had three fatals in a row in one week, wow, that was too much to handle. A fifteen year old who drowned, a sixteen year old who hanged himself, and a mother who was crushed by a dump truck right in front of her husband and daughter. Boy, those are some faces that I'll never forget. And so much of it involved kids. Kids who died and kids who survived."

"Remember, Rev, those are all reminders of people who were helped as well as people who died. You made a difference. You made the whole terrible ordeal just a little easier for the relatives and friends. That's what you have to think about."

"I know that, Bud. Maybe I'm getting selfish, but I'm just starting to feel like it's not worth all the grief and pain that I end up adopting. I feel good about helping and doing a job that few can or want to do, but . . . well . . . I guess I have to decide where my grief threshold is. And part of the problem is that it bothers me to think that I may not be tough enough to handle it."

"Well, Rev," he said in a philosophical voice, "it takes more guts to recognize your limitations than it does to pretend that you have no problems. You gotta know when to put on the brakes."

That was Bud's way of saying he'd understand if I decided to quit. He was far more intelligent and profound than most would have expected. The bouncing gung-ho Blue Knight was not a robot or a mindless Department flunky. He was perceptive enough to not patronize me or discourage me. The balance he maintained in his advice was inspiring. This was a man who could have been in a much higher-paying occupation and who would be a success at any endeavor. Yet he chose to be a cop. He believed in what he was doing. Upholding the law wasn't a trite concept to him.

We talked way into the night. I told him about how discouraging it was when the Department refused to reimburse our gasoline. "Hardnose" Hinckley was another point of failure in my chaplain ministry. Bud couldn't understand why Hardnose disliked me, but he felt sure that he'd change his mind in time.

I brought up several minor concerns and I was dying to talk about my conscientious objector beliefs, but I was afraid to risk our friendship. I was convinced that Bud wouldn't be able to accept my convictions. Plus, he'd probably feel like I'd deceived him.

The radio had been deathly quiet for a long while. At 2 A.M. we were discussing the one time issue of my 007 book. We were on a road that was literally the edge of the County. It was winding through a wooded area that had street lights every half mile. We were about as far away from the station as we could possibly be, and the nearest back up was several minutes away.

As we came around a turn in the road we could see a street light on the left about two hundred yards ahead. A van was stopped on the road just before the street light. Bud was talking as we slowly drew closer to the stopped vehicle.

"It wouldn't surprise me," he said, "if Hardnose made up that whole business about . . . ," he squinted as he tried to get a better look at the van, ". . . about your 007. Hey . . . I believe that's the Cooper's van."

As we closed in on the van, I could see that it was at an angle, with the front turned slightly to the right shoulder of the road. That kept us from seeing the driver's door as we came up on it.

The street light cast shadows around the van, but I could see the yellow lightning streak on the right side. It was the van that the youngest Cooper had been driving when Bud stopped him and hassled him.

Coasting up to within twenty yards of the van, a series of nightmarish events took place in split second time. The only way to describe them is to lock them into frozen pictures.

The mountainous silhouette of Jerry Cooper stepped from behind the left side of the van. A sawed-off pump shotgun was in his hands.

Bud had just placed his right hand on the switches of the emergency lights. I watched in horror as red lights flashed and the shotgun exploded. It was like the flash of a camera, except more yellow and red. The windshield disintegrated. I was showered with glass and particles of dashboard. I was thrown left into Buds shoulder, then right against the door, and then forward into the dashboard.

As a reflex, Bud had jerked the wheel to the right, sending the cruiser down a small hill and into a pine tree. Because we'd been going only 5 miles per hour, the distance covered and the impact were minimal.

I shook my head and glass flew everywhere. I was in the floorboard of the car and had one leg sticking out and under my door which had opened on impact. I couldn't feel any pain. Something was dripping off my left eye brow and my ears were buzzing, but I didn't see any bullet holes.

Bullet holes? That jarred some sense into me. I looked at Bud. He was laying on the seat, on his right side. He looked awfully uncomfortable. Then I saw the blood flowing over his face and onto the seat. "Oh no Lord," I prayed, "don't let him die."

Before I could continue my prayer, I saw some movement out Bud's window. I raised up some and saw a sight that would send shivers through any sane man. I saw the huge frame of Jerry Cooper easing down the hill with his shotgun poised to finish the job he'd started. His leather vest with its studs and chains sparkled from the streetlight. His spiked hair gave him a demoniacal specter. I felt fear like never before. I could taste it. It took my breath away and made my heart hammer like a machine gun. I was petrified.

He had obviously set this up to get Bud. He probably never expected anyone to be with him since they usually patrol alone. "Maybe," I thought, "he still has no idea that someone else is with Bud. Maybe I could slide out and run into the woods. But what about Bud? He needed medical help, but first he needed to be saved from Cooper."

My mind clicked into its hunter mode. There wasn't time for debates and arguments. This was real life survival. We would both die unless I did something to stop it.

The release switch for the shotgun was on the other side of the steering wheel out of my reach. So I slid my hand under Bud to get his pistol. The seat was sticky with blood and his weight was almost unmovable. Yet somehow, I felt my fingers wrap around the grip of the revolver, my thumb flip the thumb release, and I slid it out from underneath him.

Without daring to take another peek, I crawled out the door and circled it so that I was squatting between the door and the front wheel. I gripped the gun tightly in both hands and held my breath to listen.

I could hear Cooper's steps as his foot crunched twigs about twelve feet away from the cruiser. I readied myself. I should have prayed, but there wasn't time.

I heard two sounds that signaled it was time to act. First, was a moan from inside the cruiser. The second was the chambering of a shell in Cooper's shotgun. Kershunk!

The moment I heard that, I sprang up in a crouch position and leveled my gun at a very surprised Cooper, who was only three steps from the other side of the cruiser. His surprise turned to reaction as he started to point the shotgun at me. My eyes were glued to that ugly gun.

I fired three times. I don't really remember squeezing the trigger three times. I just shot the gun. Also, I don't remember any deafening explosions or jarring recoil. I just shot the gun. I didn't aim for the head or the heart or to kill. I just shot the gun.

Cooper was knocked back off his feel like he'd been kicked by a mule. He landed on his left side with his arms and legs twisted in unnatural positions. The shotgun marked the spot where he'd been standing.

I kept the gun pointed at him as I stepped around the cruiser. An eerie stillness enveloped the shadowy scene. I was afraid that he might get up. I'd seen it plenty of times in the movies. But as I inched up to his crumpled form, I knew he wasn't going to get up. He was too twisted and too still. I thought about checking his pulse, but decided to keep my distance.

Then I had a bolt of panic strike me as I thought, "What if he's not alone? Should I get back behind the car? Should I check out the van? Should I get some help? Yeah, that's what I need to do."

I went back to my seat in the cruiser and grabbed the mike. Before I depressed the key, I took a deep breath and looked around. The red lights atop the cruiser were still rotating and casting flashing red shadows on the trees. Bud was breathing, but he looked terrible. I twisted around so that I could see the van up the road. It sat there, dark and foreboding, like a Satanic chariot waiting for it's master's return.

"Chaplain 5."

Nothing. The car had choked out, but there should have been enough juice in the battery to handle the radio. Or were we in one of the famous "Dead Spots." where we couldn't transmit?

"Chaplain 5, with a 10-33." Emergency traffic.

"Chaplain 5 go ahead."

"I'm on Larsen Heights Road about three miles south of Route 14. We have shots fired. Scout 540 is down and a suspect is down. I need rescue two times and some backup. There may be some other suspects in the area. Are you direct?"

"10-4, Chaplain 5. Rescue is being notified. All units, I'm calling a Signal 13. All units respond. Officer needs assistance on Larsen Heights Road, three miles south of Route 14. Proceed code 3."

There was a flurry of activity as units marked enroute to us. They sounded like music. I could hear the anxiety in their voices. It would be just a matter of minutes before someone would be there to help.

Bud made a muffled grunt that caused me to take my eyes off the sinister van and get a good look at my injured partner. He lay there with windshield particles sparkling all over him. Something else glistened on the left side of his head. It was blood oozing from a three inch gash just above his temple. His face was covered with blood, some of which was already beginning to dry. As I looked closer, I could see that he was bleeding form his upper left shoulder also. Just below his collarbone was a wound that slowly seeped blood. His breathing was easy, free from gurgling or wheezing. I was afraid to move him and run the risk of opening the wounds further. Besides, lying on his right side on the seat, he was about as comfortable as he could be in the cramped cruiser.

I straightened up and leaned back in the seat. A wave of exhaustion swept over me as my legs and arms went limp. I dropped the gun on the floor and closed my eyes for just a second.

When I tried to open my eyes, the lids refused to separate. The combination of being tired and their being covered with dried blood, made them feel as if they were glued shut. I must have slipped off into some form of unconsciousness, because I could hear noises and the distinctive voice of Sergeant Scott.

As my eyes finally pried apart, I was astonished to see that I was at a circus. Then I realized that it wasn't a circus, but a crime scene swarming with police and rescue medics. What surprised me even more was the discovery that I wasn't in the cruiser, but on a stretcher. Medics were working on me. One was putting a gauze bandage over my left eye while another was taking my blood pressure.

Looking around I saw familiar faces, spotlights, and dozens of rotating red lights. I heard motors, shouts, and radio traffic. Most of the Department had come to the scene. I saw the Chief, the Assistant Chief, ID, IA, PR, and twenty blue shirts. This was a big deal. It was almost amusing to think that I was part of this "Big deal".

Real life shootings have nothing in common with television shootings. On TV a cop can kill a crook at ten in the morning and still meet a beautiful girl for lunch. In the real world, he'd be lucky to meet her for breakfast the next day. The interviews, investigations, and paperwork are endless. Anytime a cop fired his gun, he had to be cleared, and the shooting had to be proven "righteous" or justifiable. Oddly enough, I felt relieved when they started to load me into an ambulance, because I knew that I'd be spared the third degree for a little while.

Before they closed the door of the ambulance, Sergeant Scott leaned in and said, "How you doing, Rev?"

"I think I'm all right. I'm not hurting anywhere. How's Bud?"

"They took him away several minutes ago. The EMT said he'd be fine. All the wounds were non-fatal. They'll have to remove a pellet from his shoulder and sew up his head, but he'll be O.K."

"So will this guy," said one of the medics, "the doctor said to bring him in for observation. Probably spend the night at the hospital."

"Well, Rev, the fella's from IA will probably be by soon to get a statement from you. They need to get it while it's still fresh in your mind."

"Don't worry about that, Sarge. This will be fresh in my mind for the rest of my life."

"For what it's worth, you saved yours and Bud's life. The Chief is already talking about a medal for valor. Just remember that you did what you had to do. Whether Cooper lives or dies, you did the right thing."

I almost sat up. "You mean he's not dead?"

"No, he's still kicking. They've taken him away to the shopping center where a Medivac chopper is waiting to take him to the trauma center. They have surgeons standing by to operate on him when he gets there. You put two slugs in his chest and one in his right arm. He's mean enough to live through that."

The next 48 hours were more of a blur, and in some ways, more of a nightmare, than the shooting had been. My life would never be the same again.

The incident became the crucible through which every aspect

of my life would be judged and compared. Like those who returned from the war, it became the event that all others were related to. Things either took place before or after the "shooting". No longer could any experience stand on its own.

In the emergency room they removed three pieces of glass from the left side of my forehead and put a couple stitches on each laceration. The doctor then gave me a shot of something that must have put me to sleep for four or five hours.

When I awoke, my wife and Sam Hicks were in the room with me. After a few moments of hugging my wife, I got caught up in the competition of seeing who could be the most reassuring.

"Ya done good, Rev. Bud's gonna be just fine," said Sam.

My wife chimed in, "Honey, I know you feel bad about it, but you saved yours and Bud's lives. I'm proud of you."

"Oh, don't worry about me," I said in my most macho tones. "I'll be just fine. I'm just glad that Bud is all right. The whole thing seems like a bad dream right now. I'll grapple with it later."

And so the conversation went. Not just that one, but every discussion I had with anyone else was an empty superficial justification for gunning down a human being. Whether or not I'd done the right thing conscience wise was something I had little time to meditate on. Within minutes of waking up, I was pulled into an odyssey of interviews and meetings that made self-evaluation impossible. To cope with the onslaught of attention I received, I encased my conscience in lead with serious considerations towards never releasing it again.

Bud was sitting up in bed when I visited him. He had a gauze turban on his head and two tons of it wrapped around his shoulder. A 7-11 Big Gulp was in his right hand and a "hello world" grin formed a crescent connection between his rosy cheeks. We only got to talk for a few minutes because I was wanted at Headquarters.

"I've waited all this time to get a chance to drop Cooper, and you beat me to it, Rev. That ain't fair."

"Well, if you'd been paying attention, you could have gotten off the first shot. Instead you got caught with your mouth open."

We laughed as if it had all been a daily occurrence. We both knew that we'd carry scars that the doctors never saw.

"Well, I guess I need to thank you for saving my life. And I guess that since you're a hero now, you won't be out riding with us peons anymore." He said with false regrets.

"Before I ride with you again, Bud, I want a 50 caliber machine gun mounted on the hood, loaded and ready for war."

We joked some more and I promised to have a pizza sent to him that night. He swore that the hospital food would accomplish what Cooper failed to do. As I turned to leave, he said, "Don't worry about IA. I assured them that if the Chaplain did it, it had to be righteous."

All that day and the next are summed up with one word. Meetings. I had two meetings with Internal Affairs. At one they recorded my statement and at the other they had me write it out. I was a little paranoid as I wrote out my statement because I knew it would be compared to the recorded one and I didn't want there to be even a hint of contradiction. There wasn't, of course, but then I wasn't thinking as clearly as I normally did.

I had meetings with the Chief, the psychiatrist, and the Public Relations officer. All of which was SOP for shootings. Since I couldn't be placed on administrative leave pending the outcome of the investigation by IA, they asked me politely to not ride with any officers for a few days. That made me laugh. I had no plans to ride with anyone ever again, but I didn't tell them that.

Dozens of reporters wanted to talk to me. It was hard to hide my phone number since the church had a three-inch display ad in the Yellow Pages with my home phone listed. So I gave interview after interview over the phone. For the sake of my family, I refused any reporters who came to my home.

Words like "hero", "exceptional bravery", and "courageous" were being used about me and that was terribly disconcerting. I didn't feel brave. I felt awkward and hypocritical. Not to the point of being morose, but to the point of being confused. Church members were calling and visiting, and without exception, they were congratulating me. Cops from the station came by my house to shake my hand and tell me that I was "a heck of a Chaplain". The problem was that I enjoyed the recognition that made me feel guilty. I suppose the fact that Cooper lived made it easier to deal with, but what about the convictions that I'd completely ignored. Everyone was telling me what a great job I'd done, and I liked it. I was proud about saving Bud's life and it was gratifying to know that I would not retreat from danger. Yet, I had compromised my conscience, but, then again, the alternative was unthinkable.

At 2 in the morning, exactly 48 hours from when the shooting happened, I was lying in bed praying. Through my superior ability to rationalize, I had placed the incident into a special category that I mentally labeled 'Abnormal Experiences'. I decided to think of it as an exception-to-the-rule situation that, like lightning, wouldn't strike twice in the same place. After asking for forgiveness and clearing my conscience from guilt, I moved on to the topic of my continued involvement as a Police Chaplain.

I was not involved in idle chit-chat with God. I was spreading my heart out on the table like a deck of cards. I wanted guidance. I wanted to know that my heart was properly motivated whether I remained a Chaplain or withdrew to the security of sanctuary life.

In the darkness of my bedroom, with my wife and children deep in slumber, I did something that I did only with my children. I slipped out of my bed and got on my knees to continue my prayer. I felt the need to physically humble myself before God. Usually, we see ourselves as too spiritually sophisticated to do such things, but that night, it seemed like the only appropriate way to pray.

An hour later I closed my prayer with these words:

"And now, Father, if it is your will, end the floundering in my life by helping me discover what I need to do. I know you don't speak to men from burning bushes any more, but could you somehow, someway, give me a sign to direct my path. Make my heart sensitive so that I will recognize the sign when I see it. And give me the courage to obey your will, whatever it may happen to be.

"I offer this petition in the name of your Son and my Savior, Jesus Christ. Amen."

My knees popped when I stood up, but my heart felt relieved. I crawled into bed and felt ever muscle relax to accept the sleep my body so desperately needed.

The phone rang. I picked it up before the second ring.

"Hello."

"Chaplain? I need to talk to you. Can we meet somewhere?" said a gravel voice, heavy with emotion.

"Sure," I said with reservation in my voice, "who is this?"

"This is Charles Hinckley. I'm sitting at home with my revolver in my hand and I need you to tell me why I shouldn't blow my brains out." As he said that his voice broke and he began to cry. Hardnose Hinckley crying? Hardnose Hinckley asking me for help?

"Sarge, can you meet me at my office in ten minutes?"

He paused a moment before answering. "Yeah, I guess I can." His voice was so soft that I could barely hear him.

"O.K. Sarge. Leave your gun at home and come straight to my office. I'll be there when you get there. We're gonna take care of everything, O.K.?"

"O.K., I'm leaving now."

As I leaped up to get dressed, it suddenly dawned on me what had happened. So I stopped, looked up, and said, "Thank you, Father, for answering my prayer so quickly."

About the Author

Mike Root was born in the nation's capitol. After attending schools in Georgia and Arkansas, he returned to the Washington, D.C. metropolitan area to accept a position as minister of the Fairfax Church of Christ. In his eleven years there the church has grown to become one of the largest in the area. For eight of those years he was a volunteer Police Chaplain with the local police department. He holds degrees from Harding University and George Mason University. He has been a guest speaker for numerous seminars and lectureships, and has been listed in *Outstanding Young Men of America* three years.